# DEVIL'S BACKBONE

A MIAMI JONES FLORIDA MYSTERY

A.J. STEWART

JACARANDA

Jacaranda Drive Publishing

Los Angeles, California

www.jacarandadrive.com

Cover artwork by Streetlight Graphics

ISBN-13: 978-1-945741-49-4

*To the fine folks of Spanish Wells and Eleuthera, Bahamas.*

*And Heather. There's no point in being there if you're not.*

# CHAPTER ONE

I CUT A LONELY FIGURE AT THE BAR AT LONGBOARD KELLY'S. THE courtyard was bathed in sunshine, but none of the umbrellas were open because there was nobody out there, and Mick didn't feel the need to have the logos fade away for no reason. At least that was my theory. Mick had never mentioned the topic, and there was no one else around to discuss it, so my bored mind was taking liberties.

Muriel was somewhere in the back counting stock or doing bicep curls or whatever it was that kept her in shape, and Mick was absent from his own establishment for the first time in living memory. I probably shouldn't have been there either, as it was a workday and all, but I needed a six-pack in my cooler for my afternoon appointment.

"Poor puppy," said Muriel, carrying a couple of bottles of liquor into the bar. "You lost all your play friends."

I shrugged.

"You want a beer before you go?" she asked.

"Drink alone?"

"You make it sound so sordid when you say it like that."

"Hemingway did it, and look what happened to him."

"Hemingway took his own life after three months of abstinence. You're thinking of Bukowski."

I really wasn't. "What happened to him?"

"He drank constantly and lived into his seventies. Got leukemia."

"That's hard luck. I think I'll just take the six-pack and go."

"Sure." She took a six-pack from under the bar and loaded it into my cooler. "When's Ron back?"

"He might never come back, the way he's talking. You know he actually said they were having a 'whale of a time' in Cape Cod."

"You serious?"

"About the whale?"

"About him not coming back."

"Nah. They'll be home end of the month."

"You're gonna give Mick a heart attack saying things like that."

"Where is Mick?"

"Out. That's all I know."

I took my cooler and waved Muriel goodbye, then I wandered out to my car. It wasn't overly warm, but the humidity was getting nasty, so I put the AC on and headed out.

My destination was only twenty miles away but a slow forty-minute drive south and west. I parked far from the gate to the grounds. I knew a lot of folks who came here didn't move as well as I did, but given the few cars in the lot, it was moot charity. Truth was I liked to move that extra bit every chance I got, just to keep the old machinery working.

I was collecting the cooler from the back when I heard my name.

"Miami Jones?"

I turned to look at the owner of the voice and got a face full of khaki. He wore light khaki trousers and a matching shirt, and his vest and bucket hat were the same color but a shade or two darker.

"Can I help you?"

He stepped toward me as he closed the door on his generic sedan. I watched his hands for a weapon, which felt unnecessarily nervy.

"You know who I am?" he said, looking around as if a paparazzo might jump from the bushes at any moment.

I gave him another look. He was an old guy dressed up like a fisherman, just a little too much so, like it was a Halloween thing.

"No," I said.

He stepped closer. He was a good six inches shorter than me, so I got mostly hat.

"Really?" he said.

"Yeah, really."

"You don't watch much cable."

"I don't own a television."

He frowned, and it took him a minute to process this little nugget.

"How do you not own a TV?"

"Pal, you got something to say? 'Cause I got somewhere to be."

"Yes, right, of course. Well, my name is Rusty Reels."

I nearly choked on my own saliva, but now that he'd said it, I realized I did know him. I recalled him from the times I sat in a sports bar to watch a football game and one of the televisions in the corner that no one was watching would stay on some outdoor sportsman's channel.

"The fishing guy," I said.

He smiled. "You do know me."

"I wouldn't go that far. What is it you want, Mr. Reels?"

"You know I host a highly rated fishing program." It was more a statement than a question. He paused to let me acknowledge it, but when I didn't he continued.

"But I'm also one of the top athletes in the world of competitive sports fishing."

I frowned. Athlete was pushing it. "Sports fishing?"

"Bass, mainly."

"Okay."

"I've been invited to a big-money tournament: the Bonefish Classic."

"Bonefish? Is that different from bass?"

"You don't know much about fishing, do you?"

"I know mahi-mahi rocks on a fish sandwich. The rest I leave to Mick."

"Who?"

"Doesn't matter. Why are you telling me this?"

"I have reason to believe the Bonefish Classic is going to be fixed."

"Fixed?"

"Yeah, you know, crooked. I have reason to believe that some of my competitors and the organizers are in cahoots to funnel prize money between them."

"Did you just say cahoots?"

"Are you listening to me? They're cheating."

"How much money are we talking?"

"First prize is two hundred and fifty thousand."

"Dollars?"

"Not pesos."

"That's a lot of money for fishing, isn't it?"

"There's more money in it than you know."

"Clearly."

"The Bassmaster Classic has a total prize pool of a million bucks."

"I'm in the wrong game."

"I hope not. I don't need your help as a fisherman."

"What do you need my help for?"

"I need you to go to the site and check it out, find out who's corrupt and, if possible, put a stop to it, or at least hand it to the authorities."

"All right, Mr.—"

"Reels."

"Yeah, of course. I can take a look at your case. If you make an appointment and come to my office, we can discuss it further."

"I can't do that."

"Why?"

"I think I'm being followed. I don't want them seeing me at a PI's office."

"My office is in a building with a bank and a lawyer and a bunch of people. There's no reason for anyone to think you're visiting me."

"They'll figure it out."

"Well, I don't generally conduct business in the parking lot of a cemetery. Which is a thought—how did you know I was here?"

"I followed you. I'm telling you, these people have eyes everywhere, and I need your eyes looking at them." Reels pulled an envelope from one of his many pockets and handed it to me. "I need you there tomorrow. That's a plane ticket. You'll be met at the airport and taken to your accommodation, and you can take it from there."

"Whoa, airport? Where is this tournament?"

"Spanish Wells. Eleuthera."

"The Bahamas?"

"Yes."

"I can't drop everything and go to the Bahamas tomorrow."

"I'll pay a thousand a day plus expenses."

I took a deep breath, in through my nose, out through my mouth. Truth was I had nothing better to do, and a kay a day plus was nothing to sneeze at.

"Please, Mr. Jones, help me out. The integrity of my sport is at stake."

Calling anything that involved the participants lugging a cooler of beer a sport seemed a stretch, but the money was real.

"All right, Mr. Reels, I'll take your case."

# CHAPTER TWO

I left Rusty Reels to drive away, took out the small cooler, and ambled toward the entrance to the cemetery. The first time I had visited the South Florida National Cemetery, it had not long opened and was mostly fields of grass, but the number of headstones had grown every time I visited over the years.

The moisture in the air seemed to rise from the grass below my feet as I walked to my destination. Lucas was sitting on said grass, leaning back with his face to the sun. He didn't open his eyes but sensed my approach.

"MJ," he said.

"Lucas." I opened the cooler and handed him a beer. He must have sensed that, too, because he held out his hand to take it. He waited for me to open mine and sit down, then he poured some of his beer onto the base of the headstone.

"Cheers, old man," he said.

I poured some of my beer onto the grass as he had. "Cheers, Lenny."

Lucas and I saluted Lenny Cox's grave, then each took a sip.

"How's the big smoke?" I asked.

"Getting tiresome, to be honest."

"You're not thinking of leaving the marina, are you?"

"I'm not in a hurry to do anything, mate. How about you? How's the house coming along?"

"Close but no cigar." My house on Singer Island had been the victim of arson, and it had been a long process from rubble to rebuild. "They're painting this week, so I'm told."

"Let's hope it stays in one piece for a while."

"Let's hope. I am thinking about keeping the builder on retainer though."

"And your lovely wife?"

"Danielle's out of town. Apparently our president and the prime minister of Britain are visiting Tallahassee, so she's been seconded to protection detail."

"So you're a bachelor again."

I thought about the apartment I was staying in. A guy I met while watching football at a bar on Singer Island offered the use of his place while he was summering up in Vermont. It was a nice two-bedder with an ocean view in one of those obnoxious towers that had appeared along City Beach.

"I may be giving a bad name to bachelordom."

"Microwave meals and empty beer cans."

"Nothing of the sort, I'm afraid."

"You're eating and drinking at Longboard's."

"There you go."

Lucas sipped his beer and brushed his hand along the side of Lenny's headstone. "You got much work going on?"

"Oddly enough, I was just approached in the parking lot."

Lucas raised an eyebrow.

"What do you know about a guy called Rusty Reels?"

"The fishing guy?"

"That's him."

"What's he need a PI for?"

"He's involved in a competition, and he thinks it might be rigged."

"Huh. Where's this?"

"Spanish Wells. You know it?"

"I do. Sleepy little place. It's a lobster town. No resorts. Funny place for a tournament."

"Why?"

"Well, let's just say the folks there can be tough to get to know. A touch wary of newcomers, you might say."

I offered him a grin. "Sounds like someone I know."

"So is it deep-sea fishing?"

"You tell me. It's called the Bonefish Classic."

"Bonefish? Odd, but makes sense."

"Odd? Why?"

"They're not exactly trophy fish. Plain silver to blend in with the sandy bottoms and turtle grass, and they're not that great to eat because, well, it's all in the name."

"Right. So why does it make sense?"

"Bonefish love the shallows, and there are plenty of sand banks around Spanish Wells."

As Lucas opened us each a second beer, I searched for Rusty Reels on my phone. He looked to have some kind of mini empire going, with TV shows on the Outdoor Sportsman's Channel and a range of rods and associated fishing accouterment, including a clothing line that looked to be more of the khaki he had been wearing in the parking lot. There were a lot of pictures of him on a sleek boat with a stool-like seat at the bow.

I showed Lucas the screen. "You know this boat?"

"Bass boat. What all the big competitors use. They often use Grand Prix starts, all lined up, and they speed off to all parts of the lake to find the best fish, so they have nice big engines and low draft, and they go like stink."

"Is that what they would use in Spanish Wells?"

"No idea. I've never seen a bonefish competition before, but when I've gone after bonefish there, we've used flatboats. Similar but sans the big old motor."

"You got anything like that at the marina?"

"Nah. Those aren't South Beach material. Really designed for inland waters, lakes and so on. You wouldn't want to be on the ocean if a decent chop came up."

"This Reels guy seems to have been pretty successful in the competitions."

"He used to be, won a lot back in the day. But I'm not sure these days. I don't get to many tournaments anymore."

"You ever compete?"

"Nah," said Lucas. "Me and Lenny did our fair share of fishing, but we ate what we caught and caught no more than we could eat."

We sat in the warm grass and toasted Lenny again. It had been a long time since my old mentor had died, and I didn't think of him as often as I had in the years after his demise. Some days I felt bad about that, but he would have told me to get on with life and put my time and effort into the living. But on fine afternoons in South Florida, drinking in a graveyard felt like the right thing to do. Even in death Lenny reminded me of what was important.

Lucas sipped his beer quietly, and I called my office and left a message for Lizzy to let her know I had gotten a job and would be out of the country for a few days. I gave her the name of our new client, but I didn't ask her to write up a contract. She knew her job better than I did.

We finished our drinks, and each touched Lenny's headstone one more time and then wandered out. Before heading for his truck, Lucas slapped my back.

"Hey, when you're in Spanish Wells, give my regards to Ken Corrigan."

Lucas would expect to run into someone he knew if he walked down a street in Mumbai. I, on the other hand, was surprised when someone recognized me in West Palm Beach, and I had played professional baseball. But I nodded anyway and walked away, wondering where I had left my passport.

# CHAPTER THREE

I<small>T TURNED OUT MY OFFICE MANAGER</small>, L<small>IZZY</small>, <small>HAD STORED MY PASSPORT</small> in the safe in our office after I had left it sitting on my desk. I felt like a ten-year-old whining to his mother he couldn't find his shoes, and Lizzy treated it exactly that way, offering a mini-lecture on looking after my stuff.

It was the following morning that I realized I didn't own a duffel or a backpack to take with me, having put such items in storage while I was waiting for my house to be rebuilt. I found an old carry-on suitcase in a closet in the spare room of the apartment and hoped my benefactor wouldn't mind me borrowing it. I contemplated going for a run on City Beach, but something about air travel sat uneasily with me, and I couldn't get the feeling out of my guts. It wasn't the flying so much as all the other bother: parking, check-in, security, always running late or feeling like I was, then waiting around for hours with nothing to do except sit in an airside bar that had all the charm of a doctor's office.

As it was, I got a clear run to MIA and was through security with days to spare. The bar was closed for renovations and the line for coffee was like something at Disneyworld, so I grew old on a seat at the boarding gate that was purposefully built with no lumbar support to make the seats on the aircraft feel luxurious.

We walked across the tarmac to board the twin-prop aircraft, and I could see my fellow travelers getting that excited look they got when a vacation was within reach. I was told my little wheelie was going to be too big for the luggage bins on board, so it was tagged and left at the base of the stairs to the aircraft.

The plane might have held seventy souls, but was only half full, so I sat beside no one and chatted to the flight attendant occasionally and watched the ocean turn from dark and foreboding to the most amazing turquoise, like a mane of color leeching from the island of Eleuthera into the inky black of the Atlantic.

The airfield at North Eleuthera was a casual affair, tourists ambling off like chickens escaping a truck accident, and a line of fluorescent-clad staff directing them toward the cinder block terminal. Inside the building was utter chaos, even with only thirty arrivals. The customs area comfortably held about a dozen people, but there were about twenty airport and customs staff and then even more ancillary workers and hangers-on who seemed to provide no service to anyone but were permitted to wander at will.

My passport was stamped, and no photo was taken. I was pointed back out onto the tarmac for reasons I couldn't fathom. I wandered out with a few other travelers, and we stood in the baking sun, heat rising from the asphalt and pulsing from the sky, with all the humidity of a bread oven.

A woman in an official-looking uniform yelled at us with a voice that could penetrate body armor. None of us moved, having heard her but not understood a word. She looked at us like we were broken parts and then repeated her tirade. I got the impression we weren't supposed to be back out on the airside of the airport, but that might have just been years of TSA brainwashing talking. Then she pointed at a trailer that held our luggage.

I took a chance of further verbal abuse and walked over to the trailer, pulled my little suitcase from the Jenga pile of luggage and then glanced at the woman in the uniform. She nodded and pointed me back into the terminal, this time through a door that led out onto the street.

About ten guys asked if I needed a ride but they all did it with such disarming smiles that I would have happily gone with any of them. But I noticed the big guy with a linebacker's build leaning against a pole with a piece of card that read Jones, so I moved his way. He saw me but made no effort to meet me halfway.

"You looking for me?" I asked.

"You Mr. Miami Jones?"

"I am."

"Then you looking for me. My car's this way."

We walked past a dozen minivans parked against the chain-link perimetric fence, ready to whisk the arrivals away to wherever the heck they were going. My driver stopped by a beat-up burgundy Camry. He got in the wrong side of the car, which turned out to be the driver's side, and I remembered the Bahamians drove on the left. I tossed my case in the backseat and got in.

We drove for twenty minutes or so through a tunnel of low, dense foliage. My driver said nothing, and I watched the scenery go by. We passed nothing that resembled a town, and the air rushing in through the open windows was warm and almost edible.

We arrived at a small dock where an island version of a park-and-ride had been set up. There were no stores, just a broad concrete dock with a small pergola and some benches. Across a half mile of water, I could see an island with buildings that resembled a town.

The driver stopped right in the middle of the dock and directed me to the side where a skinny guy in a blue speed boat sat waiting as if waiting was a well acquired skill. The skinny guy nodded, and the driver frowned.

"You know where you're going?" he asked.

"Sure. Jump on."

The driver did not jump on. He looked at me, and I jumped on as best I could while carrying a suitcase. I longed for my old duffel. But like a lot of things I longed for, it wasn't with me.

The skinny guy fired up the outboard and reversed from the pier and then he spun the boat around and headed out along the coastline. I glanced back at the docks, but my driver was gone. My new driver also didn't say anything, but the wind rushing across the bow made it challenging. On the water, the air was cooler, and it felt good to blow the cobwebs out.

We edged along the coast in a channel, not heading across to the island town. Then once we were north of the small island, my driver —captain didn't seem to fit—cut west around a sandbank. As we sped along the length of the island, I could see a beautiful sandy beach and nice homes set back from sea walls. At one point, there appeared to be bleachers on the sand, as if several hundred people might arrive just to sit and watch the scene. We were well out from the shore, and in close it looked shallow and the most magnificent blue. It was the kind of color the tourist brochures in Florida often used Photoshop to achieve.

About two-thirds of the way along the beach, my driver cut hard toward shore, and he gently eased off the throttle as we neared the sand. He switched the engine off and raised the outboard some, then we coasted until we bottomed out a good twenty yards short of the beach.

The driver pointed a long finger toward a stout building surrounded by trees about fifty yards back from the sand.

"How do you suppose I get there?" I asked.

"Walk, man." He smiled and pointed over the side of the boat.

Fortunately, I was dressed for the occasion in cargo shorts and boat shoes. I slipped the shoes off, sat on the edge of the boat and spun around, then dropped into the water. I was expecting to go waist deep, so my knees jarred when I hit the sandy bottom and the water was only half way up my calves.

I held my shoes in my mouth by the laces, and the driver passed me my suitcase, which I lofted above my head. I was getting the impression this part of the Bahamas was a do-it-yourself kind of place. I sloshed through the warm water until I reached the beach, where I dropped the case down and turned to wave to the driver. He was pushing his boat back off the sand with an oar, and once he was sufficiently deep he lowered his outboard into the water, revved it up, and sped away across the sparkling sea.

The sky was the same color as in South Florida, but the water was something else. I glanced along the beach. It was clean but for the odd batch of sea grass. It looked like erosion was an issue by the number of seawalls that had been erected between the sand and the lawns of the houses above.

My accommodation had no such sea wall. It was either yet to become a problem at this end of the beach, or the owner was ignoring reality. The house was farther back than most of the others, and I couldn't drag the wheels across the sand, so I carried the case in one hand and my shoes in the other, up onto the thick grass and along a flagstone path to the back patio.

I contemplated going around to the front, but having been dropped off at the rear, I figured testing the back door was worth a shot. The patio was a small brick affair with a cheap plastic chair facing the water. A plain white door was placed in the middle of the back of the house, and I couldn't help but think sliding glass doors would better take advantage of the view. That's what I had at home on Singer Island, offering a prize view across the rear lawn to the Intracoastal Waterway. We had rebuilt the house just as it had been, a one-story ranch in a line of two- or three-level wedding cakes. I liked the simplicity of it, and it seemed the owner of my new digs took simplicity to an even higher level.

I tried the door and found it open, so I stepped inside. It was dark and warmer than outside and musty like last winter's coat. I left the door open to let some air in and searched for a light switch. Once revealed, I saw it was more an old shack than a beach residence. There was a small kitchen with a bar fridge and a single hot plate, a round dining table with two plastic chairs that matched the one outside, and a rattan futon.

I did a quick walk-through and found a bedroom with a full-size mattress and a single sheet—all that was required and nothing more. What I didn't find was any kind of air conditioning. The air inside was still, and I felt myself stewing. I opened the fridge for a drink and found it empty and as warm as everything else. There was no television, no AC, no food, no water, and not much else to recommend the place. Lucas would have loved it. Lenny too. But they were built of sterner stuff than I, so I resolved to have a chat with my client about the provided accommodations.

# CHAPTER FOUR

---

AFTER WATCHING THE WATER SPARKLE FOR A FEW MINUTES, I GREW restless and contemplated going for a run along the beach. I was already sweating by standing still and wasn't sure what state I would end up in and if there was any kind of shower to be had afterward, so I changed into board shorts and a Pats T-shirt and went for a walk instead.

I wandered barefoot along the beach past a variety of sea walls that suggested battling beach erosion was not a coherent government policy but rather every homeowner for themselves. The tide seemed to be going out, and I sloshed along in the warm shallows, little silver fish gathering around my feet when I stopped to take in the picture-postcard view. I wondered if they were baby bonefish or something completely unrelated.

I reached a point where a street dead-ended at the beach but about four feet above sea level. There was no seawall, as there was no homeowner's property at the road's end, so someone had used heavy carpets to hold down the land eroding with every high tide. There was a trailer full of kayaks up on the high ground, and beside them another private property, also with no sea wall, and a wood picnic table overlooking the sand.

I was looking at the picnic table when I heard the scream for help. I spun around and scanned the water. Several hundred yards out I saw a woman kneeling on a stand-up paddleboard. She wasn't waving for help exactly but just held her arms out wide. For a moment I watched her, not sure if I had understood her call correctly. She didn't look in trouble.

"Hello," she yelled. "Help."

I realized the ebbing tide was taking her farther out to sea. There was no way to tell how deep the water was, but she was acting like it was the Bering Strait.

I looked around the foreshore and locked onto a bright orange kayak lying in the grass beside the picnic table. Unlike the ones on the trailer in the street, this one had a paddle lying on it. I dragged the kayak down onto the sand and into the water. By the time I was sitting down on it, the woman's board had drifted around, and she was now facing out to sea.

A couple of quick pulls on the paddle and I was cruising across the water, just inches above the bottom. Regardless, it was faster than running through water, which was always a slog. I got into my rhythm and felt the muscles in my shoulders open, having been coiled up in the airplane.

It took only a couple of minutes to reach her board. The first thing I noted was that she was a redhead, and the second thing was she had no paddle.

"You okay?" I asked.

"Do I look okay?"

"You look like you lost your paddle."

"It fell into the water."

I glanced around. "Where did you drop it, roughly?"

"I didn't drop it. It fell."

"Okay. Any idea where?"

"In the water. It's gone."

"They do float. We might find it."

"Look, are you going to bring me in, or am I going to have to sit here and listen to your stupid commentary?"

I felt like going with the latter but reined myself in. People often acted unlike themselves when they were under stress.

"We're going in. If you lie down on the board, you can hold on to the handle at the back of the kayak, and I'll paddle you in."

"I'm not lying down. I'll get wet."

"That can happen out on the water."

"If I wanted to get wet, I would have swum back to shore."

I said nothing to that, instead checking the hatch in the front of the kayak to see if I could find anything to help. Whoever owned the kayak came prepared. There was a small lifesaving float—like a soft orange brick—tied to a long yellow rope. I took the rope and fixed it to the handle at the stern of the kayak, then I took two strokes backward to ease in beside the board.

"Can you get a move on? We're floating to China here."

"Pretty sure if we keep going that way, we'll hit North Carolina one day."

"Thank you, Magellan. I don't want to go there either."

"Good barbecue, but fair enough. Take this and hold on."

I passed her the float, then turned the kayak and began paddling. There was a sandbar forming closer in that reached out from the beach like a witch's finger, and I headed for it.

"Hey, can you not splash me with your paddle?"

I took a deep breath, in through my nose and out through my mouth, and focused on the beautiful water and white sand. I paddled more carefully so as to not get my charge damp in any way, and against the tide it took a few minutes to reach the end of the sandbar.

I slipped off the kayak into ankle-deep water and dragged it onto the sandbar, then I turned back toward the water when something caught my eye.

"Will you look at that?" I stepped away into the water and picked up a paddle floating there. "Your paddle?"

"Who else would it belong to?"

I shook my head and tossed the paddle onto the sand, and I noticed a man walking onto the sandbar in our direction. I pulled the paddle board onto the sandbar, and the woman was able to step from it onto soft but mostly dry terra firma.

"You all okay out here?" asked the man as he reached us. He wore Ray Charles sunglasses, and his black skin glistened with a light sheen of sweat. My pasty skin was positively dripping.

"Lady was in a bit of distress, so I'm bringing her back in."

"Thanks," he said.

"I'm staying way down there," said the woman, pointing along the beach. "How am I supposed to get the board back now?"

"Well, you've got your paddle back, so . . ."

"Is that supposed to be funny?"

"More logical than funny."

"I'm not getting back on that water."

I sighed. I was starting to melt, and my patience had drowned just off the sandbar. "I suppose I could bring it back for you," I said. "I just need to return this kayak first."

"You stole a kayak?"

"I borrowed it."

"Likely story."

"Actually, it's my kayak," said the guy in the sunglasses. "So I'll take it."

"All right," I said. "Thanks."

"You sure you're okay?" he asked the woman.

"I'm standing out here in the heat with you two when I could be drinking a Chardonnay in my air-conditioned house. Does that sound okay?"

I offered the guy a smile, and he raised his eyebrows. The woman started walking along the sandbar, so I picked up the board and the paddle and followed her. The guy wisely sat on his kayak and paddled away.

The woman stormed ahead, so I followed her footprints. By the time they cut up the beach and through the long grasses on the fore-shore, I was more sweat than flesh. Beyond the beach grass was a lawn that led to a house with a wide verandah. It looked like something from Florida and of a different species to the place I was staying.

I dropped the paddleboard at the base of the stairs and was about to toss the paddle next to it when I heard the woman's voice. She was standing behind a screen door in the house with a glass of water in her hand.

"Not there," she said. "Someone will trip on it. Put it over there."

I did as I was told and dragged the board to the side of the yard, then turned to her and leaned on the paddle.

"I couldn't trouble you for a glass of water?"

She snorted. "You think I'm letting you in my house? Are you crazy?" She stepped back and closed the door, and I heard the lock turn.

"Thanks," I said.

I headed back toward the beach and had reached the tall beach grass before I realized I was still carrying the paddle, or rather using it as a crutch. For a moment I thought about taking it back and dropping it beside the board, but I found my reserves of good-will had run dry, so I tossed the damned thing way into the beach grass.

As I got back to the beach, I noticed a little farther down the bleachers I had seen from the boat. They were the kind of temporary things that were erected at fairs and junior baseball tournaments, and they looked horribly out of place on a beach. There was no volleyball court or any such facilities that might justify their existence, and I didn't have the brain capacity to think it through, so I turned and walked away.

When I reached the house where I had borrowed the kayak, the guy in the sunglasses was sitting at his picnic table. He smiled and held out a bottle of water that looked like the elixir of life, which I supposed it was.

I stepped over and took the bottle and without a word downed the entire thing.

"Thank you," I said. "I needed that."

"I can tell. You delivered your cargo okay?"

"Yeah. She's gonna organize a parade in my honor, just not today."

"No good deed."

"Something like that. And sorry about taking your kayak."

"No problem. That's why it's out here. I appreciate what you did, even if she didn't."

I turned and looked at the water. It called to me, azure and sparkling.

"You look like you could do with a beer. Why don't you take a dip while I grab a couple from the fridge?"

I didn't need any convincing on either front. I stumbled into the water and realized I was going to have to walk for about five minutes to reach even waist deep, so I just plopped down where I was and lay back and let the water consume me. It wasn't as refreshing as I had hoped—the shallows were heating up like pasta water on a stovetop—but it was cool enough. When I got out, my savior was back at his table with two cold beers.

"You want a towel?"

"No, sir."

"Didn't think so. Cheers."

We touched bottles, and I took a long pull. It was ice cold and pulsed through my body like refrigerant.

"I needed that."

"I know. You visiting?"

"Kind of."

"Kind of? Well, have you had Bahamian beer before?"

"I've drunk Kalik back in Florida."

"This is Sands."

"What's the difference?"

"The label."

"Well, I could get used to it, that's for sure." I took another sip and nodded at the house. "You live here?"

"I do. With my family."

"Paradise."

"Yes, it is." He held out his hand. "I didn't introduce myself."

"Miami Jones," I said, shaking his hand.

"Miami?"

"Yeah, it's a long story."

"Is it a good one?"

"Depends which version I tell."

"Fair enough. I'm Kenrick Corrigan."

"Corrigan?"

"Yes."

"They don't call you Ken do they?"

"They do, all except my mother."

"Ken Corrigan."

"That's right."

I laughed. "You don't know a guy called Lucas Burnside, do you?"

"Yeah, I know Lucas."

"He asked to be remembered, if I should happen upon you."

"And you did."

"Apart from your friendly paddle-boarding neighbor, you're the first person I've met here. What are the odds?"

"With those guys? Pretty good."

"Right. You do know him."

"I do. Through my dad. He's a good man."

"One of the best," I said.

"And what about you?"

"I just try to be the best man I can be."

"I'm sure. But I mean, you're visiting, kind of. So are you here for the tournament?"

"The fishing thing? What do you know about it?"

"I know it's a song and dance. I know folks around here don't really care for an influx of outsiders, but most of the hubbub is actually happening over on Harbour Island. But they do like the money coming in, and certain quarters are happy about the publicity."

"Where's Harbour Island?"

Ken pointed out past where I had performed my rescue of sorts.

"Out around that point, on the other side of North Eleuthera. It's a barrier island that forms a sound over there."

"So why's the tournament here?"

"Mostly because of the shallows you just paddled across, but Harbour Island is where a lot of the resorts are in Eleuthera. You could say it's where the money is. It's certainly where most of the tourists are. But not you."

"I'm not a big fan of tourists, or the places they go."

"Then Spanish Wells might be for you. Where are you staying?"

"A little shack up the beach there. It's sparsely stocked though. Is there a supermarket on the island?"

"Food Fair is on the main street. You got a cart?"

"A cart?"

"Golf cart. It's how most folks get around town."

"Not yet."

"You could try the rental place; not sure if they'll have anything given all the tournament visitors, but it's worth a shot. It's on the docks, south side of the island, where you would have come in on the ferry."

"I didn't come on a ferry. I came in a speedboat."

"To the dock?"

"To the beach." I pointed in the general direction.

"Huh. Different."

I finished my beer. "I should probably go find this store if I'm going to get any dinner."

"Stay and eat with us. I'm doing burgers."

"Are you sure?"

"Absolutely, man. My wife will be home soon."

Ken and I went up to his house and prepped dinner. Their place was small and basic. All they needed but nothing more—except that it sat on a beach in paradise.

Ken made up some burger patties while I rummaged through his fridge and rustled up a salad. I made my patented lemon vinaigrette, which I had stolen lock, stock, and garlic clove from Muriel, who had gotten it from public television.

We were standing out back heating up the grill when a car pulled up and a police officer got out. She was short with her hair pulled back and a don't-mess-with-me face, which broke into a broad grin as she approached us. She kissed Ken, which made me rethink our entire approach to policing, then she turned her keen eye to me.

"Baby, this is Miami Jones. He's visiting from Florida, and he performed a rescue out on the flats today. Miami, this is my wife, Elise."

"It's a pleasure to meet you," I said. "I hope you don't mind my barging in on your dinner."

She glanced at the table where I had deposited the salad.

"Mr. Jones, welcome to our island. And I assume that salad is your handiwork?"

"It's Miami, and, yes, ma'am, I made it. How did you know?"

"Well, Miami, my husband is a many great things, but a maker of salad is not one of them. If you gentlemen will excuse me, I'm going to get out of my uniform."

Elise Corrigan walked into the house, and Ken dropped the patties on the grill.

"So your wife is a cop?"

Ken smiled. "She is. Corporal Corrigan, although she is known on the island as Corporal Elise to save confusion."

"What confusion?"

Ken reached into his pocket and flipped open an ID.

"You're a cop too?"

"I am. Corporal Ken Corrigan."

"Two Corporal Corrigans. I can see how that kind of alliteration might get out of hand."

Ken laughed. "You worried now? You're in the house of two cops."

"Not really. My wife is an agent with the Florida Department of Law Enforcement."

"Nice. But she's not with you?"

"She's on security detail protecting the governor of Florida while the US president and British prime minister visit."

"Of course she is."

"How many officers do you have on the island?"

"Five. Four corporals—with one undergoing evaluation for promotion." He nodded toward the house. "And our boss, Superintendent Bridges."

"Seems like a lot for a sleepy place. You got a Cabot Cove murder problem or something?"

"No. We look after all the islands over here plus help on North Eleuthera and sometimes with our colleagues on Harbour Island. It's not the sort of policing you do in Florida though."

"Oh, I don't do any policing in Florida. I leave that to the professionals." Usually.

As we sipped our beers by the grill, two small kids appeared from nowhere. They clearly belonged because they ran over to Ken and hugged his legs.

"How was school?"

"We did painting!" said the boy.

"I played basketball and scored a point!" said the girl.

"Fantastic," said Ken. "Kids, this is Mr. Jones."

The two kids dropped into line to face me. "Hello, Mr. Jones," they sang.

"Hello," I said.

"This is Paul and Shayna," said Ken. "Who are going to wash up for dinner."

The kids smiled and dashed inside, and I resolved to instill a similar discipline in my office.

"Nice kids," I said.

"They are."

"School run this late?"

"They've been at a church activity. Kind of like daycare."

"Is the school far?"

"No, just down the road. Near the police station, actually."

"Are you married, Mr. Jones?" I turned to find Elise had snuck up beside me with a beer in her hand.

"Ah, yes. I am. I was just telling Ken that my wife is in law enforcement."

"Ah. And do you have kids?"

"No, no, we don't."

Ken slid the burgers off the grill and took them to the table, where the kids sat waiting quietly. I wondered if it was possible to order them like that. He offered me a patty, and I built my burger while he fixed two for his children.

"So what is it that you do, Miami?" asked Elise.

"I'm a private investigator."

"Oh, very interesting. Is it like *Magnum PI*?"

"Well, there's a lot of boring database work that they wouldn't put on television, but I have people who do that stuff."

"So what do *you* do?"

"Whatever I'm told."

Elise nodded. "You are a wise man, Miami."

"Occasionally."

We ate burgers and drank beer and listened to the kids talk excitedly about their school day. I couldn't remember ever being that excited about school, but maybe my memories of that time had been washed away by puberty. All I recalled was watching the clock in class and playing baseball and football.

Ken recounted the story about me being a rescue hero, and I suggested the woman could have stepped off the board and walked in, so hero might have been taking it a touch far.

"And how about you, Elise?" I asked. "You on the trail of any master criminals these days?"

"As it happens, I am." She bit into her burger, and I waited to hear the juice. "We have another conch theft."

"A conch theft? Like the snail thing?"

"Well, the shell at least. You know the conch shell?"

"I can show!" said Shayna, and she dashed inside and returned with a shell bigger than her head with a coiled spiral at one end and what I recalled Lenny calling a siphonal canal at the other. It was the color of sand on the outside and a luminous pink on the inside.

"It's beautiful," I said.

"It's mine," said Shayna. "I found it at the beach."

"I like it." I glanced at Elise. "But you say someone stole one?"

"More than one. Some people who have lived here for decades, generations even, have these shells as decorations around their gardens. They've been disappearing."

"Why would you steal a shell from a garden if you can find them on the beach?"

"Why do people do anything?"

I couldn't comment on that, so I sucked on my beer. "You think it's a tourist who couldn't find one?"

"If it is, they've been here a while because it's been happening for at least a month."

"How many gone?"

"Not many. One here, one there. Maybe five we know about over the month."

"Wow."

"I know," said Elise. "It's a crime wave. Makes you want to get back to Florida, huh?"

I smiled. Then I stopped. I always wanted to get back to Florida. Except in my Florida, there was no Lenny and no Danielle and no Ron. So I didn't feel in any hurry.

The sun dropped away to the west, and the water went from ripples to glassy, but the humidity didn't ease up one bit. When the bugs started coming up from the grass, Elise said it was time to retire inside and put the kids to bed, and I decided it was my cue to exit stage left. I helped take the dishes in and then thanked them for a very pleasant evening. Ken and Elise walked me to the beach.

"I want that vinaigrette recipe," she said.

"I'll write it down and drop it off. Thanks again."

"See you round," said Ken.

I felt light as I ambled back along the beach in the dark, the glow of the beach houses showing my way.

## CHAPTER FIVE

I DIDN'T SLEEP WELL. THE HUMIDITY NEVER ABATED, AND THERE WAS NO breeze until 5:00 a.m. I lay sweating on the mattress, then eventually got up and found a plastic cup in the kitchen and poured a glass of water. It didn't taste salty, so I figured it was safe enough, even if it was warm. I sat shirtless in the plastic chair outside and was there when the birds began their predawn rituals and the light slowly turned the water from gray to blue.

Rusty Reels appeared from the beach before the sun was fully up. I wasn't sure if he knew about the lack of AC and therefore assumed I'd be awake or if it was just a fisherman thing. He was still in khaki but had traded the trousers for a pair of shorts that did him no favors. He had the kind of old legs that lacked any real muscle definition, which made his knees look too big for the rest of his body.

"Lovely morning, isn't it?"

"It is that."

He was carrying two travel mugs of coffee and handed me one. I took the top off. It was black, and the steam rose like hot breath.

"No milk?"

"Is that okay? I'm lactose intolerant."

It was way too humid for hot coffee, milk or no, so I sat it on my chair arm.

"You get in okay?" he asked.

"More or less. Didn't sleep much."

"Jet lag."

"Jet lag? The flight's an hour. Did you know there's no AC or fans in this place?"

"Is that right? I'll get onto my people about that."

"Do. So what brings you out at this hour?"

"This is when the fish bite."

"And yet you're talking to me."

"Metaphorically. It's my habit to rise early. I wanted to talk to you before you got out and about today."

"About what?"

"I got a death threat."

I sat up. "How?"

"How are they going to kill me?"

"No, how did they convey this threat?"

"Oh. Someone called my production office in Atlanta and said if I blow the whistle on what's going on here, they'll kill me."

"You need to alert the local cops here in Spanish Wells, and you should inform the FBI back in Atlanta."

"I'll have my office contact the FBI, but as for the locals here, I don't put much stock in them."

"I think you'll find them more competent than you give them credit for."

"No, I'd rather have my own security."

"Okay, that makes sense. I'd still advise you to let the police know, but bringing some security is a smart move too."

"I'm not bringing security in. I've already got it." He nodded at me.

"I'm not here as security. I'm here to investigate, remember?"

"You must do security work."

"Sure, I have, but I'm not a one-man security detail. There are pros for that sort of thing, and they don't usually work alone. I'll keep my eyes open, but you really need a team."

"All right, if you're not up to it, I'll get my office to look into it."

"In the meantime, keep your head down."

"That won't be easy. I'm a celebrity. People know me. I'm a big drawcard for this event, so the promotors are going to expect me to do meet and greets, media, that sort of thing."

"If you can't stay hidden, then stay public. Keep faces you know around, not too many but more than one."

"Well, it's not a problem today. I'm about to head off to film a segment out near Egg Island."

"Egg?"

"Yep. Should be safe enough."

"I guess so. Are you staying on the island?"

"Of course. I've rented a house at the east end near the Shipyard."

"There's a shipyard here?"

"It's a restaurant and bar. Looks over the water toward the dock at Gene's Bay."

"That must be nice for you. I bet it's got air conditioning and everything."

"Of course. Listen, the main office for the tournament is down island at the school, east along Samuel Guy."

"Who's Samuel Guy?"

"It's the main street. They've got a village set up there for the sponsors. I'm going to stay away from there until I've done my shoot today and then I'll try to keep my media commitments to a minimum."

"Good. I'll go check it out."

"If you're heading that way, drop this off with the tournament promoter, will you?" He handed me an envelope. "It's my official documentation. The guy's name is Chase Hutchinson."

Reels stood and swallowed the last of his coffee, then he put his hand out to take mine. I hadn't touched it and it was still hot, so I just picked it up with my thumb and forefinger and gave it back to him. Reels said he'd see me later and then returned down to the beach and disappeared.

I sat in place for another fifteen minutes, then went and stood under the shower. It was never hot but never cold, a lukewarm flow that cleansed but barely refreshed.

I put on a blue shirt with white palm trees all over it and some khaki shorts and headed toward the beach with my boat shoes in one hand and Rusty's envelope in the other.

# CHAPTER SIX

I DIDN'T EXACTLY KNOW WHERE THE SCHOOL GROUNDS WERE, SO I wandered along the beach past the Corrigan house, beyond the house of the woman I had helped on the paddle board, and on toward the bleachers. I had assumed they weren't permanent based on my distant assessment but found them even more temporary up close. The seats were wood boards, and the frame was metal piping held together by scaffolding fasteners and what looked like fencing wire.

The bleachers had been erected on the sand overlooking the wide-open bay, the water a patchwork of light over sand and dark over turtle grass held together by a turquoise thread. Behind the bleachers was a tall wire fence which surrounded a baseball diamond, as if the stand had been built facing the wrong way.

I followed a tight sand path from the beach until I came to a sign that read Samuel Guy All Age School. The gate to the baseball field lay open, and inside a small village had been erected. It was the kind of expo I expected to see at a marathon or triathlon, a place for sponsors to show off their wares to athletes and wannabes. Stalls under canopies and marquees were set up around the perimeter of the space like a farmer's market, but no one was selling produce. What I found interesting was no one was selling fishing gear either, at least not the stuff I expected. No rods or reels or bait or lures. I saw logos for tech gadgets and fitness apps, supplements and powders, sportswear you might see at Augusta National, and social media and streaming companies. Not a bucket of worms in sight. No cable or network TV, no khaki vests with a thousand pockets.

There weren't many people milling around yet, but those who were there were a lot younger than I expected them to be. There were more hoodies and flat peaks on caps than crusty old sea dogs, and a lot more of them were women than I usually saw at the average fishing hole.

In the corner of the field was a portable office like you might find on a construction site. There was a printed sign on the door that bore the logo for the Bonefish Classic above the word Organizer. I saw an air-conditioning unit hanging off the side, and even at such an early hour I looked forward to a brief respite.

I didn't get that far.

I pegged the guy outside the office for the organizer. To continue the theme, he looked nothing like a fisherman. I could have seen him in Silicon Valley. His gear was from a different catalog than the polos and hoodies around him. His crisp blue button-up shirt and navy blazer gave him an air of authority, which was matched by the tone of his voice as he directed people around him like a school principal.

When the last of the minions had rushed off to do his bidding, I approached and offered my hand.

"Miami Jones," I said.

He looked me up and down and didn't appear to love what he saw. Palm tree–print shirts and khaki shorts tend to give off a casual vibe that no-nonsense types dismiss. As I stood there with my hand out, I noted I still hadn't put my shoes on.

"I'm with the *Miami Herald*," I said.

The guy nodded and shook my hand with a distinct lack of enthusiasm. "Chase Hutchinson."

"You're the organizer?"

"And promoter. What is it you do at the *Herald*?"

"I'm a freelancer, mainly long-form articles. I'm working on a piece about Rusty Reels. Oh, he asked me to give you this." I handed him the envelope Rusty had charged me with delivering. Hutchinson looked at it like it contained the Ebola virus and then took it with the same enthusiasm with which he shook hands. I wasn't sure if it was me, Rusty, or just the guy's general demeanor.

He tossed the envelope with a thud into the open glove compartment of the golf cart parked behind him.

"Rusty Reels, huh?" he asked.

"Yeah, that's the general angle. But I had a few questions about the tournament."

"Right. Well, let's ride and talk."

Hutchinson got into the golf cart, so I slipped in on the other side. It wasn't your average cart. The paintwork was a glittering metallic blue, which made me think of a disco ball. Hutchinson pulled a small radio off his hip.

"This is Hutch, and I'll be at the stadium seating."

He started the cart, and it came to life with a roar that reminded me of a lawn mower. I had expected it to be electric, but the smell of gasoline was unmistakable.

Hutchinson pulled out fast and zoomed around the school building and out into the street. We headed back toward the beach, and the cart came to a sudden halt just short of the sand. I had just walked the opposite trip in about a minute, so the cart felt unnecessary.

We got out and stood by the bleachers. Calling it stadium seating was a touch grandiose. I watched Hutchinson look across the water like Billy Beane used to look across the diamond at Oakland. His patch.

"You been in this fishing business for long?" I asked.

"This is my first tournament. I came over from the USFL."

"Football?" The USFL was a second-tier spring competition that managed to attract some network coverage but few crowds.

"Yeah. We're doing something different here. Really bringing the sport into the new media world."

I didn't say anything about it being a sport, but I pictured a cooler of beer cans in my mind again. "So I take it Rusty is a headliner."

"Headliner?" He made a face like he'd just put hot sauce on his tongue. "Not really."

"How many competitors have their own show?"

"All of them."

"Really? How many fishing shows can there be?"

"You're thinking like an old guy."

"I tend to do that."

"This is a new world, not your grandpa's fishing hole."

"You don't sound like a Rusty Reels fan."

"Look, I don't dislike the guy. I'm just saying he's a dinosaur. I mean, who watches cable television anymore?"

"I don't own a television."

"Exactly."

He was the first person I had met who wasn't surprised by this fact.

"Today's generation uses different screens in different ways. They don't want to be told when they can watch, and they don't want to spend half an hour watching some old dude dropping shrimp bits into the reeds. They want to see a big one landed in a thirty-second clip, and they want to watch it whenever they are good and ready."

"Would you really call bonefish a *big one*?"

"They aren't marlin or swordfish but guess what? When you land one of those, you're miles out at sea, and no one is around to see it. But with bonefish, we can have something that fishing has never had before—a grandstand finish. Think about those grandstand golf holes in Arizona, that atmosphere. By working with a fish that likes the shallows close to shore, we can have a crowd actively watching the competition."

"So the fishing is from the shore?"

"We have two classes, onboard and wading. The wading class will be in the shallows here, just offshore, and our cameras can catch their action from here. The onboard class will be on flatboats around the sound opposite Harbour Island, and we have a camera operator on each boat, plus more cameras on pontoons on the water. Even the athletes will wear GoPro cameras. So we have the best of both worlds—the atmosphere of a live crowd plus video coverage that takes the viewer right onto the water. I have an edit suite in my office that can take live feeds and edit social posts and reels within minutes."

"What do you do with all the fish?"

"What fish?"

"The ones they catch."

"This isn't 1953. We catch and release. We care about marine welfare as much as athlete welfare."

"If you let them go, then how do you know who won? I mean, how do you stop cheating?"

"There's no cheating. Can't happen. All catches are videoed live, and we use an onboard digital measuring app. Even the waders have the app. There's no way to circumvent the system."

"You seem to have it all buttoned up."

"We do. Listen, I've got things to do, so I have to keep moving. Don't forget to drop by the competition village and check out our sponsors."

I didn't say I would, but I didn't say I wouldn't. Hutchinson jumped back in his cart and zoomed away up the street. I watched him go, then I started back along the beach, looking for a grocery store.

# CHAPTER SEVEN

I WALKED ALONG THE SAND UNTIL I REACHED THE STREET WITH THE trailer full of kayaks at the end of it, then I put on my shoes and cut up past the Corrigans' house to the main street. I walked past a small graveyard with old headstones, weathered to a dull gray, the plots poorly tended, and by pastel-colored houses, a small liquor store, and a local radio station.

I had every intention of continuing along the street until I found the grocery store, but I got waylaid by a sign tacked up on a power pole. It only had two words: Drinks and Buddas.

Drinks usually get my attention, especially when I'm walking along a hot and humid street on a tropical island, but the thing that set me off to the center of the island in the middle of the morning was the misspelling of Buddha.

The island gave the impression of being quite flat, but the hill that ran down its spine was higher than I figured. By the time I reached the gravel parking lot, I was puffing and sweating like I had run a marathon. There were five more golf carts in the lot, and I walked around them and past a food truck and into the open-air bar.

There were a couple of groups at the tables dotted around the space, and two men at the opposite end of the bar. I could smell burgers and fries and felt like I had found my place. There was no view, so the owners had stuck up little signs all over the place with pithy little quotes on them like, "May you always have sand in your shoes and a dollar in your pocket," or, "Marriage is like a deck of cards. In the beginning all you need is two hearts and a diamond. By the end you wish you had a club and a spade."

I sat at the bar, and the woman behind it offered me a wink. She was older than Muriel and not nearly in as good a shape, but her smile was just as friendly. Despite the hour, I ordered a bottle of Sands and asked if she recommended breakfast or lunch, and she ordered me a burger with island fries. The beer bottle was sweating more than me. She left me to it and slid down to the end of the bar where an old guy with a Bahamian flag kerchief around his neck leaned on one elbow. I could hear him talking but didn't understand a word. His accent took his words to a higher place that I was not equipped to go. But he wasn't happy about something, because he was shaking his head as if his football team had just lost. The bartender offered him a consoling smile and then pulled a tray of condiments from beneath the bar and came back my way.

"Are you good?" she asked.

I nodded toward the old guy who was sucking on his beer. "Better than some, I'd say."

"Oh, he's all right. He just thinks he's lost a conch shell from his garden, but it's usually his wallet that he's lost."

She walked away to refill the tables with ketchup and mayo, and I wondered about what kind of place had an epidemic of missing shells. When she delivered my burger I asked her about the fishing tournament.

"More traffic," she said.

I had just walked along the main street and seen nothing and nobody, so I wasn't sure what the traffic was usually like.

"You getting some business from it?"

She looked around the bar. "Not much. Most tourists like to go to the places on the water, you know, Shipyard or Wreckers, and most of the competitors are staying on Harbour Island."

My burger so hit the spot I considered a second. Instead, I thought about my chat with Chase Hutchinson. I wondered how any cheating could happen. It sounded like he had it buttoned up, but I also knew where there was a will, and so on. I figured I would need to get a look at the system so I could see all the angles.

My better angels talked me out of the second burger, and I paid my check and left a nice fat tip. Then I continued along the main street until I reached a small shopping mall, the anchor tenant of which was a supermarket known as Food Fair. The parking lot was full of golf carts, and I started to wonder if I needed to pick one up.

The store was bigger than I expected, but the shelves bore slim pickings. A guy stocking canned meats told me they only got what the cargo ship brought in each week, and the day after the boat came in was the day everyone shopped. Sometimes, they got certain products every week, and other times they might not appear for months. People bought what was available. That was island life. I had to agree, and I didn't mind one bit.

I picked up a few essentials and bought a bag to carry my goods in, then I kept walking past more houses that were in varying need of repair. I wandered along until I reached the gate to my shack, but I found it locked with a heavy chain that might have been ripped off a supertanker.

After considering and then dismissing the idea of climbing over the high gates, I backtracked to the first street that led down to the beach, then came back up to the shack from the sand.

Everything was as I had left it despite leaving the place unlocked, except for the note sitting on the table telling me to come to the ferry terminal dock at 8:00 p.m.

# CHAPTER EIGHT

I HADN'T COME IN ON THE FERRY, SO I DIDN'T KNOW WHERE THE terminal was. At around 7:30, I walked out onto the beach and back up the road, then across the quiet end of the main street and over the hill to the south side of the island. Because of the geography of the place, all the beaches were on the north shore, and the docks and piers were on the south. A channel ran between the island on which Spanish Wells sat—I hadn't picked up on whether that was the name of the island or the township or both, and no one seemed that fussed about it—and another that looked less populated and more lush.

I walked past small piers with no corresponding buildings, home to tourist charter boats and small fishing vessels, and a good number of tiny dinghies. I reached a point where I had to move away from the water to go around a resort that called itself a yacht haven. It had a decent-sized marina and a restaurant/bar that sat out over the water. The view looked spectacular as the sunset colored the sky purple and the lights below the bar lit the water in similar shades. The road outside was lined with golf carts, and the buzz from the people in the open-air restaurant suggested a full house.

Beyond the resort, the road cut back to the piers along the channel, and as I continued, the houses on the hill gave way to stores and marine supplies and real estate offices. I passed a small open building like a garage with no door, inside which sat four men on two well-worn sofas. A sign at the rear of the dark space said it was the Lazy Pot Coffee Shop, and an industrial-sized can of Folgers and an old coffee machine suggested this was true to a point, but the men were passing around a bottle of rum, which suited the hour better than a shot of caffeine. They collectively offered me a nod, which I returned as I walked on.

I reached an area that looked like it was busy during the day—there was a wooden shelter that reminded me of an old bus stop, and a newer building that housed a phone store and a retail outlet that appeared to rent out boats and golf carts, none of which were parked outside. There was nothing to denote any kind of ferry terminal other than the vacant bus stop. I stood by the water and wondered if I should keep walking, but farther down I saw a refrigerated seafood warehouse and lobster boats at rest—a working dock, not somewhere any tourist booster would want the incoming dollars wandering around.

I was standing by the water's edge trying to guess where I should go when I heard a psst from the darkness behind me. I turned.

"Psst."

It was coming from near a small hut that sat across a lane from the rental outlet. I stepped closer and saw a sign that suggested the tiny hut was the customs office.

"Psst."

"Will you stop that?" I said. "I'm right here."

Rusty Reels stepped out of the shadows of the hut and looked around like he was the world's worst spy.

"You alone?"

"Who do you think I know here?" I said.

"I mean, were you followed?"

"Of course not. What's with the cloak-and-dagger? Has someone taken a shot at you?"

"No. But there was another boat out watching us from afar while we were shooting today."

"Did you see who was onboard?"

"Too far away, and when my producer's boat went over to tell them to scram, they took off before he could get there."

"Okay, so why did you want to meet at a dead-quiet dock?"

"This is where the government ferry comes in. It's usually a bit busier. But I want to go and get my boat from a dock down the island and bring it back and tie up outside my rental house."

"Why isn't it there now?"

"We rented the pier before I got any threats, and the house doesn't have a dock as part of the rental."

"So how will you moor there now?"

"I'll just tie up. Anyone has a problem, they can sue me."

"Fair enough. What do you want me for?"

"I have to go get the boat from where it's tied up now. It's in a quiet area, and I want to make sure I don't get jumped."

"I did mention I don't do security alone, right?"

"I know, I know. I just haven't been able to organize anything else yet, so I just want you to follow a minute or two behind me and make sure no one's following. Okay?"

I shrugged.

"Give me a minute's head start, but don't lose me in the darkness. There's not a lot of lights down at that end."

He started walking back along the docks from where I had just come, and I took a few long gulps of briny air and waited. Docks were always places where bad things happened in the movies, but this was not that kind of place. I got the sense I could have curled up and gone to sleep, and in the morning folks would have stepped around me until I had gotten my full eight hours.

But someone had threatened Rusty, and it paid to stay alert when someone had you in their crosshairs. I let Rusty get beyond the coffee shop and then set off after him at an easy pace. I looked around and up and down and saw nothing but stillness. I passed the rum guys in the Lazy Pot without a nod, keeping my focus on a guy I hadn't noticed on one of the docks. He seemed to pay Rusty no mind, and when I got past, I glanced back and saw him amble off the wood planks and heard his flip-flops slap the concrete as he headed away in the opposite direction.

I kept my eyes moving for the rest of the way but saw nothing of interest except the bar at the resort, which was calling my name despite my rule against eateries with views. I walked past the street I had used to cross the island, and a couple of streets farther on I saw Rusty glance back and then move toward the water. I followed and felt the hairs stand up on my arms. It was dark and quiet but for the distant hum of air conditioners and not at all the part of town to be in with a death threat hanging over you. It was a wise choice to move the boat to a more peopled part of the island.

Rusty was standing on the deck of a boat when I got onto the pier. It was low to the water and flat topped like a pontoon but sharp at the front like a chisel. I heard the whine as he eased the motor into the water.

"You want me to come?" I asked.

"Nah, just toss the line here. My producer will be waiting at the other end. If you could wait until I get away from the dock, then you should probably head home too. If someone has seen us together, you might be in danger."

I cast the line onto the deck, and Rusty started the engine, and it burbled away as he backed out into the channel, then he gave me a salute and motored slowly toward the east end of the island.

I stood in place until the sound of the engine was taken by the night, not because I was looking for bad guys but because I was considering walking back to the bar at the yacht haven. I headed that way, but when I reached the street that led back across the island to my accommodation, I felt an unease in my guts. I could hear the sound coming from the bar, the clinking of glassware, and the indecipherable but joyous hubbub of a crowd having a good time.

Suddenly, I didn't feel like being in such a crowd. I didn't feel like a beer. I didn't feel like a good time, mainly because I knew my good time was so far away. I turned up the hill into the thick night, gasping for breath but resolving not to waste being in paradise. Tonight, I would retreat and lick my mental wounds, but I would make tomorrow a better day.

# CHAPTER NINE

I SLEPT WITHOUT SLEEPING. THE HUMIDITY WAS OPPRESSIVE, AND without a fan or AC, I felt as if I were basting like a Thanksgiving turkey. It was still dark when I gave up and went into the kitchen to make coffee. I wondered what kind of person had a house in the tropics with no AC but a perfectly good Mr. Coffee machine.

I took my coffee out onto the back patio and sat in the plastic chair and waited for the drink to go as cold as it would get. I really didn't need the steam in my face, but I wanted the caffeine.

The night bugs were loud, and the lapping of the water against the sand was soft. I sat for a good long while thinking about what made a place paradise and whether it could be considered such a thing if there was no one there to share it with.

I was sipping my lukewarm coffee in the predawn when I sensed, more than saw, a person approach from the beach. Despite my client having a death threat hanging over him, I didn't tense as the person stepped up quietly from the sand to the grass at the end of the yard. I figured it was probably someone looking to pinch a coconut from a tree or something. But I also figured they were less aware of my presence than I was of theirs.

"Morning," I said.

The person stopped, but they didn't run. Instead, they straightened themselves and stepped forward. As they got closer I decided it was a man, but it took them reaching the patio for me to see that they were wearing some kind of uniform. It was khaki and had a touch of the Gaddafis about it. Under the military-style peaked hat, he gave the impression of being a general or some such. He mumbled something into a radio, then stepped up onto the brick patio.

"Mr. Jones," he said. His face was so dark all I could make out were his eyes.

"Who's asking?"

"Royal Bahamas Police Force."

I sat up a touch. "Police, you say?"

"I do. So are you Mr. Miami Jones?" He moved a little closer, and I noted that he was an older guy with gray at the temples.

I was about to answer when movement caught my attention and another police officer appeared from beside the house. This guy was much younger and looked less like a supreme leader and more like a cop in black trousers and a blue shirt.

"Sir?" said the older cop to me.

I turned back to him. "Yes, I'm Miami Jones. What brings you fellas out on such a jock-rottingly humid morning?"

"We can discuss that at the station."

"The station?" I started to get a moderately bad feeling that, in all honesty, should have arrived a minute earlier than it did. "Why don't we discuss it here? I was just about to catch the sunrise."

"Are you refusing to cooperate?"

"Am I under arrest?"

"Not at this time."

"Then there's nothing to refuse, is there? I'm happy to help you boys out, but I don't yet see any need for me to get out of my chair."

"If you prefer, I can arrest you for breaking and entering." He gestured toward the shack behind me.

"My vacation rental?"

"For which I am sure you can supply a rental agreement?"

My bad feeling got a little worse. I looked at the old cop in his pressed uniform and got the real feeling that he was a no-nonsense guy and wasn't interested in joining me for a coffee. My part-time nemesis and sometime friend Detective Ronzoni of the Palm Beach Police Department had taught me that it was better to pat the dog before it growled, not after it had bitten you, so I put my coffee on the ground and slowly stood. I asked if I could get my shoes and wallet, and the young cop followed me inside to collect those items along with my phone.

The young cop told the old one that the front gate was still locked, so I dropped in behind the older officer and followed him back out onto the beach. The young guy brought up the rear, the way cops do when they're escorting a suspect.

We stepped down onto the sand, and I noted how much cooler it felt right by the water, and the impression was only reinforced when we climbed back up to the side street and walked back to the main road, the humidity growing with each step. I made a note to investigate sleeping on the beach in the future, tides willing.

There was a small police car parked outside the gates to the property. I had half expected a golf cart, but this wasn't much more. I got in the back of the car with the older cop. It didn't smell like a cop car in the States—they smell of sweat and fast food and long stakeouts and a thousand backsides. This car smelled of tanning lotion.

I sat back and waited for the young cop to drive us the short distance. I had no idea what was going on, but I was going to learn more at the police station than sitting on my patio.

And they might have a fan.

I walked into the station house behind the older cop and saw Kenrick Corrigan standing at the duty desk. He offered me a sheepish look, and I raised my eyebrows.

The station was small with an open type of floorplan, a few desks and filing cabinets. The window louvers were open but offered no benefit, and a pedestal fan stood at attention in the corner, moving the air around and making the space tolerable for human habitation.

The older cop pointed to a seat in front of a tidy desk, and I took it since it was right in the wind tunnel of the fan. I figured there was no interview room, which was welcome news since interview rooms rarely have fans, and AC didn't appear to have been invented yet.

He took off his hat and hung it on a coat rack, but he left his uniform coat on. It looked too heavy for the occasion, especially coupled with a neck tie, but there wasn't a drop of sweat on his face. I wondered if he drank coolant instead of Gatorade. Ken Corrigan stayed at the duty desk with his back to me, and the younger cop left the station again. The old guy sat behind his desk and pouted at me like a disapproving grandfather.

"I am superintendent Archer Bridges," he said in a deep baritone. "So what is it that brings you to our island, Mr. Jones?"

"I'm here for the fishing tournament."

"The Bonefish Classic?"

"Yes."

"Are you a keen angler, Mr. Jones?"

"No, Superintendent, I am not."

"Strange that you would attend a tournament of no interest to you."

"I didn't say the tournament wasn't of interest. I said I'm not a keen angler."

"Those two would go hand in hand, would they not?"

"To a fan, perhaps."

"If you're not a fan, I ask my question again. What are you doing here?"

"Okay, Superintendent. I'm a private investigator from Palm Beach County, Florida. I was hired to investigate some irregularities with the tournament."

"What irregularities?"

"My client had concerns about whether the competition was above board."

"Above board?"

"You know, whether it was fair."

"Yes, I know what above board means. So who is your client?"

"That's confidential."

"You're not a lawyer, Mr. Jones. There is no client privilege in the PI business."

"It's good form, regardless. Clients don't tend to work with investigators who have flappy lips, and at this point you've given me no reason to share confidential information."

"Let me put it this way then. Do you know Mr. Rusty Reels?"

My bad feeling meter hit red. "I do."

"How do you know him?"

"Okay, you got me. He's my client. Now, do you want to tell me what this is all about?"

The younger cop, who had picked me up, came back into the station and strode over to Superintendent Bridges, whispered something to him, then stepped back behind me.

"Mr. Jones," said Bridges, "you are under arrest."

"For what?"

"For murder."

# CHAPTER TEN

I DIDN'T PROTEST, BUT I DID ASK WHO IT WAS I HAD ALLEGEDLY KILLED. Superintendent Bridges jinked his head, and the young cop led me back to the cells without a word. He took my wallet and phone and then asked for the laces in my boat shoes.

"Just take the damned shoes." I kicked them off and stepped into the cell. It was much brighter than I expected it to be. There were two cells side by side, and both had sand on the floor. Despite being bright and airy, the humidity was like the brig on a square rigger.

"You guys going to tell me who's dead?"

"The superintendent will be with you again shortly."

"Is it Rusty? Is that who it is?"

He said nothing more as he turned and walked back into the station house. I paced for a while as dawn turned into day, then I gave up on working out the nervous energy and sat on the cot and tried to fathom what was going on. I had barely spoken to a soul since arriving, and two of the souls had been cops. Rusty had been alive and well when I left him, and he was only moving the boat less than a mile in a placid channel. He was being met at the other end. It seemed impossible that something had happened to him. Except for the death threat.

I sat in the cell for a couple of hours. I wasn't given food or water, and no one offered me a phone call. On television they called it *letting the suspect sweat*, but I needed no help to do that here.

I was scribbling football plays into the sand with my big toe when I heard a commotion coming from the front office. Someone was not happy, and they were voicing it. People were often not happy in police stations.

The young cop appeared with the tournament promoter, Chase Hutchinson, in tow. Hutchinson was fuming, and he was cuffed. The young cop opened the second cell and shoved Hutchinson inside. Clearly Hutchinson had resisted his invitation to attend the station.

"Shoe laces," the cop said.

"They're slip-ons," spat Hutchinson.

"Okay then." The cop undid the cuffs and then locked the cell and left. Hutchinson rubbed his wrists like he'd been shackled for a month and cast his moody eye at me. I nodded with a fancy-meeting-you-here smile.

"What the hell did you do?"

"I spoke to you," I said. "Now I'm in jail."

"Someone's gonna pay for this," he said through gritted teeth. "This is outrageous."

He paced back and forth, and I thought about telling him to relax, but I decided he would get there on his own. He looked out of place in his pressed trousers and blue shirt. Unlike me, he clearly hadn't received a predawn visit.

Eventually he stopped pacing and sat on his cot. They were on opposite sides of our cells, so we were facing each other through the bars.

"They ask you anything?"

He said nothing. He stayed mute for the next few hours, so I left him to it.

It was somewhere near lunchtime when Ken Corrigan came back to the cells. He nodded to me but moved to Hutchinson's cell and unlocked it.

"The Minister of Tourism called from New Providence. You're free to go for now."

Hutchinson looked like the Cheshire Cat. He stood, brushed off his trousers, and offered me a wink, then he strode out of the cell. Ken Corrigan left the cell open and stepped over to mine.

"Mr. Jones," he said.

"Corporal Corrigan."

"Would you like some lunch?"

"Is there a menu?"

"I'm going to Eagle's Nest to get a sandwich. I can get you one."

"I'd appreciate it. Anything's fine."

Ken left me alone for about twenty minutes, then returned with a sandwich, chips, and a bottle of water. He left the cell door open and sat down next to me on the cot.

I took a long gulp of water and opened my sandwich. Tuna salad never looked so good. I ate a bite and then took another gulp of water.

"I don't want to get you in any trouble," I said, "but what is the superintendent's story? I mean, he's really got it in for me, and I know they all say this, but I really didn't do it."

"We don't get a lot of murders here."

"That's a tick for Spanish Wells. But he seems pretty fixed on one version of events. In my experience it's better to stay as open as possible for as long as possible or you miss things."

"Let's just say the superintendent is fighting history."

"What does that mean?"

Ken shrugged and bit his sandwich.

"Can you at least tell me who it is I'm supposed to have killed?"

"You really don't know, do you?"

"I've got my suspicions at this point, but, no, I don't know for sure."

Ken wiped his mouth with a napkin. "The superintendent will be interviewing you again as soon as he has all his ducks in a row, but I think you've figured out whose death we're investigating."

"Rusty Reels?"

Ken nodded.

"So he's really dead?"

Ken bit his sandwich and nodded again. "We believe so."

"You believe so? Is there some doubt?"

"I can't say anything more. But the super will be in soon. In the meantime, because you'll be interviewed under caution, I've been instructed to allow you a phone call."

I slowly finished my sandwich and thought about who I should call. In ordinary circumstances—if being in jail could be called ordinary—I would call Danielle. But she was on detail in Tallahassee and probably didn't even have her personal phone on her. Those protection details were funny about distractions like that. I could leave a message that might not get answered for an hour or a day. And if she got back to me, she would call my cell phone, which had been confiscated. I couldn't call Ron, since he was on Cape Cod, and I couldn't remember Lucas's number. I wondered whose number I could remember. These days I just tapped an icon on a screen, no dialing required. There were only two numbers in this world apart from my own cell I could remember by heart, and my childhood home in New Haven wasn't going to do me any good at all.

So I called the only other number I could remember. Ken lent me his phone but didn't leave the cell. He opened his chips and ate as I punched in the number. I tossed my chips to the side. I didn't need a mouthful of salt when I wasn't sure the moment my next taste of water might come.

"LCI," said the woman who answered. That's what it was to the outside world. To those of us who worked there, it was Lenny Cox Investigations, despite my having owned it for more than a decade.

"Lizzy, it's me."

"Whose number is this?"

"It's a long story."

"That involves you being in some kind of trouble."

She knew me too well. "Kind of. Look, I'm in jail."

"That's considerable trouble, even for you."

"I know."

"What did you do?"

"Nothing."

"That's what they all say."

"You're not helping."

"Is that why you called? For help?"

"I need you to call Danielle and let her know."

"Of course. She'll want to know why you're locked up though."

"I've been arrested for the murder of our client."

"Mr. Rusty Reels?"

"The same. You got my message."

"Of course. I've written up the client agreement, but I guess he's not going to sign it now."

"It doesn't look that way."

"Do you have counsel?"

"Counsel?"

"A lawyer, Miami."

"No, not yet."

"They've interviewed you without counsel?"

"They haven't really interviewed me since I got arrested. I think they're letting me sweat."

"Well get a lawyer, and don't say another thing until you do."

"Okay."

"Where are you exactly?"

"In the cells at the police station in Spanish Wells."

"Okay. I'm on it."

"Okay. Thanks, Lizzy. I'll speak to you soon."

"You hope."

She hung up, and I passed the phone back to Ken.

"Who was that?" he asked.

"My office manager and spiritual guardian."

"You a religious man?"

"No, so she's got her work cut out for her, and she knows it."

"She's right, you should retain a lawyer."

"You guys have a public defender?"

"Not here. In Nassau. But they'll only help once you're charged and appear before a magistrate."

"What about in questioning?"

"There's no requirement for the government to provide a lawyer for that, but you can find your own."

"Then what do people here do?"

"People here don't get arrested for murder."

"But if they get arrested for anything?"

"Honestly, it's mostly drunk and disorderly or petty theft, and the evidence is usually in their breath or their pocket."

"No one ever needs a lawyer?"

"Not often, but if they did, they'd probably hire one in Nassau."

"You have no lawyers on the island?"

"Yeah, we have a couple. Mr. Sands is just down the street."

"Sands? Like the beer?"

"Yes. It's a common name in the Bahamas."

"Can you call him for me?"

Ken shrugged. "If that's what you want." He stood and took our lunch debris away, then locked the cell door and walked into the front office.

# CHAPTER ELEVEN

Corporal Corrigan returned about half an hour later to say he had walked down to see this Mr. Sands and that he would visit that afternoon. I thanked Ken and then did what people do in jail.

I waited.

Time moves slow when you have no purpose and no timepiece. I did a couple of sessions of pacing, and Ken brought me a couple of refills of water before my attorney showed up.

He looked like something from a British drama. He was white and oily skinned, and his handshake was soft and wet.

"Hewitt Sands, Esquire," he said.

"Miami Jones, convict."

He didn't seem to get the joke. He wiped his gray hair across his head and mopped his brow with a kerchief that he took from the breast pocket of his gray suit. The suit looked five sizes too large, as if he had lost an enormous amount of weight or the loose fit kept him cool. The whole look reminded me of a birch forest in winter.

Sands sat heavily on the cot as if he wasn't expecting it to be so far down, then he mopped his brow again and reached inside his circus tent-sized jacket and pulled out a pen.

"It's warm in here," he said.

"I hadn't noticed."

"You should ask for a fan."

"Is that required under the Geneva Conventions?"

He frowned. "I don't think the Geneva Conventions apply in this case."

This guy was where bad comedy went to die.

"Young Ken tells me you've been arrested for murder." He wiped his face with the kerchief once more, but the fabric was waterlogged.

"That's what he tells me too. So what's the deal?"

"Did you do it?"

"Is that a relevant question for my defense?"

"I don't know."

"Well, no, I didn't do it. They haven't told me anything yet, and they haven't formally interviewed me."

"Okay. I recommend you just tell the truth then."

That was a hell of a defense strategy.

"What happens from here?"

"They will interview you, eventually."

"How eventually? How long can they hold me without charge?"

"I don't know. Until you appear before a magistrate."

"And how long until that happens?"

"Depends. The circuit magistrate might visit, but more likely you'll appear in Nassau."

"So how long will that take?"

"As long as it takes. The court will get to you in due course."

"Due course? There's a lot of *I don't know* in that story."

"It's not really my area."

"You are a lawyer?"

"Yes."

"And you don't look like you started this gig yesterday."

"I have been a member of the Bahamian and British bars for thirty-seven years."

"You do many homicide cases in that time?"

"No, none. For that, someone would usually hire a firm in Nassau."

"What kind of work do you do here?"

"Me? Conveyancing, mainly. Real estate. I have a brokerage down the street."

"Awesome. I'll hang at dawn."

"What?"

"Nothing. I'll need you to sit in on any police interviews, as a witness if nothing else."

"Sure, just not between four and five this afternoon. I've got a home showing with a couple from Savannah."

"I'm sure the police will be happy to work their investigation around your schedule."

"I'm not so sure they will."

I just shook my head.

Having filled me with confidence, Hewitt Sands, Esquire, left the building. I considered doing some pushups or jumping jacks to work out the rising sense of hopelessness, but that felt a little too prison yard workout for me, so I just sat on my cot and stewed. The irony was not lost on me that what I was doing was in fact what most prisoners did when they were not working out in the prison yard.

I sat for a couple more hours, wondering what it actually was that a prisoner serving a sentence did with their time. Working out or sitting and stewing were the only two obvious options, and after only a few hours I was ready to climb the walls. Then Ken Corrigan came back to the cells and suggested the obvious third option.

Food.

He asked if chicken and chips would be okay for dinner.

"Am I going to be here for dinner?"

"Um, yes. The superintendent is finalizing some information, so he won't be interviewing you today. I'm afraid you'll be in overnight, at least."

"At least?"

"I can't say anything more, Miami, but he's building a case."

"Against me?"

Ken shrugged. "So, chicken and chips?"

"Sure, whatever. And if I need a bathroom?"

"If you need it now, you can use the office one. But overnight, we'll bring in a can."

"That sounds awesome."

"Our cells are not designed for long-term holding. I suspect if you're in custody beyond tomorrow, they'll move you to New Providence."

Ken left and returned sometime later with a plastic bag that smelled fantastic and two bottles of water. He didn't stay to eat with me this time. I figured he would probably dine at home with his family, and I couldn't hold that against him. I would have chosen to dine with his family too.

I opened the foil tub and found roasted chicken and french fries. I used the plastic knife and fork to eat, and it reminded me of eating on a plane—confinement and plastic cutlery—only aircraft usually landed somewhere I wanted to be.

I drank the better part of the two bottles of water—the second was warm before I even got to it—but still felt little need to use the bathroom. I was perspiring every bit of moisture I could ingest.

At eight o'clock, I heard Ken doing the rounds, shutting the louvres and storm shutters. He brought a fan out to the cells and sat it just out of reach but pointing at my cot; then he turned it on. The relief was palpable. He then unlocked the cell and let me use the bathroom in the station. He refilled my two bottles from the faucet, and when I was back in the cell, he brought a can in, which was quite literally a steel bucket with a wood seat attached. He set it in the far corner, then locked the cell again.

"Elise is on early shift tomorrow, so she'll see you then."

"The station isn't staffed overnight?"

"We rarely have guests."

"All right then. I'll see you in the morning."

I heard the lock on the front door of the station bolt into place as Ken left and then there was nothing but still air. I heard a laugh in the distance, and it made me think of Alcatraz. When I had played baseball in the Bay Area, I had visited the long-closed prison, and I had listened to tape recordings of prisoners talking about their sentences there, and how the single toughest time was on nights like New Year's, when they could sit in their cells and hear the sounds of people partying across in San Francisco. More than anything this served to reinforce what they had lost.

I wasn't in Alcatraz, and I hadn't done anything wrong, so I should have been more confident than I was. But Ken had said a case was building, and I knew it was possible it could be made against the wrong guy. I would not have been the first innocent man sentenced to prison.

Which made me wonder how innocent I was. For the murder of Rusty Reels, I certainly was, but in the bigger scheme of things, who could tell? I thought about all the times I had skirted the law or even flat out broken it and never gotten caught. Now I was in lockup for something I didn't understand but knew I didn't do. As my mother used to say, the universe has a paddle for everyone's backside.

The question I couldn't yet answer was how big the paddle was going to be.

# CHAPTER TWELVE

I WAS DOZING ON THE COT WHEN I HEARD THE BOLT SLIDE ON THE FRONT door the next morning. With the benefit of a fan, I slept better in jail than I had in the shack by the beach. I sat up and rubbed my eyes and waited for a few minutes before Corporal Elise appeared.

"G'morning," she said.

"Morning."

"You sleep okay?"

"Pretty well."

"Most people don't say that."

"Most people in jail don't have a clear conscience. Plus, I didn't have a fan in my last digs."

"Hmm. I'm going to have to take that back now, I'm afraid."

"That's okay. I'm done sleeping."

Elise removed the fan and when she returned asked if I had used the can.

"No."

"You want the bathroom?"

"If you don't mind."

She let me out and pointed to the bathroom, then she went into another room. I used the facilities and then splashed water across my face, and when I came out the station was empty, so I ambled back into the cell and closed the door behind me.

When Elise reappeared, she had some toast and a cup of coffee. She pulled the cell door open with her foot and put the breakfast on the cot beside me.

I thanked her and sipped the coffee. "You often let prisoners roam around the station without supervision?"

"We're on an island in the middle of the ocean. Where you gonna go?"

"Good point."

"Plus, while I don't believe for a moment you are an innocent wallflower, I sure don't think you killed that man."

"You don't? Why?"

"You ate at my home. I watched you."

"You think one dinner, and I'm a trustworthy guy?"

"No. I think you're a smart guy. One who wouldn't have gone back to bed after he killed someone. I think you'd be long gone."

"You'd be right. That doesn't seem like the sort of thing I'd hang around after."

"But not everyone agrees with me. Watch yourself, okay?"

"I'll do that."

She closed the door but didn't lock it, and I ate my breakfast like a man who had all the time in the world.

As it turned out, I had about an hour. My attorney arrived in a different but equally outsized suit and a collection of handkerchiefs the envy of a magician.

"It's sticky in here," he said.

"Indeed."

"So do you want to go over your story?"

"I don't have a story. I just have what happened and what didn't happen."

"What would you like me to do?"

"Sit beside me and intimidate the cops with your presence."

Hewitt Sands, Esquire, stood a little taller at the idea of intimidating the police, or anyone at all, I suspected.

"Well, I'll wait in the office then," he said eventually, clearly desiring to be close to a fan.

Ten minutes later, Elise Corrigan returned and opened the cell. "The superintendent would like a word now."

"Can you ask him to wait a few minutes? I've got to clean my andirons."

She smiled. "A word to the wise. That kind of comment won't win him over."

"Damn. And that was my objective for the day, too."

I walked past Elise, and she directed me back to the same seat at the clean desk from the previous day. Superintendent Bridges sat waiting for me. Sands sat off to the side. The young officer was at a desk to my right, pretending to work.

"Mr. Jones," he said, "are we treating you well?"

"I don't have much to compare it to, but I can't complain."

"Good. I want to ask you some questions about your relationship with Mr. Rusty Reels."

"Go ahead."

"You claimed yesterday that you were working for him."

"He's my client, yes."

"And I assume you have some kind of contract signed by Mr. Reels?"

"My office made up a contract, yes, but you won't find Rusty's signature on it because we never got around to that."

"Do you normally work without a legal contract?"

"More often than my office manager would like. I'm a handshake-agreement kind of guy."

"Who has no proof that he was working for his alleged client. So how do you claim Mr. Reels came to hire you?"

"He approached me about four days ago."

"At your office?"

"No, at a cemetery."

Bridges frowned. "Explain."

"I was there visiting a friend. Rusty approached me in the parking lot."

"Any witnesses to this meeting?"

"Not that I know of."

"Convenient. Why would Mr. Reels approach you in a cemetery rather than go to your office?"

"He said he didn't want anyone to see him. He was concerned about being followed."

"Oh, I see. And he could be followed to an office but not a cemetery."

"I didn't say it was logical."

The superintendent shuffled his papers. "Would it surprise you to know that Mr. Reels was already in the Bahamas four days ago?"

"It would. How do you know?"

"We may be a small country, but we do keep a record of such things."

"On little bits of paper that don't appear to have any kind of filing system behind them. So that makes me wonder how you really know that."

"Mr. Reels appeared at a fishing equipment show at Paradise Island, Nassau. People took video. It's on the internet."

"When was this?"

"Last Saturday."

I did the math. "Five days ago? He could have flown back to the US the following day."

"He was seen by some fans out fishing the following morning. Not in the US. And we have no record of him leaving on any flights. Can you explain that?"

"No." I glanced at my attorney. His face was covered by a hand-kerchief. "But Rusty organized my flights, my transfers, and my accommodation. He gave me the ticket."

"That ticket was purchased with cash in Fort Lauderdale. No licensed taxi or transfer company at North Eleuthera Airport has any knowledge of you, and you didn't use the government ferry to cross to St. George's Cay."

"That's what this island is called? At least one thing is cleared up."

Bridges gave me his poker face. "And your so-called accommodation is a privately owned property used by a part owner in a lobster boat. He only uses it during the season, and he doesn't rent it out to anyone. He knows nothing of you."

"Well, I didn't organize any of that, so I can't speak to it."

"At this point, Mr. Jones, we have you arriving with a cash ticket, no known transport, and breaking and entering into a private residence."

"Calling it a residence is a bit much. It doesn't even have AC."

"But it is breaking and entering."

"The place was open when I got there, so there was no breaking."

"I can assure you that is the least of your worries. What were you doing at the ferry dock the night before last?"

"Rusty asked me to meet him there."

"He called you on your phone?"

"No, he left a note at the cabin."

The superintendent looked at his young officer, who shook his head. "We have no evidence of such a note. Do you have it on you?"

"You made me clean out my pockets. You know I don't."

"So, you claim you were meeting Mr. Reels but have no evidence of such. Why were you meeting him?"

"He said he got a death threat."

Bridges sat back in his chair. "From whom?"

"He didn't know."

"How did he receive it?"

"It was called in to his production office in Atlanta."

Again, Bridges looked at his young officer, and again the guy shook his head. I was beginning not to like the kid.

"His office didn't mention any such thing when we contacted them. Don't you find that strange?"

"Maybe you're not asking the right questions."

"Oh, I think I am. You claim you met him at the dock at night because he got a threat. Is that your story so far?"

"Yes." I looked again at my attorney. He was scrolling through his phone.

"And why would a man who got such a threat want to meet after dark at a quiet dock?"

"I don't think he knew it would be that quiet. It was the main ferry terminal, right? During the day I assume it's pretty busy."

"It is, but it doesn't explain why he wanted to be there at all."

"He wanted to move his fishing boat. It was moored down at the western end of the channel, and he wanted to tie up in a more public spot outside his rental house, which was at the east end. He wanted me to make sure he was safe while doing it."

"You went together down to his mooring?"

"Yes."

"Would it surprise you to know that you were seen arriving at the dock alone and then following Mr. Reels leaving it—not with him but following him several hundred meters behind—and no one saw you talking together."

I nodded. "The guys in the coffee shop. Yeah, they saw me, and that's what they saw. I arrived alone, spoke to Rusty outside the Customs Office, then he asked me to follow him so I could keep an eye out for anyone else trying to follow him."

"Really? You don't find any of that strange at all? Because I do. And so will a jury."

"You want to tell me what happened to Rusty?" I asked.

"Do you want to tell me?"

"I don't know."

"You followed him from the dock. Then?"

"We went to his boat. We untied it, and he motored away."

"He suddenly wasn't worried about this threat anymore?"

"Not alone on his boat. And he said his producer was going to meet him at the other end."

Bridges shook his head and made a note. "So why were you out near Royal Island?"

"I wasn't. I don't even know where that is."

"So how do you explain Mr. Reels's boat being found a few hours later floating off the resort at Royal Island?"

For a moment I didn't say anything. The truth was I couldn't explain it, and it seemed there was a lot more I didn't know.

"You're saying that Rusty went out to sea after leaving me?"

"I'm saying that you went out to sea with him, killed him, and then left his boat out there, hoping it would float away into the Caribbean."

"What did you find, exactly?"

"I'm not sure I'm willing to share that right now."

"Then I can only assume you're comfortable with a mistrial. I might not know much about Bahamian law, but I do know it's based on English law, and that means I have a right to a fair trial, and I also have a right to know what the evidence is against me. Isn't that right, Mr. Sands?"

Sands looked up from his phone. "What? Yes, I suppose it is." He looked at the superintendent as if he was asking permission.

"All right, Mr. Sands," said Bridges, looking at me. "We received a call the night before last on our after-hours number that a boat had been found floating off Royal Island."

"Who called it in?"

"Some workers at the island resort. They found no one on board and what they suspected were bloodstains on the deck. We then sent a boat out and confirmed this and the ownership of the boat. It belonged to Mr. Rusty Reels."

"And within a few hours, during the middle of the night, you managed to link that back to me. How?"

"We already knew where Mr. Reels was staying—this is a small island, and he is well known—so we went there and found evidence that linked to you."

"But how did you know where I was?"

"Corporal Corrigan said you had told him you were in the shack at the end of the beach. No other home down that end could be considered a shack."

"What was this evidence that linked me to Rusty?"

The superintendent opened his desk drawer and removed a pair of latex gloves, which he put on. Then he pulled out an evidence bag with what looked like a diary or notebook in it. He opened the bag, removed the book, and opened it. Then he showed me the page.

It was a handwritten notation: *Cheating? Miami Jones.*

"See," I said. "He hired me to investigate the cheating."

"That's one way to look at it."

"What's the other way?"

"He thought you were behind the cheating."

"That's crazy. I don't have anything to do with the tournament. I didn't even know it existed until a couple days ago."

Bridges pulled a folder out of his drawer and took out a photograph printed on a letter-sized page, which he slid across to me. It was an image of me and Chase Hutchinson, the tournament promoter. I was handing Hutchinson a large envelope.

"Who took that?"

"Perhaps Mr. Reels had a real investigator on the job."

"It's nothing," I said. "It was Rusty's paperwork for the competition."

"Paperwork? Then how do you explain that yesterday when I spoke with Mr. Hutchinson, he said he had left the envelope in his golf cart, and when we inspected the cart, we found said envelope, inside of which we found five thousand dollars cash."

"I didn't know what was in it."

"Convenient, again. But the only person who can verify anything you say is now dead."

"How am I supposed to have killed him?"

"We believe you hit him with something, then pushed him overboard."

"And left his boat out there?"

"Hoping it would drift away and be considered an accident."

"If I left the boat out there, how did I get back to the island?"

"We believe you had a second boat waiting out there. A witness saw you returning to Spanish Wells late last night."

"Someone says they saw me?"

"Correct."

"Who?"

"A local person. So you see, Mr. Jones, we're not as bad at this as you banked on us being. Or maybe you just got unlucky with the tides not taking the boat well out to sea before you could get away. At this point it would benefit your defense if you just told us where you dumped the body."

"Wait, what? You don't have the body?"

Bridges tugged at his cuff. "Not yet. But we know the tide patterns, so we'll find him eventually. But it would make our work easier if we knew where he went in the water, and the magistrate will look upon you positively if you provide that information."

"Unfortunately, since I didn't do anything to Rusty, I can't help you."

"That is a mistake, Mr. Jones."

"The mistake is yours, Superintendent. I don't know why Rusty was out there, but I can assure you I will find out."

"No, Mr. Jones, you won't. You will remain here until we can arrange transportation to Nassau, where you will be held until you appear before a magistrate." He turned to the young officer. "Corporal, please escort Mr. Jones back to his cell."

# CHAPTER THIRTEEN

I SAT IN THE CELL FOR A COUPLE OF HOURS WONDERING HOW IT WAS I could look so guilty of something I had no part in. It wasn't like I had woken up drunk with no memory of events—I knew for certain I had not harmed Rusty Reels—so I just needed to pull at the threads of the story until the gaps started to appear.

My biggest problem was access to information. I knew what Superintendent Bridges had told me, but I didn't know if that was the full story, and I had only gotten the details as seen through his particular lens. Everything in life can be looked at from more than one direction, and truth—unlike fact—was in the eye of the beholder. But sitting in a jail cell hampered my ability to investigate. I needed Danielle, and she was at the disposal of the governor. I had no doubt she would drop it all and come if I needed her, but I put a pin in that idea while I tried the think of a plan B.

Then plan B walked in the door.

I heard her voice coming from the duty desk inside the station.

"Excuse me, but who is in charge here?"

"That would be the superintendent, but I am sure I can help you," replied Elise Corrigan.

"No, I need to speak with the superintendent immediately."

"What is it regarding?"

"It is regarding the US citizen you are currently holding."

For a moment I heard nothing and then it was Superintendent Bridges who spoke.

"How can I help you, Madam?"

"Are you in charge?"

"I am. Superintendent Bridges."

"Superintendent Bridges, my name is Lizzy Staniforth, and I am an associate of Mr. Miami Jones. I need to see him most urgently."

"I see. Are you a member of the bar in the Bahamas, Ms. Staniforth?"

"No, Superintendent, I am not. It may be a requirement to be a member of the Bahamian bar to appear before a magistrate, but a suspect who has not been convicted of any crime has the right to visitation to facilitate their defense, and such visitation is not the sole domain of lawyers."

"Yes, well, I'm not sure about all that, but I am afraid you can't just barge in here and expect free reign. There are procedures."

"You're telling me your procedures are to deny due process? I understand. I will call the US Embassy in Nassau and let them know a US citizen is being denied said due process, and I am sure they will put me on hold while they connect me to the right person. When I'm on hold, I suppose I'll just while away the time on social media, perhaps on the pages of the Bahamas Department of Tourism, where I will have no choice but to let other Americans know they risk spending time in a jail cell without being allowed any visitors simply by coming here."

"Madam, I am sure this ugly American thing you do will be very effective at your hotel, but this is a police station."

I heard the phone ring, then a moment later, Elise say, "Superintendent, it's for you."

There was silence for a long while, then I heard the superintendent say, "Corporal, please confirm with the prisoner that he knows this person."

Corporal Elise stepped into the cell area and looked at me.

"She works for me," I said.

Elise left and then not a minute later returned with Lizzy in tow. They couldn't have looked more different if they tried. Elise was black and buttoned-up in uniform and without makeup, while Lizzy was as pale as Wonder Bread, wearing solid black everything, and had lipstick the color of a stolen Ferrari.

Elise unlocked the door and let Lizzy in, then she pulled it closed but left it unlocked.

"Call if you need anything," she said before walking back into the station proper.

"Lizzy, what are you doing here?"

"Do you want to reconsider that question?"

"I mean, I didn't expect you to come to the Bahamas."

"Danielle is protecting the president, and Ron is doing whatever it is people do in Provincetown. Leaving my boss to rot in jail didn't feel like a great career move."

"Well, thanks for coming."

"What have you gotten yourself into?"

"I really don't know, Lizzy. But how did you get in here? It didn't sound like the good superintendent was going for your story."

"No, the nasty tourist was always plan B. Plan A was having Danielle call her friends at the FBI, who called their friends at the Bahamas police in Nassau."

"Good thinking."

"Yes, but nepotism will only get us so far. The rest we'll have to do by ourselves."

"I'm not sure how much I can do from inside a cell."

"Start by telling me everything."

I recounted all I could, from Rusty Reels approaching me in the cemetery parking lot to being invited to the station house. How I got the plane ticket, who collected me at the airport and delivered me to the shack, who I had spoken to and when. I outlined the evidence that had been outlined to me. I gave her the details of my attorney, so-called, and she made notes of everything.

"Okay, I'm going to start with this lawyer, find out where things stand legally. What they can and cannot do."

"Not sure how much use he'll be."

"He'll be as useful as I need him to be." She stood, and I called for Corporal Elise.

"I'll be back," said Lizzy, and in a waft of perfume that suited the island but not the room, she was gone.

A few minutes later, Superintendent Bridges appeared at the door to the station.

"Is she really your employee?"

"Yes."

"How does she know Deputy Commissioner Mackey?"

"I have no idea, but have you ever heard the phrase like a dog at a bone?"

"Yes."

"Well, she's a tiger."

Bridges pursed his lips and walked away.

I sat and waited half an hour. Lizzy strode in as if she had been granted a backstage pass, and she let herself into the unlocked cell.

"They don't seem too worried about you running for it."

"Like I said, I met two of the local cops before things went pear-shaped, so they kind of trust me. Plus, they made the point that we're on a small island in the middle of the ocean. So what's news?"

"Your attorney is a buffoon."

"I agree."

"If he's the best the court can appoint, then I can only assume they get a lot of mistrials."

"They don't appoint defenders. He was the only option on short notice. He won't be back?"

"Oh, no. He'll be back. Sooner rather than later if he knows what's good for him. Listen, I'm off to find somewhere to stay. I'll be back shortly."

"I think you'll find the island is booked out because of this fishing tournament."

Lizzy did her approximation of a smile. "We'll see."

# CHAPTER FOURTEEN

---

IT WAS LATE IN THE AFTERNOON WHEN HEWITT SANDS, ESQUIRE, returned to the police station. I was coming out of the bathroom with Ken Corrigan when he blew in the door. He looked like an ice cream that was dribbling down the cone, except he was the color of a beet.

"Mr. Sands," said Ken. "What can we do for you, sir?"

He diverted his eyes from Superintendent Bridges. "Um, I have a briefing document."

"This isn't a courtroom, Mr. Sands," said Bridges. "Just speak."

Sands glanced at the door as if he was going to run for it, but his escape plan was scuppered when Lizzy appeared in the space. She didn't say anything, but it appeared she didn't need to. Sands gulped, opened his briefcase, and pulled out a document.

"Petition for the release of suspect—"

"I told you, Mr. Sands, this is not a courtroom. You do not petition anyone here. Just tell me what you want."

"I want you to release Mr. Jones, Superintendent."

Bridges laughed. It wasn't a gut buster, but it was more than you usually get from a dad joke.

"You want me to release a murder suspect? You have considerable standing on this island, Mr. Sands, so I wouldn't choose to erode it by making a fool of yourself."

Sands looked as sheepish as was possible to be, but he cast his eyes to his paper and read.

"As per the briefing document, the police have no evidence to hold Mr. Jones at this time. You have no evidence that Mr. Jones was ever on the boat, or anything tying Mr. Jones to the location. You have no witnesses placing Mr. Jones on the boat, and you cannot contradict Mr. Jones's version of events."

"I have blood on the boat, and we are analyzing fingerprints, Mr. Sands, and the rest is coming."

Sands read for a second. Then, he said, "You have blood on a boat where fish are caught and gutted. You have no evidence the blood in question belongs to anything but a fish."

Sands didn't look up. "Furthermore, you have no basis on which to suppose a crime has been committed at all. You have no victim and no weapon, and you have no, um, motive. In summary, all you have at this time is a man taking a walk on a warm summer evening and being arrested for it."

Sands stopped talking but didn't raise his eyes to meet the superintendent's. Just as well because Bridges looked ready to shoot laser beams.

"Mr. Sands, I am entitled to hold Mr. Jones as I see fit, and you are free to petition the magistrate as you wish when the matter reaches the court."

Sands started reading again as if what he had in front of him was more an FAQ than a court document.

"My client will petition the court if necessary but would prefer to save the police the embarrassment of exposing a prejudicial and premature arrest to the magistrate, which may subsequently harm the prosecution."

Bridges pinched his eyebrows at Sands, then he turned his gaze to me.

I shrugged. "I'm sure Deputy Commissioner Mackey won't see it as that embarrassing."

Bridges looked back to Sands. "Mr. Sands, your client is a foreign national and therefore a flight risk."

Sands glanced at Lizzy.

"Go on," she said.

Sands cleared his throat. "I would suggest that you keep his passport until your investigation is concluded."

Bridges took a deep breath. "The man has no abode. He was in his previous accommodation illegally. Without an address I cannot release him."

It was like watching two ranchers negotiating over a prized bull, or at least a nice lamb, except it was my liberty at stake.

"He has an address," said Lizzy from the doorway. "He'll be staying with Mrs. Minette Albury."

"Mrs. Albury? Does she know this?"

An old woman with a walker slid around Lizzy. "Yes, Archer, I do."

The superintendent stood to attention. "Mrs. Albury, are you sure about this? This man is accused of murder."

"Miss Lizzy has explained everything to me, and I believe Mr. Jones is a good man, and he should not suffer the same persecution as Our Lord and Savior Jesus Christ."

I watched Bridges. The Jesus comparison felt like major league hyperbole, but it was in service to my aid, so I rolled with it.

Bridges turned slowly to look at each person in the room. I don't know if he got the sense he was the only one on his side or if he was still thinking about Deputy Commissioner Mackey, whoever that was, but he let out a long, slow breath.

"I will release Mr. Jones into the care of Mrs. Albury, pending our investigation. I will be keeping Mr. Jones's passport, wallet, and phone until our investigation is concluded. I will require Mr. Jones to check in with this station each day. Corporal Elise, please write up the paperwork." Bridges turned to me. "Don't get comfortable, Mr. Jones. As soon as I have the evidence I need, I will be coming for you."

"Understood."

I stood in place until Elise had done the paperwork, then Hewitt Sands read it over as if I needed expert counsel to read a get-out-of-jail-free card. I signed the paper, and Elise gave me a smile that she made sure Bridges did not see. She handed me my shoes and then found my little suitcase that they had collected from the holiday rental that wasn't.

"Mr. Jones," said Bridges.

I turned to him as I reached the door.

"Don't leave this island."

# CHAPTER FIFTEEN

THE FACT THAT I WAS HAPPY NOT TO BE IN JAIL DIDN'T MEAN I understood where I was going. We left the police station and walked for a good twenty minutes, covering all of two hundred yards in that time. Mrs. Albury was no spring chicken, and her walking frame took its sweet time getting anywhere.

As we dawdled along Samuel Guy, Lizzy informed me she had approached the church for help, and once she heard the story, Mrs. Albury had generously offered a room.

"We're sharing a room?" I asked.

"Heavens, no. Mrs. Albury says she has room for both of us in return for a little yard work."

Her home was in a cluster of weather-beaten houses inland at the east end of the island. She had a small front yard that wasn't so much grass as weed and in need of a mow.

Mrs. Albury gave us the two-cent tour. Her home was modest but orderly. There may have been a need for a little maintenance outside, but the inside was dusted within an inch of its life. We walked through a small reception room and along a tight hall. On one side was a kitchen, and opposite was Mrs. Albury's bedroom. A second bedroom was at the back of the house, and Mrs. Albury invited Lizzy to drop her bag in there.

Mrs. Albury pushed the rear door open, and we descended wooden steps into another weedy yard with a small shed at the rear. I looked around at the surrounding houses as we slowly made our way across the yard. All the houses were similar in size and vintage, some showing signs of hurricane damage never repaired and others freshly painted and turned into vacation rentals.

I pulled the doors to the shed open. It was hot inside, and the building exhaled stale air. The shed was filled with a golf cart that looked in worse condition than my first car. There was a layer of dust covering every inch of it.

Mrs. Albury pointed out a camp cot that she said her late husband used on fishing trips, and she said I was welcome to push the cart out to make space.

"It doesn't start?"

"No, dear. I wish it did, but my husband maintained it, so it hasn't run in a decade."

I put the cart in neutral and released the parking brake, then I put my back against the rear and pushed. They're not big vehicles, but they are heavy. There was no driveway, so I pushed it onto the packed ground that suggested there had been one once upon a time.

The women beat a retreat from the sun while I set out the cot. I found a fan in the corner and tested it. The breeze it made licked the sweat from my brow, and I sat on the cot and cooled down as I surveyed my surroundings. The shed wasn't any bigger than the cell I had come from, but freedom created its own space.

Lizzy came out with a pillow and sheet. "I know it's not much, but I didn't have a lot of notice."

"It's not jail, so you've done well. Thank you."

We walked back inside, and Lizzy showed me the bathroom. I splashed my head with water to cool down, then I joined them in the kitchen.

"I think you might need this," Mrs. Albury said, placing a small glass on the Formica table. I looked at the caramel-colored liquid and took a sip. It was rum and not from the top shelf, but I drank it anyway.

Lizzy sat opposite me and opened her notebook. "The police are going to continue investigating this thing, so we need to do the same. The only way I see you getting home is for us to figure out what really happened."

"Agreed."

"Where do we start?"

"The cops said that I got to Spanish Wells without a trail—my ticket was cash, and neither my airport pickup nor the boat that took me from the dock to the island were registered taxis or shuttles. Who were they? We find them, maybe we find out if they were hired by someone with an ax to grind with Rusty."

"Or you."

"Maybe. But if someone had an ax to grind with me, wouldn't I be the one who's dead?"

Lizzy shrugged and made some more notes. "Then there's this house you were staying in. If Mr. Reels didn't arrange it, then who did?"

"The cops said the owner doesn't rent it out but only uses it during lobster season."

"Maybe someone knew it was empty."

"Sure. But who?"

"Can you explain to Mrs. Albury where the house was?"

Mrs. Albury eased herself into a seat. I described the big gates and told her it was toward the other end of the island, and although the island was less than two miles long, I didn't get the impression Mrs. Albury ventured that far very often.

"I know the house," she said. "And you're right, dear, the man who owns it had it handed down from his father. They were both lobstermen. The boy's name is Merrick."

"Boy?" I asked.

"Yes, he's, what, about forty now."

"Right. And he only comes when the fleet is operating?"

"That's right. I think he lives in Nassau now."

"And he doesn't rent it out?"

"If I recall correctly, it's not the kind of place that would be easily rented."

"Yep, that's the place. But someone opened it. There were storm shutters inside."

"No, he wouldn't leave those off. But if someone was down there, Mrs. Trout would know."

"Mrs. Trout?"

"Yes, dear. She runs the little bakery opposite Food Fair. It's just a few hundred meters from your shack. If someone was there, she would know."

"Then I suppose I should go and see Mrs. Trout."

"Tomorrow," said Lizzy. "Right now, you've got some grass to cut."

"Right. I'm on it. Where's the mower?"

"In the shed, dear," said Mrs. Albury.

I didn't recall seeing a lawn mower, but I trudged out to find it. It didn't make itself apparent as I looked around the small space, and I began to wonder if Mrs. Albury was remembering a mower she had owned a long time ago. Then my eyes fell upon something not on the floor where I had been looking, but hanging from the wall. It looked more like a torture device than a lawn-care tool. It had a long thin handle with rotating blades at the bottom. I hadn't seen a manual mower since I was a kid, and that wasn't my dad's. If my father had been forced to use anything other than his gasoline-powered mower, he would have left the grass to go wild.

I took the mower down and pulled it out to the backyard. Then I eased it around to push it. It was like moving a camel that didn't want to go anywhere. A lot of effort for very little return. I pushed harder than I had shifting the golf cart and found keeping it constantly moving was a touch easier than getting it going, so I didn't do rows and tight turns at each end, rather I went round the yard like I was making crop circles.

I was a heaping mess by the time I was done with the yard. I took a break to get my breath back, then I dragged the thing around to the front and repeated the pain. When I was finished, I dropped to the hard ground. I hadn't felt this poorly in a long time, and my mind flew back to college and the summer football training I did at the University of Miami. I had lost my lunch more than once on the practice fields in Coral Gables, running suicides until we collapsed. I hadn't worked that hard now, but I also wasn't twenty anymore.

As I sat gasping in the front yard, I noticed it was decorated around the perimeter by a ring of large conch shells half stuck into the ground, mouths open like Venus flytraps. In a couple of places there was a shell missing, giving it the look of a boxer's smile.

I pulled the mower back to the shed but didn't have the strength to hang it, so I left it in the corner, found a faucet in the backyard, and hosed myself down. I didn't get changed, and instead, I stood outside until I was as dry as the humidity would allow.

When I got back inside, Lizzy told me to wash up for dinner. There was a bowl of salad on the table, and the kitchen smelled of roasting chicken. I washed my hands in the kitchen sink for good form as Mrs. Albury poured three glasses of iced tea.

"Those are conch shells around the yard, aren't they?" I asked.

"Yes. My husband and I used to collect them. Back in the day they were a dime a dozen, as they say."

"There seemed to be a few missing," I said as we sat at the kitchen table and Lizzy served dinner.

"Did you think so? I thought I might be losing my marbles."

"I don't think there's anything wrong with your marbles, Mrs. Albury."

She patted my hand. "Thank you, dear."

"I heard a few people mention that they'd had shells go missing."

"Missing, you say? A serial shell stealer on our island?"

We ate our chicken and salad and sipped tea. I would have been partial to a beer, but that didn't appear to be on offer, and the rum looked to have been a one-shot deal. But I wasn't in a complaining mood. Imprisonment changes your perspective, and I suspected that was true whether you deserved to be there or not. It was nice to eat a home-cooked meal with other humans.

When we had cleaned up from dinner, we chatted at the table for a while, then Mrs. Albury announced she was going to bed. Lizzy said she would do the same and finish her book, so I figured I'd head out to my bunkie. As I opened the back door, Lizzy stepped into her room.

"Lizzy," I said, "thanks again."

"Anytime, boss."

"I owe you one."

"One?" she said. Then she stepped into the bedroom and closed the door.

I wandered to the shed, set the fan going, and lay on the cot. I could smell cut grass. A guy didn't smell cut grass in a cell. I took it in, and as I closed my eyes, I resolved not to take those little things for granted as much as I usually did.

# CHAPTER SIXTEEN

THE FIRST ORDER OF THE MORNING WAS TO INSPECT THE GOLF CART FOR signs of life. I figured it might be useful to get around as we investigated Rusty's death, but it would also be handy for Mrs. Albury once we were gone.

It was clear it was going to need a new battery and some gas, and probably some oil. I was no mechanic, but the good thing about old golf carts is that they were pretty basic machines. Near the school, I had noticed a marine maintenance store with a collection of golf carts in various states of repair out front, so I walked down there to ask the experts.

The guy there was in coveralls with the sleeves cut off. He was working on a golf cart that had a small truck tray on the back. I told him who I was, where I was staying, and what I wanted to do.

"You're the fella who's been spending time at Her Majesty's pleasure."

"Her Majesty?"

"In the cells."

"Yeah, right. That was me. But I didn't do it."

"Well, you're out, so . . . but, yeah, I know the cart you mean. It'll need a full checkup, but a little gas and a fresh battery should be enough to get it back here."

He filled a small can with gas from the pump out front and then procured a battery from inside his workshop, along with a small electric pump. He handed me the pump and left me to carry the can, so to speak, then he hefted the battery onto his shoulder, and we walked back to Mrs. Albury's.

"You got a name?" I asked.

"Phil," And that was all he said for the duration of the walk. We got to Mrs. Albury's, and Phil replaced the battery and put the old one on the floorboard. Then he filled the gas tank. As he worked, I plugged in the pump and went around the vehicle and filled the tires with air.

When we were done, Phil turned the key, and the cart started with a pop of black exhaust. "Gimme an hour," Phil said, and he tore away.

I went inside and found Mrs. Albury and Lizzy eating toast. Mrs. Albury offered me coffee, but it was already too warm for that, so I took a glass of iced tea.

"What's the plan?" Lizzy asked.

"Might go and talk to this lady at the bakery."

"Mrs. Trout," said Mrs. Albury.

"Right, Mrs. Trout. What time does she open?"

"When she's ready," said Mrs. Albury, without a hint of sarcasm.

I was itching to get going. Lizzy might have gotten me released, but the threat of a murder charge still hung over me, and I was keen to get it resolved—in my favor—and I knew the police were not on that track, even if the Constables Corrigan seemed to believe me incapable of such a crime.

After an hour or so I walked back up the road to see how Phil was progressing with Mrs. Albury's cart. He was standing in the forecourt wiping his hands on a rag while talking to another man. As I approached, the other guy nodded goodbye and walked away.

"How's it look?" I asked.

"For how long it's been sitting, not too bad. No major rust, and that's a killer here. She keeps it garaged, huh?"

"In the shed."

"Yeah, that's helped. I filled it up and gave it some oil, but the bearings are close to shot, so it'll get around for now, but they'll need fixing."

"You have bearings?"

"Yep."

"If I do a little running around in it I could bring it back this afternoon, if you think it will make it that far."

"Don't go out to the Sand Bar, but if you're just around town, you'll be fine."

I patted my hip pocket and felt nothing. "I've just realized I don't have my wallet."

"I can put it on a tab for Mrs. Albury."

"No, I'll cover it."

"Then pay me when I've done the bearings."

"Deal."

Phil gave me the keys, and I motored slowly back to the house. The carts on the island were mostly gas powered, so unlike the electric ninja carts found on most golf courses in the US, these made a noise like a small aircraft taking off. I pulled in beside the house and killed the engine and waited for the clicking and clacking to settle down before I got out.

Mrs. Albury and Lizzy were standing at the front door. "You're a bright spark," Mrs. Albury said. "You got her going."

"You can thank Phil more than me. There's a little more work to do, but she'll be like new by day's end."

"I don't really have anywhere to go, dear."

"It'll get you to Food Fair, if nothing else."

"True enough."

"Which reminds me. I'd like to go and chat with Mrs. Trout. Do you mind if I use your cart this morning?"

"Go ahead, dear. Maybe you can get me a couple of things while you're out."

I asked Lizzy if she would come with me to talk to Mrs. Trout, and she went to find her shoes. I sat in the cart for longer than was necessary, and when Lizzy returned, she had applied makeup heavy enough to appear on Broadway. As she sat on the bench seat of the cart, I asked her if she had any money.

"The cops kept my wallet."

"I have the company credit card."

"I think Phil would prefer cash."

"We'll find an ATM."

"Let's hope so. I wouldn't mind some carrying around money if that's okay."

"It's your business, Miami."

"It doesn't have my name on the door, and I couldn't tell you how much we have in the bank."

"We're doing just fine."

"I know that. If we weren't, you'd have let me know. But that's sort of my point. Now hold on. This thing starts with a kick."

I pressed the accelerator gently, and the cart lurched forward before settling into a throbby rhythm. Lizzy gripped the upright that held the plastic canopy. There were no doors on a cart, so falling out was a possibility on the bumpy roads around Spanish Wells.

When we reached the Food Fair, I pulled into the lot. There weren't many vehicles, but those that were there were all golf carts, apart from a solitary pickup truck that sat outside the Commonwealth Bank.

I parked, and Lizzy went into the bank. I looked around the small mall. There was a computer store, and on the opposite side from the grocery store was the Eagle's Nest restaurant, from which Ken Corrigan had gotten me food during my incarceration. Their chicken and fries was good eats, so I made a mental note of their location.

When Lizzy came out, she handed me a hundred Bahamian dollars—the currency was pegged to the greenback, so US dollars were accepted as local currency, but the banks didn't dispense them.

"I've got more if you need it," she said.

"Thanks, Mom."

She gave me her pouty face. "You find the bakery?"

"Maybe." I pointed across the road to a house with a sign hanging from a shingle that simply said Bakery.

We left the cart and crossed the road on foot. A path led to the front door, which I knocked on and then tested the knob. It was unlocked, so I stepped inside. It was indeed someone's house, but the front room had been converted into a small store. There was a table in the middle of the space with a range of fruit cakes and loaves on it and then a counter that held a few loaves of bread that looked unfamiliar. Everything was literally homemade, not the homemade that most grocery stores liked to claim.

We stood looking at the goods for a long minute until an old woman appeared from the rear of the house. She didn't look surprised to find us there, but she didn't appear in any hurry to serve us either. She put a tray of fudge on the counter and then waited silently, as if speaking would interrupt our capacity to select a bread.

"Mrs. Trout?" I asked.

"Yes, that's me."

"My name is Miami Jones."

"How can I help you?"

"We were wondering about the small house down the street, the shack with the big gates."

Mrs. Trout frowned and glanced at Lizzy. They were chalk and cheese. Mrs. Trout wore no accouterment and a plain housedress with an apron over it. In the dim light, Lizzy's black clothing disappeared, and her makeup glowed.

"Do you make everything?" Lizzy asked.

"I do."

"This nut bread looks good."

"It goes very well with a cup of tea."

"I'll take one of those, please. And this fudge. You'd like some fudge, Miami?"

I did not want fudge. I don't particularly have a sweet tooth. "Sure," I said to Lizzy's glare.

Mrs. Trout bagged up a loaf and some caramel fudge.

"We're staying with Mrs. Albury," said Lizzy.

"I see. You'll be wanting a couple of these scones then. She loves those."

Lizzy told her to bag a half dozen as I marveled at the best upsell technique outside of a McDonald's.

"You're the young man who was with the police," said Mrs. Trout.

"That's right."

"They say you killed a man."

"They are wrong. But I am going to find out who did."

She rang up our purchases. "You were asking about the house down the street?"

"Yes," I said. "Mrs. Albury said it was owned by someone called Merrick."

"That's right." She passed the paper bag to Lizzy, who handed her some cash. Lizzy unwrapped the end of the fudge, broke off a piece, and handed it to me. I hesitated. I didn't care for candy. She raised her eyebrows as if no was never an option, so I took the fudge and popped it in my mouth.

"Holy cow," I said. "That's fantastic." It was like mainlining caramel, and it dissolved in my mouth and instantly seeped into my bloodstream.

Mrs. Trout gave a nod like none of this was news to her. I looked toward Lizzy to get some more fudge, but having given me a taste, she wrapped the fudge up again and dropped it back into the paper bag. She was going to make a great drug dealer one day if life ever took a desperate turn for her.

"Have you seen anyone down at Merrick's place?" Lizzy asked.

"I did, as it happens," said Mrs. Trout. "Four or five days ago. There was a couple of men down there, which was strange."

"Strange, why?" I asked.

"Merrick comes for the lobster season. He doesn't summer here. And these boys were opening the house up."

"Did you recognize them?"

"No, they weren't local."

"How do you know?"

"It's not that big an island, young man."

"Can you describe them at all?"

"They were black, that much I can say."

"Aren't most people in the Bahamas?"

"In the Bahamas, yes. In Spanish Wells, no. But other than that, they were just a couple of men. I've never seen them before, and I haven't seen them since."

"Nothing memorable about them? Hairstyles, clothes?"

"One wore a T-shirt with a happy face on it. That's all I can recall."

"A happy face?"

"You know, the yellow, smiling thing."

"Yes, I know it."

We thanked Mrs. Trout and returned across the street. Lizzy said she wanted to grab a couple of things for Mrs. Albury, so we went into the Food Fair. We got Mrs. Albury some margarine and some potatoes, and a jar of pasta sauce. We didn't have a bag, and plastic ones were banned in the Bahamas, so the woman at the checkout offered us a small box to carry our purchases.

When we got back to Mrs. Albury's, she informed us that she was due at a lunch at the church and that we were invited. Lizzy was in, but I deferred, saying I wanted to get the cart fixed up.

I dropped Mrs. Albury and Lizzy off at the church hall and then continued onto Phil's garage. He said it would take a couple of hours, and I told him I would be fine on foot for a while, then I set out to visit my church.

# CHAPTER SEVENTEEN

MANY PEOPLE FOUND SOLITUDE AND PEACE IN A CHURCH. I FOUND MY version of that sitting in bleachers. I wandered down to the beach and along to the temporary stand. No one was sitting there because there was nothing to see but sand and water, but for me that was the whole point. I climbed about three-quarters of the way up and sat.

I had started my lifelong habit shortly after my mother died. I was in school, and my father lost his way after he lost the love of his life, and I found my mind clearest when I was sitting alone in the bleachers at my school ballpark. The size of the bleacher or the stadium was never relevant. I had found my time to think at high school fields, college ballparks, and even major league stadia. The only criterion was that I could sit high in the stand looking down on the world.

Usually, it was green grass and red clay that I saw. Now there was sand and turquoise water, and I found this view equally meditative. I took a deep breath of ocean air and let my mind wander. Sometimes, the harder I thought about something, the less clarity I got. It was like being on the mound, pitching at a big-league hitter. The harder I tried to throw, the worse I performed. Pitching wasn't really about strength but about technique, clearing your mind to let your body do the thing it had done a thousand times in practice, pushing away the pressure of the moment and relaxing into it.

It was easier said than done in a ball park during a big game, but it wasn't all that hard sitting by the sea. I let my own predicament take a back seat and thought about Rusty Reels. He was a famous guy—at least in the world of fishing—and he therefore had enemies. Every famous person did, and the level of fame could be very low in picking one up. I had collected one or two myself over the years.

I wondered what it was Rusty had discovered that warranted killing him. He had suspicions about the tournament, but in hiring me he had shown he didn't have anything concrete yet. Had that changed? Had he seen something since I had arrived? If that were the case, it was strange he hadn't mentioned anything to me at the dock. Had he seen something that night?

Something had dragged him away from his plan to return the boat to a mooring outside his rental house. I couldn't fathom why he would have ventured out to sea after leaving me. I wondered then if he had made it back to his house before going out again. I needed to talk to his producer, who was meeting him when he moved the boat.

Then there was the money that I had allegedly given Chase Hutchinson. Why would Rusty have asked me to deliver cash? Had someone switched it out before the police found it? Or was Rusty testing the waters, confirming whether Hutchinson was indeed facilitating bribes?

I stepped down from the bleachers and turned around and walked back up the street along the baseball field. I crossed home plate and headed for the promoter's office. As I opened the door to the portable cabin I was hit by the frigid air inside.

Chase Hutchinson caught my eye as I closed the door. It was fair to say he didn't look pleased to see me. He was barking orders into his radio and started shaking his head at me before he finished talking.

"I've got nothing to say to you."

"I didn't do anything," I said.

"Don't care. Go away."

"I'm being set up."

"Still don't care. I was in jail because of you." He half-whispered the last part, as if it were a source of great shame.

"No you weren't. You were in jail because whoever is setting me up is doing the same to you." I wasn't yet sure that Hutchinson wasn't the one doing the setting up, but I didn't think voicing that opinion was going to help. "You don't want to know why?"

"The Minister for Tourism wants this thing to work, so I've got someone watching my back."

"Only until they make something stick. Or decide that you need to end up dead like Rusty."

"Are you kidding?" His expression suggested he hadn't considered this possibility, and it was taking up all his processing power now that he was.

"No, I'm not. A man is dead, and a lot of things don't add up, but your tournament is at the center of it all, and that means so are you."

Hutchinson thought about it for a long moment. His eyes darted from side to side as he did, not focused on anything in particular.

"What are you going to do?" he asked.

"I'm going to find out what's going on and who's behind it. Like you, I just spent time in jail because of them, so I intend to turn the tables."

"What do you want from me?"

"The police said the envelope I gave you contained five thousand dollars."

"That's what they told me."

"But you hadn't opened it, and you left it in the glove box of your cart. Is that right?"

"Yep."

"You weren't expecting a payment from Rusty?"

"Hell no."

"Not an entrance fee?"

"No. This is an invitational event. No fee. And even if there was, we don't do cash. We only use cryptocurrency. One of our sponsors."

I had no idea what that meant. "Could someone have switched the envelope?"

"Maybe, but it looked the same and felt the same to me."

"Do you hire many locals for the event?"

"Quite a few."

"Any black guys?"

"What country do you think you're in?"

"You haven't noticed that Spanish Wells is mostly white?" I said.

"I have. But most of the people we've hired are from North Eleuthera, and over there most of the population is black."

"What are they doing?"

"Most of them were involved in the setup last week—setting up this village, the bleachers, various things."

"And where are they now?"

"Back in Eleuthera. We finished the setup days ago, so there's nothing much more to do until tomorrow when the event starts, then most will come back next week for the teardown."

"Do you recall anyone wearing a smiley face T-shirt?"

"No. But all our people are given tournament staff T-shirts to wear. It's good publicity to have lots of people with the logo on it, plus we know who our people are."

"All right. I'm going to keep digging. I might be back."

"Should I be worried?"

"Just keep your eyes open."

# CHAPTER EIGHTEEN

I MADE MY WAY BACK TO PHIL'S, WHERE THE GOLF CART WAS READY. HE told me his price, which was more than I had in cash, so I gave him the hundred I had and told him I would return with the rest shortly. He seemed okay with this plan. I wasn't sure if, like the police, he figured we were on an island with nowhere else to go, or whether folks here were just good to their word.

I drove the cart back toward Mrs. Albury's, but as I passed the church, I noticed Lizzy standing outside a large shed next door with a gaggle of parishioners. She saw me and waved me over, so I pulled a lazy U-turn.

The ladies were about to enjoy coffee and cake, and I was invited to join them. We sat at a long trestle table in what I discovered was a large multi-purpose building. There was a basketball court marked out on the floor.

Lizzy passed me a cup of hot coffee, which I had no intention of consuming, and a piece of carrot cake, which I would.

"Did you learn anything?" she asked.

"I don't know yet."

"I did."

"What did you learn?"

"I know who owns the burgundy Camry that collected you on arrival."

"You do?"

"Yes. It's a rental car, owned by a guy called Carl. He runs a small lot near the airport."

"How on earth did you discover all that?"

"You'd be surprised what the church phone tree knows. Basically everything that goes on in a small place like this."

"Huh."

"There's something else." Lizzy introduced me to four or five ladies at the table whose names I didn't catch but Lizzy rattled off as if they were lifelong friends.

"These ladies have all had conch shells go missing from their yards."

"You don't say."

They did say. All at once. The table erupted into stories of missing shells and garden surrounds that now looked sad and broken.

"Can't you just replace them? They wash up on the beach, don't they?"

"Not so much, not these days," said one woman.

"We all used to dive for them, but those days are long gone," said another.

"You dove for them?"

"Certainly. In our younger days they were more common, less fished out. Now mostly commercial fishermen take them, and they don't get to grow to the size we used to find thirty or forty years ago."

"Are they worth a lot?"

"Not that much," said Lizzy. "I did some quick research, and it seems queen conchs are worth more, maybe a hundred dollars or so, max."

"That's a fair bit for a shell."

"The big ones are rare."

"It's a puzzle," I said.

"It is," said Lizzy. "I've volunteered your services as an investigator to find out what's going on."

"You've volunteered me? What's it pay?"

"It pays room and board, coffee and cake, and access to an intelligence network the envy of the CIA."

I couldn't see a way to say no to that, or a table full of women who might have had a few miles on the clock but looked capable and determined. I figured those were necessary traits for people living on an island not connected to any kind of mainland, subject to the weather and vagaries of shipping and supply chains and a potentially intermittent source of power and refrigeration.

"I'd like to chat to this guy who owns the Camry," I said.

"I'll see what I can find out," she said. "But as I said, he's on North Eleuthera, not this island. However, there is someone we should speak with who is on this island."

"Who's that?"

"The police witness to you returning in the boat after Mr. Reels went missing."

Lizzy had a name and an address, which was to say, a description of where the witness's house was, since no one on the island seemed to pay attention to street names or numbers.

After we were done with coffee and cake, we delivered Mrs. Albury home, then Lizzy and I headed out to find the witness.

I had suggested going alone, but Lizzy thought, given my precarious position within the police investigation, that my turning up alone might be considered witness tampering or some such, so together we rode along the south side of the island, past the docks and the Lazy Pot and all the piers that lined the channel. We cruised around the yacht resort and passed the bar called Wreckers, then I slowed as Lizzy cast her eye up the hill.

She directed me up a street to a green house with a covered patio that overlooked Russell Island to the south of the channel.

I knocked on the door, and when it opened, I was surprised to see a guy about thirty-five standing before me. He was fit and strong looking and by a considerable distance the youngest person I had met so far, outside of the police force.

"Sorry to bother you," I said. "I'm Miami Jones. This is Lizzy Staniforth."

"Yeah, I've been expecting you. Come in."

As we walked into the living room, I said, "You were expecting us?"

"Yes, one of the ladies at the church called."

I raised an eyebrow at Lizzy.

"I'm Augustus Pinder," he said.

"Augustus," I replied.

"It's a family name. People call me Captain Augie."

Augustus had some serious gravitas to it, and Augie sounded like a dog's name to me, but then I went through life with Miami, so I wasn't in any position to critique.

He invited us to leave the cooled indoors and sit out on the sweltering patio, then he offered us lemonade, which I took more readily than the coffee.

"What are you the captain of?" I asked as I sipped my lemonade.

"A boat," he said, matter-of-factly.

"Right, but what kind of vessel are we talking?"

"I have a lobster vessel in the season, but this time of year I run a charter boat."

"Charter?"

"Fishing, day tours, that sort of thing."

"Bonefishing?"

"I can take people to do it, but I have a twin engine outboard designed for deeper water. To bonefish you need a flatboat, or we can wade in."

"You know about what happened to Rusty Reels?"

"I do."

"Then you also know they arrested me for it, before letting me go."

"I do."

"Part of the evidence was your testimony about seeing a boat come in late the night Rusty died."

"That's right."

"Can I ask you how you came to see a boat come into port so late?"

"Back pain."

"Back pain?"

"Yes, I get pretty regular back pain. Cost of a life spent lobstering, I suppose. I have medicine for it, but there's a limit to how much of that I'm prepared to take, so some nights the pain wakes me. Usually, I come out here and sit for a while."

"You were sitting out here that night?"

"Yep."

"And what did you see, exactly?"

"I saw a dinghy come in from the south cut."

"What's that?"

"You see that patch of green to the east there? That's Charles Island. No one lives on it. Then south of us here that's Russell Island. Russell is connected to St. George's Cay—that's what we're on now—by a bridge just down below us. There's a channel that comes in from the south between Charles and Russell that then joins the main channel along the south side of Spanish Wells."

"And that would be coming from the area where Rusty went missing?" I asked.

"Yep. You go out that way for Royal Island or Meeks Patch, and the southern parts of North Eleuthera."

"Did you see who was driving this dinghy?"

"Not more than to say it was one person at the tiller."

"Do you know the boat at all?"

"There's any number of aluminum dinghies down there. Locals use them to get across to Eleuthera or do a spot of fishing, and a few of the bigger yachts at the resort have them as tenders. But this one didn't come from the resort."

"How do you know that?"

"Because locals don't tie up at the resort."

"How do you know it was a local?"

"Because I've seen the same boat come in at a similar hour a number of times in the past few months." He sipped his lemonade.

"It wasn't the first time this same dinghy came in from that way?"

"No, not the first time."

"Did you mention that to the police?"

"I don't think so. They didn't ask."

"What would a person be doing out at an hour like that? Fishing?"

"Possible, but unlikely. You have to really know these waters and be paying fast attention not to run aground out there. There's all kinds of sand bars that you can't see at night. And you don't really catch anything after dark around here that you can't get during the day."

"What were they doing then?"

"Don't rightly know. Maybe someone coming across from North Eleuthera."

"Don't boats come from the east if they're coming from Eleuthera?"

"Mostly, if they're coming from Gene's Bay. But if you were coming up from Bluff or Current, you might come in the south cut. But I don't know anyone who would need to do it at midnight."

"It is a strange time to be out," I said. "The town seems to close up pretty early."

"It does."

You said the police didn't ask you if you had seen the boat before, but how did they know to ask you about it at all?"

"I mentioned it when I joined the search for the missing man the next morning."

"You were involved in the search?"

"Of course. Most of the charter captains were."

"And you didn't find anything?"

"Not a brass razoo."

"What do you think happened to him?"

"I assume you didn't kill him?" He gave me a quizzical grin.

I looked him in the eye. "No. He was a client. He thought something funny was going on with this fishing tournament, and it looks like he might have been right."

Captain Augie nodded. "I have no earthly idea what he was doing out there, but I don't think he was up to any good."

"Why?"

"They say he was an experienced fisherman, on TV and stuff. He had to know how treacherous the waters around here can be, especially if you're unfamiliar with the area."

"Could it have been an accident, not foul play?"

"Maybe. The waters were calm that night, but if you're motoring along and hit a sand bar, you can get tossed overboard, easy as you like. But . . ."

"But what? There was blood on the deck. Maybe he hit his head when he hit a sand bar?"

"Story doesn't add up. See, if you hit a sand bar, either your boat gets grounded and stays in one place, or it capsizes. And if by chance it works its way off the sand, it's going to keep going until it runs out of fuel if there's no one on board to pull back the throttle. Boats aren't like jet skis. They don't stop moving if you fall off."

"And that didn't happen here?"

"No, it was spotted drifting off Royal Island. The motor was going, but the throttle was in neutral, and the gas tank was three-quarters full."

"Which explains why the police think someone took him out and then fled."

"I guess so."

"But it probably wasn't the person you saw in the dinghy. Not if they've come in and out before."

"That I can't say."

I finished my lemonade and thanked Captain Augie for his time, then he walked us out. As we stepped outside, I turned back to him.

"You say you're a chartered captain?"

"Yep."

"Can I hire you to show me where Rusty's boat was found, help me get the lay of the land, or water as the case may be?"

"Sure," he said. "You busy tomorrow?"

"Nothing I can't move."

"Then meet me at the pier at the end of 8th Street in the morning."

# CHAPTER NINETEEN

THE FOLLOWING MORNING OFFERED A COUPLE OF CLOUDS TO GIVE THE
sky some depth and throw occasional shade on the azure sea
around Spanish Wells. I took the cart along the south coast until I
found 8th Street. Next to an open patch of grass, I found the pier
where Captain Augie was getting his boat ready. I noted the hull
was painted with the name *Exotic Days* and a picture of a sea turtle.

"Can I just leave the cart here?"

He shrugged. "Why not?"

I couldn't argue with that.

"Just leave the key so they can move it if they need."

I wasn't sure who *they* were, but I left the key in the ignition,
expecting never to see Mrs. Albury's cart again. I confirmed that
Captain Augie had received the credit card payment from Lizzy the
previous evening, and he said he was sure it was fine. Then he
untied the lines on the dock, and we motored out into the channel.

We eased past the town of Spanish Wells on one side and the
mangrove green of Russell Island, then we reached the south
channel where Captain Augie had seen the dinghy come in. He
turned south, then once we had passed through the cut, he sped up
and headed out to sea.

It was hard to see what he meant about treacherous waters. I was no sailor, but I could spot the alternate patches of color that designated different depths, and the whole thing looked so picture perfect that it was hard to imagine anything bad happening on such placid waters.

Captain Augie put on some tunes, and I started to get a sense of how this kind of work might appeal. After a short burst to the southwest, he eased off the throttle and started pointing out landmarks. To the west, Royal Island, to the east, another island oddly called Meek's Patch, then farther east, running all the way to our south, was North Eleuthera.

"And south of that?" I asked.

"A couple hundred kilometers and then Cuba."

We cruised to the south end of Royal Island, and Captain Augie pointed out the beach at the resort.

"Doesn't look very big," I said.

"It's not. Maybe hosts eighteen people, tops. You can hire the entire island for a week for about a hundred and forty thousand."

"Dollars?"

"Yep."

"US or Bahamian?"

"Same difference."

I let out a low whistle. "The boat was somewhere here?"

"Give or take," he said.

"How would someone see a boat at night from the resort? Nav lights?"

"Cops said the nav lights weren't on. Some boys at the resort were heading home to Bluff," he said, pointing due east.

"That's a town?"

"Yep. Small township on North Eleuthera."

"And these guys work at this resort."

"They do."

"I need to meet them."

"This is a private island."

"And I'm accused of a murder I didn't commit. That trumps trespass. You want me to swim in?"

"I can drop you at the dock and wait."

"Good man."

Captain Augie eased his boat into a small half-moon bay with a pristine beach and a dock at one end.

"This guy got a name?"

"Barnard."

I stepped up onto the dock and wandered toward the shore. Across the beach I could see a handful of villas with wide verandahs overlooking the water. As I reached the shore I noticed a second beach on the other side of the spit of land I was on. It looked like a swimming bay and was so symmetrical it appeared manmade. Ahead I saw a larger building like a clubhouse at a golf course. What I didn't see were any people. There was no one on the beaches or the lawn, or on any of the verandahs.

Then I saw someone. A man in black trousers and a white tunic approached me at a pace I would call casual hurried. He strode over to me and offered a private-island kind of smile.

"Can I help you, sir?"

"I certainly hope so. I'm following up on the disappearance of the man off your island the other night."

"The police already conducted their inquiries."

"I'm a private investigator." I handed him one of the cards Lizzy had brought over with her. I didn't add I was also the prime suspect, and I was banking on my name not having traveled this far yet.

The guy gestured for us to walk around the clubhouse, and he led me up a service track toward a block of utility buildings. We stepped into a small aluminum cabin that could have been an office or a storage shed. It turned out to be both, with a hint of lunchroom thrown in.

I was offered a seat but not a glass of water, and the guy in the tunic didn't relax at all, despite having removed me from the potential eyeline of any of the well-heeled resort guests.

"What is it you require?" he asked.

"What is your name?"

"My name?"

"Yes. Is it a secret?"

"Mr. Fleck."

I nodded. It sounded like the name of an assassin as much as a butler, so I resolved not to upset the guy.

"I'd like to speak with the men who found the boat if I might. Just a couple of minutes. I believe the first man's name is Barnard."

I had no idea if that was his first or last name, or if he was one of those Brazilian footballer types who wandered around with a single tag.

"Yes, and Courtenay. Let me see if they are available. Please wait here and do not wander the grounds."

Mr. Fleck left me alone for about a minute, then he returned. He didn't have time to go find anyone, so I assumed he had used a radio.

A couple of minutes later there was a knock on the door, and Mr. Fleck called, "Come," and an old man stepped into the cabin. He was broad and slightly hunched in a blue button-up shirt.

"Courtenay, this is Mr. Jones. He has some questions about the boat you found the other night."

"I told the police everything."

"Please, it will only take a minute," I said. I gestured for him to take a seat at the lunch table, and he glanced at Mr. Fleck, who gave him a curt nod and then stood back like a mob bodyguard.

Once he was seated he didn't look at me. I got a good look at his salt-and-pepper hair. He kept his eyes on the table and rubbed his fist with the thumb of his other hand.

"It's Courtenay, right?"

"Yes, sir."

"I'm not a sir. I work for a living. Call me Miami."

Courtenay nodded but said nothing.

"What do you do here?"

"Maintenance."

"Late at night?"

"I also do dishwashing."

"Okay. Can you tell me how you found the boat?"

"We were going home."

"You and Barnard?"

"Yes, sir."

"Where do you live?"

"The Bluff."

"Over on North Eleuthera."

"Yes, sir."

"It's Miami."

"Yes, sir."

"How long have you lived over there?"

"All my life."

"And Barnard?"

"He stays with his aunt."

"In Bluff?"

"Yes, sir."

"You were going home, and you found a boat?"

"Barnard saw it. I was driving."

"This was late at night."

"Yes, sir."

"Is it dangerous to cross those waters at night?"

"Not if you've lived here your whole life."

"Fair enough. You saw lights, or . . ."

"No. Barnard saw the hull in the moon glow."

"It didn't have lights?"

"No."

"Then what did you do?"

He shrugged. Either that or sitting down made him uncomfortable. "We took a look."

"You don't sound like you were keen on that."

"I don't put my nose in where it's not wanted."

"But a man overboard?"

"You don't know what you'll find."

"What did you find?"

"Nothing. A fishing boat and no one on board."

"And you brought it back here to the resort?"

"No."

"No? Why not?"

"Not for me to do that."

"What did you do?"

"Barnard called the resort office and told them to alert the police."

"And you waited out there?"

"Yes, sir."

"And then what happened?"

"The police came. Two young lads. They asked us what happened, and we told them, and they let us go."

"And you went home."

"Yes, sir."

"Do you know what happened to the boat?"

"No."

"Was there anything memorable about it?"

"No."

"Okay. Well, thank you, Courtenay."

"That's it?"

"Is there more?"

"No."

"Then that's it."

"Thank you, sir."

The old man stood and replaced the chair and then left without a word.

The other guy must have been waiting outside because a young man stepped in directly. He wore a beautifully tended Afro-style hairdo and a linen shirt. He had a welcoming smile that made me feel that he would be better suited to greeting paying guests than Mr. Fleck.

"Barnard, this is Mr. Jones," said Mr. Fleck. "He has some questions about the boat you found the other night."

Barnard sat at the round table and lost his smile.

"Hi, Barnard, I'm Miami."

"Hi."

"What do you do here, Barnard?"

"I'm the entertainment coordinator."

"I imagine that covers a lot of territory."

"It does. We offer a curated experience to our guests. Sometimes we perform local dance routines, sometimes I'm hosting casino nights, and another night I might be playing flamenco guitar."

"You play flamenco guitar?"

"I do."

"Impressive."

"Thank you."

"Is this relevant?" said Mr. Fleck.

"Social niceties are always relevant, Mr. Fleck. Now, Barnard, can you tell me how you came to find the boat?" I asked.

"Yes, I had finished working after a late dinner. Our guest family had spent the day—"

Mr. Fleck cleared his throat.

"Well, they had a late dinner, and I had played background guitar for their drinks and desserts. Courtenay and I were returning home from the service dock—"

"To Bluff?"

"Yes."

"Where you're staying with your aunt."

"How do you know that?"

"Courtenay. He said he'd lived there all his life. And you?"

"No, I'm from Exuma. But I hope to perform in Nassau soon, and maybe even the US one day."

"But for now, you're here."

"Yes, this is my second season at the resort. And I stay with my aunt when I'm here."

"Nice to have family for things like that. So you were heading home from the dock . . ."

"Yes, and we can't have been more than five hundred meters out before we saw it."

"You both saw it?"

"Well, I guess I must have seen it first."

"Courtenay wanted to take a look?"

Mr. Fleck coughed. "I don't believe that's what he said."

If I had this guy at my police interview instead of my useless attorney, I might not have ended up in jail. "Thanks, Mr. Fleck. I'll ask the questions. Barnard?"

"Well, no, I guess it was me who wanted to check."

"Courtenay wasn't eager?"

"He's the sort of person who likes to keep to themselves."

"Okay. But you took a look."

"Yes."

"Courtenay said there were no lights on the boat."

"No, none. The engine was on, but it was in neutral. It was just floating there."

"Was there anything on the deck?"

"What do you mean?"

"Any fishing gear or anything?"

"Not that I saw, but Courtenay wouldn't let me get on board."

"He wouldn't let you?"

"He said we should keep off. Because of the blood."

"What blood?"

"On the boat. There was something splattered across one side of the deck."

"You said there was nothing on the deck."

"Sorry, I thought you meant like rods and stuff. But there was something on the white deck."

"And you thought it was blood."

"That's what Courtenay thought. He said we shouldn't touch it because it was people like us that ended up getting blamed."

"People like you?"

"Black men."

"I see. Blamed for what?"

"For whatever happened out there."

I nodded. Courtenay wasn't wrong in his thesis. But instead, I had gotten the blame.

"You called the office here?"

"Yes. The night reception. Courtenay doesn't have a mobile phone."

"And then what did you do?"

"We waited out there. Courtenay said we couldn't tow it in because we would have to touch it."

"And guys like you get the blame."

"Are we getting the blame?"

"No, Barnard, you're not. Courtenay was smart to not touch anything. The police don't think you guys were involved."

"And what about you?"

"I think the police are right about that."

"Good. Did they find anyone?"

"No, they didn't." I looked at Mr. Fleck, and he raised an eyebrow to ask if I was done.

"Just one more thing," I said. "After the police let you go, where did you go?"

"Home."

"To Bluff."

"Yes."

"Not Spanish Wells."

He frowned. "Why would we go to Spanish Wells?"

"No reason. Barnard, thanks for your time."

We stood, and Mr. Fleck opened the door, and Barnard left. Mr. Fleck held the door open, suggesting it was time for me to go through it too. So I did. He led me away from the resort buildings deeper into the island.

"My boat is the other way," I said.

"No, Mr. Jones."

We walked for a good five minutes along a sandy path through the scrub. Away from the shore there was no breeze, and it was hot. It felt desolate, and for a moment I considered whether Mr. Fleck was indeed an assassin. Then we stepped to the shore of a long, wide bay in the center of the island. It was a massive natural harbor, shallow but well sheltered.

Mr. Fleck walked me to a secluded dock where a couple of dinghies were tied up, along with Captain Augie's boat.

"Good day, Mr. Jones," said Mr. Fleck, and he strode away.

"Friendly guy," I said as I stepped onboard.

"If you've paid to be here."

"You ever come here?"

"Not since the resort was opened. There was a place built here in the '30s that went to ruin, and we used to come and play here as kids, but it's a bit rich for my blood now."

Captain Augie turned east, and we motored to another island where some tourists were on the beach feeding animals.

"Are they pigs?" I asked.

"They are."

"How?"

"Well, there's a cay in Exuma where they had pigs, and the story was they swam away from a shipwreck and colonized. People started to go see them and then people started feeding them. The pigs were smart, and they realized if they swam out to the boats as they came in, they could get the best food, so swimming with pigs became a thing."

"Good for the pigs, I suppose. Free food."

"Only people started tossing the food onto the beach, so the pigs ate up tons of sand with it, and the sand apparently killed them."

"That's a bummer. So how does that explain the pigs here?"

"Oh, that's for the tourists. These were brought in by a guy who sells food on the island. Hot dogs, mainly. Only he supplies skewers to hold it, so the pigs don't eat the sand."

"That's generous."

"You don't kill the golden goose. Isn't that what they say?"

We drifted out from the beach, and Captain Augie pointed toward North Eleuthera again. "You can see the township of Bluff from here."

I saw a handful of small buildings but hardly a metropolis.

"What's that down to the south?"

"That's Current. You've heard of Current Cut?"

"No."

"It's a tight gap between North Eleuthera and the island of Current. The tides shoot in through the gap, and you can snorkel or scuba through at speed. I'm told it's fun if you don't get washed out to sea. Anyway, down at the point there is the township of Current."

"If the dinghy you saw in the south channel was coming from out here, what's the best bet for where it was coming from if not dumping Rusty Reels in the water?"

"Well, there's nothing at Egg Island or Meeks Patch, and we can assume it wasn't coming from Royal Island if it wasn't seen by the same guys who found the dead guy's boat. So that leaves North Eleuthera. But if they were coming from Gene's Bay—that's where you get the ferry across—they'd come the same way as the ferry, through the east end of the channel. So that leaves Current or Bluff. But honestly, there's not much there. No bars or restaurants, not much even in the way of shops."

We motored around Meeks Patch and headed north, and he showed me a map with all the islands on it. I noted that the bay beside us was called Old Jean's Bay.

"I thought it was Gene with a G."

"That's how I always learned, but some maps have the J. Take your pick."

We headed around the east end of Spanish Wells and past the terminal for the ferry I didn't catch. As we moved around the shallows, Captain Augie pointed out the areas where bonefishing could be done from shore.

"What do you think of the tournament?"

"It's a point of contention, I suppose. Folks here like things simple and quiet, and the lobster industry has provided that for a long time. But times are changing. Lobster isn't as plentiful as it was. Call it climate change if you want, but the waters aren't what they were. Tourism becomes more important, it brings in money, but it means the island has to change, and like I say, many people don't like that."

"What about you?"

"Lobstering is hard work. Out on the ocean for up to six weeks at a time, it's good money but tough on a family."

"How long you been doing it?"

"Since I was fourteen."

My jaw dropped. "Fourteen! You started fishing on those big boats at fourteen?"

"Not fishing, lobstering, and, yeah, I bought a share in my boat at fourteen."

"You bought into a boat at fourteen?"

"Yep. It's a co-op thing."

"Who gives a fourteen-year-old money to buy into a lobster boat?"

"I saved a bit, and the bank gave me the rest."

"A bank lent a fourteen-year-old money to buy into a boat?"

"It's a good bet for the bank. At least it was back then. Maybe it's not so easy now. Like I say, times have changed."

"They always do. But what about school?"

"Once I got into a boat, I was done. I know what you're thinking, but let me ask you: How much of what you learned at school after fourteen do you actually use? You already knew how to read and write and spell. How to add up numbers and multiply the catch by the price to figure your take. What was all that stuff after?"

I thought on that. If I were a physicist or an engineer or a doctor, I would probably use what I learned later in school pretty often. But I wasn't any of those things, and neither were most people. After fourteen I learned a few handy pitching variations but not much else that I used these days. Not until I met Lenny, and he taught me everything else I needed.

"Who buys the catch?"

"You heard of Red Lobster?"

"The crustacean or the restaurant?"

"Restaurant."

"I know it." I preferred local joints myself, but I saw them around. South Florida wasn't the land of chain restaurants for no reason.

"Well, we provide most of their lobster."

"I imagine that's a lot. You say the money's good. So why do this charter thing?"

"Like I say, lobstering is hard on the body and on the family you leave behind. I'd like to see my kids growing up, you know? I'm hoping I can transition to chartering full-time so I can be home every night. I know my back will thank me. So will my marriage."

"The Bonefish Classic will help you with building this business?"

"Some. To be honest, they're saying the event is in Spanish Wells, but most of the competitors and fans are staying on Harbour Island."

"Did we pass that?"

"No. It's around the point, on the other side of North Eleuthera. I can take you over for a look and a bite of lunch if you like."

"Let's do it."

# CHAPTER TWENTY

As Captain Augie edged along the coast of North Eleuthera, I thought about Rusty Reels. There were a lot of threads leading nowhere, and the number of threads was growing by the hour—I felt like I was about to end up with a patchwork blanket. What had Rusty seen? Why had he gone out to sea when he had told me he was simply moving the boat? Did someone lead him out there, or had he been ambushed when he reached the other end of the channel? Why was he staying in Spanish Wells if all the other fishermen were staying on Harbour Island? And was *fishermen* the right word when at least a few of them were women?

I posed that last question to Captain Augie. He looked thoroughly confused.

"What else do you call them?"

"Well, I don't know, but how can it be fisher*men* if many of them are women?"

Captain Augie shook his head. "Is this what you big-city guys spend your time thinking about?"

"You have no idea. It's a minefield out there."

"Well, I've never had a woman who just caught a big wahoo get miffed by being called a top gun fisherman."

"But how many didn't even come fishing because they believed it wasn't for them, simply because of the word that was used?"

Captain Augie frowned, and I got the sense I was about to explode his mind, so I smiled and looked out at the water. The channel we were in was turquoise but either side was a touch more foreboding. We were only ten yards from a ragged cliff face that was a good twenty yards high, and farther out the water looked brown, and it cut in different directions for no apparent reason.

"Devil's Backbone," said Captain Augie. "It's a reef off the north coast here that runs in a long line like, you know—"

"A backbone?"

"Something like that. Makes this area really treacherous, especially in a keelboat. Shallows farther out make you want to stick to shore, but then the devil gets you. Been plenty of shipwrecks here over the years. Lots of speedboats run aground, too, if you're not paying attention."

I was paying attention now. "I'll let you focus."

"We'll be all right, don't worry. Conditions are good, and tide is high, and I've been through here a thousand times. We stick to the channel, we're golden."

I became mesmerized by the bottom of the channel that dropped into a deeper blue the farther we went, and before long, there was no bottom to see and no way to discern where this channel was.

But Captain Augie changed the tunes to a little Brad Paisley and stood with one hand on the wheel like it was just another day at the office. It wasn't the world's worst office.

After about ten minutes we eased around the top of Eleuthera and edged away from the reef, and the water opened up into a massive sound.

"Any reefs in here?" I asked.

"No, but plenty of sand bars."

He headed south until he moved in closer toward a series of beaches that lined the island. There were no buildings, no vacation homes, no resorts. We motored past a couple of wooden pontoons that had been erected in the water.

"These shallows are great for bonefishing," he said. "They've put up these pontoons to film the competition."

"These are camera positions?"

"That's what I'm told. They put them in a few months ahead so the fish would get used to them. The locals use them for swimming platforms."

"Why not?"

"Exactly. Now you see those islands there to the east. They protect this sound and keep it shallow because on the other side of those barrier islands is the Atlantic. And that island in the middle there, that's Harbour Island."

Captain Augie eased the boat around and then opened her up, and we sped across the sound toward Harbour Island. As we got closer I could see that this island was different. There were lots of buildings—both on the water and inland, and the size of the buildings and the marinas out front suggested money.

We cruised past piers and marinas and resorts with swimming pools and waterfront restaurants until we reached somewhere that Captain Augie knew. He pulled the boat into a dock, and a guy in a well-pressed polo shirt and shorts came running up like a valet.

"Aug," he said.

"Simon. How's things?"

The guy called Simon said something in return, and I heard the words, but I didn't understand them.

"Okay if we tie up for a bit? I'm just showing my client around the resort."

"No sweat, Aug. If we need the spot for a big boat, I'll move her down the pier there."

"Thanks, brother."

Simon ran off to do his thing, and Captain Augie and I clambered up onto the dock. I could see at least twenty boats tied up, many of them fishing-type vessels like Augie's, but there were a couple of large ocean-going cruisers shaped like torpedoes.

Captain Augie led me off the dock and then up through lush gardens and around huts with small patios and water views. We came upon a collection of golf carts all emblazoned with the resort logo. The guy there was dressed just like the one on the dock and felt even more like a valet.

The two men shook hands and chatted quietly, and the valet dude shot me a look, then pointed Captain Augie to a golf cart. Augie gestured for me to get in, and we zipped off through the gates and out of the resort.

"Friend of yours?" I asked.

"Yep. So the main town here is called Dunmore Town, but most people just call the whole place Harbour Island."

We sped by houses and B&Bs that gave the area the feel of a slightly run-down Martha's Vineyard. Before long, we were on the main drag, and we hit a traffic jam. The town held more golf carts than PGA National, and the narrow street was filled with the acrid buzz of small gas engines. We labored past restaurants and more accommodations than seemed necessary for such a small place. There were the usual stores selling useless items that no sane person would buy back in their hometown but felt the desperate need to own when on vacation. Lots of candles and macramé and art, and even one place specializing in conch shells that American tourists weren't permitted to import into the US.

As I looked around at the tourists in their golf carts looking for another place to blow their dough, I noted how different it was from Spanish Wells. If this was Martha's Vineyard, then Spanish Wells was Block Island—not definitely different or that far apart but running at a different speed and for a different crowd.

Dunmore Town looked like an okay place to drop anchor for a while, but I couldn't get past the fact that it was trying to be something it wasn't. It was a touch run down and rough around the edges while trying to put on pretensions to attract the wealthy clientele out of their waterfront resorts and spread the economic joy into the small community.

We did a short lap of what passed for downtown; then Captain Augie headed back toward the resort. On the way he cut left, and we headed down a street that ended at the sand. We walked out onto the beach.

"The famous pink sand beach of Harbour Island," he said, as if reading from the tourist brochure.

It was a fine-looking beach, wide and long, and littered with beach chairs and umbrellas and areas cordoned off for the private use of whoever was paying. It might have been the light, but I couldn't see pink in the sand. It was just another gorgeous beach in a country that had more than its share of them.

We headed back to the resort and deposited the cart with the valet, then we walked through the gardens to a restaurant that overlooked the marina below. There was an indoor dining room with overhead fans that were beckoning me, but we sat outside under an awning with a view of both the pool and the sound.

Captain Augie was the height of professionalism and ordered a cola, but I was paying and sweating buckets, so I ordered a beer and a water. As we perused menus I looked around and decided that we were not in Spanish Wells anymore. Apart from being in a resort— of which Spanish Wells had the solitary yacht haven—the clientele was of a different vintage. On the other island the only people I had met who were younger than me were police. Here, I was the oldest guy by a long shot. The pool, the patio, and the dining room were all filled with young people. When the server returned with my beer, I ordered a burger and wondered when it was that I had started using the term *young people*.

As we sipped our drinks, I heard Captain Augie chuckle under his breath. I asked him what was up.

"You're more Spanish Wells than Harbour Island," he said.

"You think?"

"You don't strike me as a resort kind of guy."

"I'm about to pay ten bucks for a five-buck beer because of the view."

"My point exactly."

As I drank my beer, I noticed a group of twenty-somethings lunching nearby. They were getting into margaritas and cocktails and having the time of their lives, but they didn't look like everyone else. There were no swimsuits among them, no board shorts or bikinis. Their clothes didn't match, but they were all well cut, as if they weren't any kind of team but they all shopped in the same fancy upscale mall. Collared shirts and crisp polos and tailored shorts.

Except for the logos. Where I would expect to see little crocodiles or swooshes or polo guys, I saw Mercedes-Benz stars and wordmarks for high-end consulting companies and merchant banks. They looked like a group of Formula One drivers who had lost their way.

But they weren't F1 drivers. Their conversation told me they were competitors in the fishing tournament. A new generation, no truckers' caps or camo. Despite seeming to talk with one another, they were all interacting with their phones, tapping screens and taking selfies and shots of their drinks and food as if it all didn't exist until it got online.

I put my beer down and wandered over and asked the obvious question. "You're with the Bonefish Classic?" I said.

I got a lot of looks up and down, taking in my board shorts and palm tree–print shirt and my distinct lack of sponsor logos. I didn't get any nods in the affirmative or any audible speech at all, but I moved onward.

"You guys hear about Rusty Reels?" I asked.

A few of them looked at each other, and one kid in a white shirt that said Accenture on the breast said, "The old guy?"

Then another in a Mercedes polo pointed at me and sat up out of his slouch. "You're the dude that killed him."

This got the attention of all of them, but the kid who had said it turned his phone toward me. "I gotta stream this."

"I think that would be a bad idea, junior."

The kid grinned. "What? You gonna punch me out, old man?"

I wasn't a fan of the *old man* comment, but I also wasn't twenty anymore, so I let it go.

"No, I don't hit little boys. But more to the point, the last guy who filmed me without permission is still paying me eight thousand dollars a month by order of the court. This is a private conversation, junior, so if you want to commit a federal crime, you go right ahead."

The kid didn't look sure about my story, which was fair enough given it was complete baloney, but he put his phone down anyway.

"What do you guys know about Rusty?"

"He's a dinosaur, man," said Accenture. "My granddad used to watch him." The guy laughed. "I mean, he's on cable. You feel me? Cable!"

I said, "I heard his cable channel had over half a million subscribers."

The kid with the phone chuckled. "Dude, last week I did a video that got twenty-seven million views over all socials."

"And he was cruel," said a young blonde woman in a Credit Suisse shirt. "All those old guys were. Did you know he'd catch a fish and then he'd kiss it, and after that he'd kill it? Can you imagine killing something you've kissed?"

I tried not to think about some dates I went on in college. "What do you do, apart from the kissing thing? You just video the fish as they swim by?"

"No, I catch and release." She said it like she owned a Prius.

"So you drag a defenseless animal around by a barb in its mouth, pull it out of the water so it begins suffocating and then you rip the hook out of its flesh with no pain relief, and toss it back in the ocean to swim away like it just spent the day at the spa?"

The woman said nothing. Another woman under an Oracle ball cap asked, "Are you with PETA?"

"No."

"Vegan?"

"Hell no."

"So you're a hypocrite."

"In my experience everyone is. But in this case I'm not the hypocrite. See, if I catch a fish, I eat it. That's the way the animal kingdom works. But if I don't plan on eating it, I don't bother trying to hook it. That's how humanity works."

The woman acting as a billboard for Oracle frowned at me but didn't appear angry. It was like she was thinking, forming her rebuttal but coming up empty. Score one, Jones.

"Look, I'm not here to defend the marine life," I said. "You wanna fish, then fish. I don't care." Then I had a thought.

"Say, what do you call yourself?" I asked the Oracle woman.

"Molly," she said. "You?"

"Miami Jones. But that's not what I meant. The term I grew up with was fisherman, but obviously you're not a man, and fisherwoman seems like such a mouthful."

"You're looking for the gender-neutral term?"

"If there is one."

"Good for you. The generic term you want is fisher. But given we use rods and reels, we're competitive anglers. It's already gender neutral."

"Angler. Good to know. So how about Rusty Reels? He had suspicions that your little tournament wasn't exactly kosher."

"What's it got to do with hot dogs?" asked the video kid.

"Hot dogs? That's what you get from kosher?"

"Well, that's what you call ballpark hot dogs, don't you? Kosher?"

"Yes, you're right on. But you also might want to jump onto your little phone there and search up the term Judaism."

The kid looked straight to his phone, and I gave him a point for being a learner. I turned my attention to the rest of the group.

"So, you hear anything about cheating?"

"Can't be done," said a guy with a foreign accent that suggested he was from Seattle, or maybe Canada. "The competition is done by length, and the fish are measured with an onboard app before release. It's all done on camera, too, one camera guy on every boat, and we all wear GoPros on our caps. Plus, there are cameras on the platforms and on the beach. Cameras see everything."

I wasn't so sure about cameras seeing everything. In my experience cameras saw exactly what the director wanted them to see.

"He's just looking for a scapegoat," said the blond woman. "To get him off murder charges."

"I was set up, but unfortunately for whoever did it, I'm an investigator, so we cracked that nut and I'm off," I said. "That's why I'm standing here with you fine folks instead of sitting in the lockup. But Rusty was my client, so now I'm looking for his murderer. Thanks for your time."

I returned to Captain Augie and found that our lunch had arrived. As we ate our burgers, the group of anglers finished their lunch and started leaving. Molly pushed her chair in and walked toward me. She stopped by me, and I wiped my mouth with my napkin.

"You said you were looking for Rusty's murderer."

"That's right."

"But you're not."

"I'm not?"

"What's the motive for killing Rusty?"

"Someone's running a crooked tournament."

"Except they're not. Lex was right; it can't be done. It would take too many moving parts to keep it quiet. So your motive is wrong, which means you don't have a motive at all, and you're going to go around in circles."

"So who am I looking for?"

"You're looking for whoever set you up. Might be one and the same, but it changes the motive a whole lot."

I had to admit it was some solid logic. I was basing everything on Rusty being right about someone fixing the tournament, and I had taken the motive directly from that. I had suspected my involvement to be random, a convenient fall guy. But what if Molly was right?

"You come up with that finishing your lunch there?" I asked.

"Yep. I'm not just a pretty face, and I'm not just an angler."

"What else are you?"

"I'm a doctoral candidate in marine science at the University of Alabama."

"Roll Tide."

"I'm not much for football."

"Well, thanks for your input. I appreciate it."

She nodded and walked off, and I watched her the whole way with my mind abuzz.

# CHAPTER TWENTY-ONE

CAPTAIN AUGIE DELIVERED US BACK TO HIS PIER, AND DESPITE HIS protests, I helped him wash the boat down. I wasn't quite ready to return to Mrs. Albury's. My mind was in a different gear on the water—slower, clearer—and I wanted to keep that feeling as long as possible.

When we were done I asked if I could buy him a beer, and he said a quick one might be okay. We wandered back to the yacht resort and walked into the open-air bar/restaurant. The whole thing sat on pilings over the water and looked across to the vegetation of Russell Island. There were a good many motor cruisers parked at the marina, but no actual sailing yachts.

"You don't want go sailing around here," said Augie as we tapped our glasses. "Too many hazards for a keelboat."

We sat and watched the gulls fighting over discarded french fries on the deck below us. A light breeze kept the humidity at bay. The girl behind the bar seemed to know Augie and pretty much everyone else, and she spoke to them in a form of English that utterly defied me.

"Do you have any idea where Rusty Reels was staying on the island?" I asked.

"He wasn't on Harbour Island?"

"No, he said he was staying in Spanish Wells. Somewhere down the east end."

"Sorry, don't know."

"No sweat. I'll tap my intelligence network."

Captain Augie raised an eyebrow.

"The church ladies," I said.

"How did you get with them?"

"I'm naturally charming."

"I can't speak to that, but those ladies aren't easily wowed by outsiders."

"My office manager speaks their language."

"Well, if he was staying on the island, they'll know."

After a day on the water, I downed the first beer quicker than prudence suggested and asked Augie if he wanted another.

"No thanks. Best be getting home."

"Of course."

"You want to come over for dinner?"

I thanked him for his generous offer but declined, suggesting I had people to see. The truth was I had people to find first.

We separated at the grass patch near his boat. He wandered off up the hill, and I returned to Mrs. Albury's golf cart, which sat exactly where I had left it.

I drove back along the dock side of the island and cut in to Mrs. Albury's house. When I came in through the backdoor, Mrs. Albury was sitting at the kitchen table, and Lizzy was standing by the sink on the phone. She pointed at me.

"Actually, he's just walked in," she said, then she held the phone out to me. "Danielle."

I nodded and took the phone.

"How's the governor?"

"He's fine, but the British PM is a bit of a flirt. I've been trying to call you. I started to worry they'd put you back in the lockup."

"No such luck. But they did keep my phone, pending the conclusion of their investigation."

"Makes sense. You okay?"

"Well fed and watered, so no complaints."

"Lizzy gave me a rundown. I had some friends do a little checking."

"I like those kinds of friends. Find anything?"

"It turns out Rusty Reels used his Global Entry card to expedite security at ATL and fly to Nassau three days before he met with you. Homeland Security has no record of him returning to the US since."

"So how did he meet me at a cemetery in Lake Worth if he wasn't in the United States?"

"Good question. Have you actually confirmed the person you met was Rusty Reels?"

"No." I asked Lizzy if she could find some images of Rusty Reels on the internet. She searched and found his website. Rusty was right there. Then she found one for the Bonefish Classic and brought up the competitor list. Again, Rusty Reels in somewhat less than living color.

"Lizzy just found him online, and, yes, that's the guy I met in Lake Worth and the same guy I dealt with here."

"He was somehow in both the Bahamas and the US at the same time. Curious."

"You got that right."

"Well, I'll see what else I can find. Tell Lizzy to call with anything—I probably won't be able to answer, but leave a message. I hope you're okay."

"I'm in pretty good hands," I said.

"All right. Stay in touch. I love you."

"I love you. And remind the British PM that you're armed."

"I think that's part of the attraction."

"I know it is."

I hung up and handed Lizzy her phone. "There's no record of Rusty returning to the US when he met me," I said.

"Could the records be incomplete?" Lizzy asked.

"Anything's possible, but it's unlikely. You don't have to check out of the country, but you do have to check in."

"What did you learn out on the water?"

"More questions, not so many answers."

"As per usual."

"Indeed. I think I need to talk to this guy who owns the Camry."

"Carl."

"Right. Did you find anything?"

"Yes, I did. Carl has a small lot near the airport, but it's like a side hustle. Or maybe they're all side hustles. Either way, he works at the airport as a baggage handler."

I recalled collecting my own damned bag off the trailer and decided Carl had time for a side hustle.

"He pulls the bags off the plane and then puts people in one of his cars."

"That's about the sum of it. There aren't that many flights each day, so I guess he's able to juggle it."

"So next question is, how do I get back to the airport? I know the cops can't legally keep me on this island."

"They took your passport."

"I can't leave the country, but this country is made up of islands. There's nothing says I can't move between them. But having said that, I don't need to bring unwanted attention to myself or our investigation, so I'd like to avoid the government ferry, and I don't know who brought me over in the boat the first time."

"Captain Augustus?"

"Augie could get me to North Eleuthera, but then I have to get to the airport."

"You should talk to young Jimmy," said Mrs. Albury from the kitchen table. "He could get you there."

"Young Jimmy?"

"Yes. He's a very entrepreneurial young man. I could call his mother for you."

"Okay, thanks, Mrs. Albury."

"You're welcome, dear. Now, about my shipment."

"Shipment?"

"An item of cargo came in off the ferry for Mrs. Albury," said

Lizzy. "We thought since you had the cart, you could collect it for her."

I eyed them both. An item of cargo could be a packet of seeds or an elephant, and I feared the latter. But when they both stared me down in return, I knew I was beat. I nodded and left.

I puttered back down to the dock and parked right by the water's edge. It wasn't as quiet as it had been when I had met Rusty there a few nights previous, but any ferry passengers were definitely long gone. The Lazy Pot was empty, the coffee crowd having left and the rum crowd yet to arrive. There were a couple of people near the boat rental place, and I saw a woman walk into a cell phone store.

I got out of the cart with an eerie feeling of déjà vu. I had no idea if there was a cargo office or if I was supposed to meet a guy, but I had been set up at this exact location once before. I didn't know if that had happened on purpose or by chance, but the coincidences were mounting up in an unnatural number.

There was a box about the size of a bar fridge sitting all alone on the dock. I walked toward it, looking around the whole time like the boogie man might jump from the shadows.

"You look like you're about to commit a crime," said a voice coming down the nearby street. I looked up to see Corporal Ken Corrigan smiling at me.

"I'm not, but it hasn't stopped me from being accused."

"Well, in this case it's not suspicious, unless you're planning on stealing Mrs. Albury's new air conditioner."

I pointed at the box. "This?"

He nodded.

"It's an AC?"

He nodded again.

"Hallelujah."

I stepped over to the box and found Mrs. Albury's name on top, with an address that simply read Spanish Wells, Bahamas.

"Can I ask you something on a semi-professional level?" I asked.

"I guess."

"What's the story with your superintendent?"

"How do you mean?"

"I mean back in the cell you said he was fighting against history."

Ken nodded.

"What's his deal? I know he's got a job to do, but he feels like the only one who's laser focused on me, and there are a lot of smart people in your station house."

"Flattery? Really?"

"I was talking about your wife, smart guy."

Ken laughed. "Come sit." He led me across the dock to the dark interior of the Lazy Pot coffee house. Since the place was empty, we each sat in a salty sofa.

"This is all before my time," said Ken.

"Before you were a cop?"

"Before I was born. Back in the early 1980s. You know much about that time?"

"Not here."

"Well, anywhere, really. You remember the war on drugs?"

"Reagan. 'Just Say No,' and all that."

"Right. Well, that came about because of the exponential growth of the Medellin Cartel in Colombia. See, until the late seventies drugs were mainly moved from South America to the US by mules, people carrying the drugs on commercial flights, either ingested or in their luggage. But a guy in the cartel called Carlos Lehder came up with the idea of flying in entire planes full of drugs. Instead of moving fifty thousand dollars worth, he could move ten million. That changed the game."

"Okay."

"But there was a problem. They had to rely on older, smaller aircraft that they had bought or stolen. Aircraft that could land on small strips in the middle of nowhere in the US. But those kinds of aircraft don't have the capacity to fly non-stop from Colombia to the US, so he needed a waypoint."

"Spanish Wells?"

"No. Certainly drugs came through North Eleuthera Airport and maybe even through Spanish Wells by boat or in the mail."

"In the mail?"

"These guys tried everything. But Lehder found an island called Norman's Cay, about a hundred kilometers due south of here. It was a private island used by a bunch of rich people, and it had its own airstrip. So Lehder bought up some of the island, then used coercion and violence to encourage the other residents to leave. Soon he had a major compound where he could fly in great quantities of cocaine and then fly or ship them out to the States."

"And no one knew?"

"Everyone knew. He was bribing people at the highest levels. Lehder even claimed to have paid five million dollars in bribes to the prime minister."

"Which I'm sure he denied."

"Of course. But the point is, these guys ran for years with complete freedom, and the Bahamas was awash with drug money. We still haven't recovered from it. It changed our lives, our culture. A sense of lawlessness and corruption is a difficult ship to turn around."

"So how does this affect me? I'm not involved with drugs."

"No, but in the early eighties the US decided that enough was enough. Drugs were on every street corner, at least that's what we heard. They cracked down on the cartels, and they forced the Bahamian government to do something about it."

"Okay."

"Around this time there was a murder. A boat was found floating south of Royal Island—between here and Norman's Cay. There was blood on the deck and a dead man on board, and evidence that another had gone overboard."

"Were they shipping drugs?"

"We don't know. None were found, as far as I heard. The men turned out to be US citizens, and it was claimed that they were just cruising through the Caribbean and were mistaken for a drug boat.

See, some local elements took to intercepting smaller boats to steal drugs and more."

"Like pirates?"

"Exactly like pirates. But they had to be careful because if they hit a shipment belonging to the cartel, then they could end up in a world of hurt."

"That's one way to put it."

"Right. The history is this. Superintendent Bridges' father was the officer in charge of the investigation."

"And the penny drops. A little."

"Well, the rumor was that some locals had hit the boat, but the superintendent's father found no such evidence. He wasn't able to prove who did it, and the US government didn't seem to push it, so the whole matter was swept under the carpet. But the rumors persisted that the super's dad had taken bribes to make the thing go away."

"Is that true?"

"It was never proven. By the time royal commissions were established to get into it all, the appetite to drag up old news was low, so a few people were prosecuted, but not many considering how much money was handed out."

"Allegedly."

"Right. So the superintendent has carried that cross for his entire career. He's been as straight as an arrow because he had to be. He had to be above reproach. But I think finding another bloodied boat out on the water might have brought back some bad memories. I don't know. Like I say, this was all before my time, and the super is not that forthcoming."

"Understandable. The sins of the father and all that."

"Right."

We sat in the darkness of the coffee shop for a while, then Ken slapped his thighs and stood. I followed, and we wandered back out to Mrs. Albury's air conditioner.

"You want some help?" Ken asked, and we each took an end and hefted the box up onto the rear-facing backseat of the golf cart. The cushions sagged, and I knew as soon as I touched the accelerator, the box was going to fall off. Ken clearly saw the same problem because he told me to hold on to it and then he walked into the boat rental place. When he returned, he carried a thin nylon rope.

"Can you bring this back when you're done?" he asked.

"Sure."

He wrapped the rope around the box, and we then each tied off an end onto the handholds on the side of the cart.

"You learn anything out on the water today?" he asked as he worked.

"You know about that?"

"It's a small island."

"So I've discovered. But today all I learned is that Devil's Backbone is a place to avoid, and that Spanish Wells is more my scene than Harbour Island."

"Despite all that's happened?"

"Despite that. I can't blame Spanish Wells or your superintendent for a series of coincidences."

"Is that what you think they are?"

I thought about what Molly the angler had said to me. "No. Coincidences happen, for sure. But not that many and not that close together."

"If you didn't do it, then someone made it look like you did."

"That's where my thoughts are headed, yes."

"Why you?"

"That's the jackpot question. There are only two options: I was a convenient scapegoat, or someone targeted me specifically."

"It's a lot of work to target you. They'd have to really hate you."

"Believe it or not there are people in this world who don't care for me. But it's a lot of work either way, so I'm trying not to get too far ahead of myself."

We finished tying off the AC unit, and I wiped the sweat from my brow. Ken had none.

"Hey, do you know where Rusty was staying?"

"I do. Why?"

"I'm hoping to have a word with his producer."

"That guy. I don't think you'll find him that helpful, but they're staying at a house called My Blue Heaven. Keep going down the road here until you can see Gene's Bay, and you'll find it."

"Thanks. So what does your superintendent think about coincidences?"

"He's pretty happy to follow the chain of evidence because, like you, he doesn't believe there can be that many that quickly. But he likes door number one, where you did it. He's waiting for prints and blood samples from the boat."

"He's going to be disappointed. The closest I got to the boat was tossing a line from the dock, and I doubt he'll get a print from a rope. But I did speak to a Mrs. Trout at the bakery. She says she saw guys opening up the shack I stayed in, but they weren't locals."

"I know," said Ken. "But two black guys in T-shirts isn't the most useful description to track them down."

"Roger that."

"Well, you enjoy installing this baby," he said, slapping the box.

It hadn't occurred that I was more than the delivery boy, and I kicked myself for not realizing it. Too many thoughts in too little a brain.

# CHAPTER TWENTY-TWO

KEN WAVED AND WALKED AWAY, AND I ZOOMED ALONG THE DOCK AND back to Mrs. Albury's. I didn't bother playing dumb and pretend there was any kind of handyman coming, so I just asked her where the AC was going. She directed me to a window in the reception room, the only room I had yet to see her occupy. Maybe it was too hot to use, but to me it felt just like the rest of the house.

Mrs. Albury came and sat in her armchair to supervise my work. I took the unit from the box and read the instructions, then I started putting together the frame.

"Mrs. Albury, you must have been around here in the eighties," I said.

"And well before, young man."

"Do you remember much about Norman's Cay?"

She turned her eyes from me. "We don't talk about that."

"I understand. It wasn't a good time. Not here, not back in the States."

"No."

"But it seems like the past is intruding into my present."

She frowned but said nothing.

"You know what I'm being investigated for."

"Yes, dear."

"I heard about another boat found out there on the water back then."

Mrs. Albury stared into middle distance as I watched the memories come flooding back.

"I'm sure one has nothing to do with the other."

"I don't know. I heard the current superintendent might be linked to it."

"Archer is a good man, so never mind that."

"And his father?"

"It was a difficult time."

"What do you remember?"

I saw the old person's dilemma, trapped between dredging up bad history and the compulsion to talk about the old days.

"I don't abide drugs," she said.

"Me either."

"But it was very bad then."

"Because of Norman Cay?"

"The cartel. Yes, they flew in and out like they owned the place, which they probably did. Everyone took their money. The police and the politicians and even the businesses that maintained their airplanes and sent them groceries."

"Do you remember what happened with the boat they found?"

She frowned deeper as if she was trying hard to crease her brow. "Bad things. Two men were killed."

"Yes. And the superintendent's father investigated it."

"Yes. That's right."

I waited for her to continue, and for a moment I thought she wasn't going to, but then she let out a sigh.

"The Americans were annoyed with all those drugs on their streets, so they wanted it fixed, but our politicians had become rich by turning a blind eye, so they were slow to change things. It took years. When those American boys were killed on their boat, we thought they might send the army in. Some people came."

"Some people?"

"A few Americans. Police or FBI or Army. I don't know. Maybe from the embassy. I can't recall. But the rumor was that Sergeant Bridges had found evidence that it was local boys who had killed the Americans."

"What evidence?"

"I don't know, dear. There was just too much money, too much temptation. There were many people in the outer islands without work, and the young ones especially were tempted to get into the drugs. It was no good."

"What happened to these local boys?"

"Nothing. No such evidence was ever produced, and the official word was that it had been the cartel who had attacked the boat, maybe assuming it was some kind of competition. And the cartel didn't care if they were blamed for things because it made them look powerful."

"And what happened about the boat, the case?"

"Nothing. Officials went with the cartel story, and the Americans must have accepted that because they left. The boat, I don't know, dear. I assumed it went back to the US."

I opened the window, balanced the AC unit in the space, and closed the window to hold it in place. Then I attached the screens on either side of the unit to plug the gaps.

"And what about the superintendent's dad?"

"He gave the official version of events and never spoke of it again."

"What do you think happened?"

"When it turned out the men were Americans, I think the cartel paid him to make it go away. And to be honest, dear, there really wasn't much of an appetite for more here on the island. We've always been independent. Apart from the world. The mood was one of if it doesn't touch our island, it isn't our concern. And it largely didn't. Most of the violence was in New Providence. People accepted that the sergeant did what he had to do."

"You all just accepted that he was crooked?"

"Sometimes justice is best served outside the statutes."

I wondered who said that. Maybe Al Capone. But I didn't take it up with her. It was a long time ago, and I was wearing my welcome thin already.

I plugged in the air conditioning unit and asked Mrs. Albury if she wanted to see the big unveiling, as if I had just performed a complete home renovation. She offered me a tired smile, and Lizzy stood at the doorway, and I hit the button to turn the unit on.

Immediately, moist hot air came out of it, and it made the room even less bearable. I waited in silence for a minute as the warm air continued to spew out, hoping that I wouldn't have to carry a defective unit back to the dock. Then just as I was about to give up, the coolant did its thing, and ice-cold air starting billowing from the window.

I looked up at Mrs. Albury and Lizzy like I had just won second prize at the school science fair.

"Very nice, dear," said Mrs. Albury, and she stood and shuffled back toward the hot kitchen.

"Should I leave it on for a while?" I asked.

"Oh, no, turn it off. Do you know how much electricity costs in the Bahamas?"

# CHAPTER TWENTY-THREE

I DECIDED IF THE AC WAS GOING TO REMAIN OFF, THEN BEING OUTSIDE was as good as being inside, so I collected the rope Ken had borrowed and told Lizzy and Mrs. Albury I was going for a little walk. My walk took me straight back to the road around the south of the island. It was actually one ring road around the island. On its north run it was called Samuel Guy or Main Street, but I had no idea what it was called on the south side where it ran along the docks.

I walked along the quiet road and enjoyed the whisper of breeze coming across from Eleuthera. The last light of the day turned the water silver, and the gathering clouds suggested a likely storm but gave no indication of where that downpour might happen.

My Blue Heaven sat overlooking the east end of the channel that led out toward Gene's Bay. The house itself was a wooden thing that might have once actually been blue but was now a battered gray. I stepped up onto a porch with rocking chairs on it and saw a warm glow through the windows.

After tapping on the storm door, I stepped back and waited. It took longer than was necessary for the door to open, and when it did I found a small man with a half-baked mustache looking at me.

"Can I help you?" he said.

"Yes, I'm looking for Rusty Reels's producer."

"No comment."

He made to close the door, and I wedged my foot in to block. That's why I never wear flip-flops out. You can't block a door with a bare foot.

"I'm not a reporter."

"I don't care."

"Rusty hired me."

"You want money? Get in line."

"No, I want to know what happened to him."

"Wait, you're the guy the police arrested. How did you get out?"

"I didn't do it, so the evidence doesn't stack up."

"Says you."

"No, says the police. That's why I'm standing at your door and not in lockup."

"Well, you can't be here. This is witness tampering."

"What are you a witness to?"

"Nothing. Go away."

"I'm not going to do that, pal. I spent time in a cell for something I didn't do, and that annoys me. So I'm going to find out who did this to Rusty, and I'm going to find out why they involved me in it, and since I can't leave this country until I do those things, I have no intention of taking no for an answer. I just need five minutes."

The guy looked down at my foot, then released the door. "Five minutes."

I shook my head. He was like one of those little dogs that barked way too much, all aggressive and hostile, trying to make up for its size instead of using it to its advantage.

The house was nicer inside. It had been renovated with white-washed shiplap and New England-style furniture. There was a large dining table covered in hard cases which lay open, exposing the camera gear inside. A couple of other suitcases sat near the door.

"Leaving?" I asked.

"Yes. Tomorrow. Nothing to shoot now."

"I guess not."

I heard the stairs on the other side of the room creak, and

another guy appeared. He was taller and muscled in the arms but carried a bulbous belly, as if he worked out but drank too much. He nodded at me.

"I'm Miami Jones," I said to the little guy.

"Mark Heston," he said. "This is Tim Paige."

"Nice to meet you boys. Sorry about Rusty."

Heston shrugged. "What are you going to do?"

"Do you have any idea what Rusty was doing out there on his boat that night?"

"Nope."

"Did he normally go out like that?"

"Nope. Never."

"He told me that he was moving the boat to a safer mooring near this place. Do you know anything about that?"

"Nope."

"Before he moved it he said you were going to meet him at this end."

"Me?"

"That's what he said. He said the mooring down the other end was too secluded."

"I don't know about secluded, but it was too far away. I told him when we arrived, but he wanted to moor it there."

"But you weren't going to meet him that night?"

"No. Maybe he said that to make you feel better or get away from you."

"Did you know anything about Rusty's suspicion that the Bone-fish Classic was being rigged?"

"Rigged? How would you do that?"

"Did you know about the death threat?"

"What death threat?"

"Rusty said someone called his office, but the cops said his office knew nothing about it. Was Rusty acting funny?"

"There wasn't a funny bone in Rusty's body," said Tim Paige.

"What did you do for him?"

"I'm the camera operator."

"You were in his boat earlier that day?"

"No. I film from another boat mostly. We get shots of Rusty out by himself or with a guide."

"Did you use a guide here?"

"No. We haven't used a guide since MoBay."

"So did you see anyone watching you the day he went missing?"

"Nothing unusual."

"There were always people hanging around, trying to see Rusty," said Heston. "Part of our job was to keep those boats out of shot."

"Did you keep anyone away that day?"

"Probably."

"But no one you'd recall."

"Nope."

"How long have you worked for Rusty?"

"Eleven years."

"Long time. What will you do now?"

"Get another job, probably. Unless we just find someone to fill in for the show. Listen, I gotta pack. Show yourself out, will you?"

Heston walked away and headed up the stairs. Paige went to the fridge and pulled out a beer. He offered me one, but I declined.

"What's his problem?" I asked.

"He just lost his meal ticket."

"There aren't more producer jobs out there?"

"Sure there are, but there are also better producers."

"He's no good at his job?"

"Depends on what you think his job is." Paige stepped closer to me so he could talk more softly. "Usually, it's just the talent that's a pain in the you-know-what. But in this case both talent and producer were pretty unpleasant."

"So why did they work together?"

"I'm not sure anyone else would do the job. I know old Heston there has applied for other jobs, but he'd never get a sniff."

"What about you? You work with Rusty long?"

"Two years."

"Will you find other work?"

"I already have other work. Rusty doesn't film all the time, and if I don't have a camera on my shoulder, I don't get paid."

"What do you think happened to Rusty?"

"I think someone got sick of him."

"Who? A coworker, a fan?"

"Someone more likely to bust your kneecaps."

"You saying he had debts? Like gambling or something?"

"I never saw him gamble, unless you call putting your future into cable TV gambling."

"How did he put his future into cable TV?"

"He doubled down, didn't he? I mean, do you have cable?"

"I don't own a television."

"So, no. And neither do I. I stream stuff because I can watch it anywhere for a few bucks, not hundreds. Cable's suffering. Mostly it's old people, isn't it? They know how it works, so they keep it."

"Can't blame them for that."

"I don't. They can have it how they want it, and it's okay with me. But most folks are jumping off, so the subscribers are down, and the ad revenue is down, and Rusty's whole empire was built on visibility from cable."

"So why didn't he just get into streaming too?"

"One, because his core audience is still on cable and two, he's like them—he didn't think the new tech was anything more than a fad. But people thought that about cable once."

"No one had it when I was a kid. We watched the networks."

"Right. Same reason we're staying in this place." He gestured around the room.

"Why are you staying here? Everyone else seems to be on Harbour Island."

"That's my point. These are Rusty's people, and this place is his speed."

"Mine too," I said.

"You do you."

"What about the kneecaps?"

"I'm just saying there's talk about Rusty propping up his empire with financing from certain non-bank lenders if you know what I mean."

"Like the mob?"

"I don't know, but that's the movies. Are those guys real? But something like it."

"How do you know this?"

"I read the industry sheets, and I hear things. Sometimes people forget there's a human attached to the camera next to them."

"I bet. So did you ever see any strange characters around?"

"This is competitive fishing. They're all strange characters. But someone who'd kill the guy? No, I didn't get that vibe. But you know, you asked about Rusty acting funny? There was one thing."

"What's that?"

"I think he might have been feeling the pressure."

"How so?"

"Drugs."

"You think he was doing drugs? Like what, opioids?"

"Something harder, maybe. I was looking for him the other day, and I wandered into his room and found needles, syringes, that sort of thing."

"You see any drugs?"

"No, but he wasn't a diabetic or nothing, so you do the math."

I gave Paige my business card and asked him to call if he thought of anything else. Then I moved to the door, and he followed me.

"One last thing. When did you arrive in the Bahamas?"

"About a week ago."

"Straight to Eleuthera?"

"No, into Nassau. I got a ferry over here."

"You did? You weren't with Rusty?"

"No, Mark and I came over to scout locations, shoot B-roll, that sort of thing. Rusty stayed in Nassau. I think he had some sponsor event schmoozing to do."

"Okay, thanks. Have a safe flight home."

"You too."

He closed the door, and I stepped down from the light of the porch to the darkness of the street and walked back to the rental store, which was closed. I left the rope on the doorstep, then headed back toward Mrs. Albury's garden shed, thinking that there was a lot of muddy water to clear before I might have a safe flight home.

# CHAPTER TWENTY-FOUR

I wasn't sure who I was looking for the next morning, and I didn't know exactly where to find them, but I had just enough information to get by.

I zipped along the dock road in Mrs. Albury's golf cart, around the yacht haven, and slowed as I reached the docks that lined the banks below Captain Augie's house. I drove past his boat, tied up and alone, and then three or four piers farther on, I noticed a kid slouched against a piling, scrolling on a phone.

When I pulled in close, I expected him to look up, but he didn't. Whatever was on screen must have been thoroughly engrossing. I got out of the cart and walked up to him and still got nothing.

"Jimmy?" I asked.

The kid still didn't look up. "Yeah." Eventually he stood—with his face still on the screen—and as he unfurled himself, I realized that unlike my summation of the twenty-somethings at Harbour Island as kids, this kid truly fit the bill. He was long and lean, like a balloon that was yet to be blown up. There wasn't an ounce of fat on him and not that much muscle, either, and his skin was both tanned and freckled.

When he tore his face from the phone, he looked at me. He couldn't have been more than fifteen, and suddenly I wasn't sure I had the right Jimmy. Putting my life in the hands of a screen-obsessed teenager didn't feel like the prudent thing to do.

"Mrs. Albury spoke to your mom," I said.

"Yeah."

"I'm Miami Jones." I didn't get any response, so I followed up with, "And you're young Jimmy?"

"Just Jimmy."

I got the attitude. He was a teen, so the hormones were running riot inside, and if my end of the arrangement had been any guide, he'd been ordered by his mother to shuttle some guy around who probably looked old enough to have been the first thing out of the swamp after the demise of the dinosaurs. But Mrs. Albury had called him entrepreneurial, so I went with that reflex.

"What's your daily rate?" I asked.

"Huh?" he replied, his eyes suddenly bright.

"Your daily rate. I pay my way."

Just as quickly the brightness faded. "My mom says I have to do it for free. She says God is watching."

"What do you say?"

"I say gas isn't cheap."

"Got that right. Let's just say that the charitable thing to do is for me to cover gas money. And since I pay cash, your mother doesn't need to know what happens between us."

A smile crept across his face, and he pocketed the phone and led me over to his boat. Although calling it a boat was being generous. It was what Lucas called a tinny, a small aluminum dinghy that was essentially a rowboat with a five-horsepower motor on the back.

We climbed down into it, and he had me sit in the middle facing back. He pulled the cord on the motor and fired it up, then we puttered out along the channel.

"You want to go to the airport, right?" he asked over the whine of the motor.

"That's right. I'm looking for a guy who works there."

"You didn't want to take the ferry?"

"No. I'd rather fewer people knew what I was doing."

He offered me a conspiratorial smile like he was up for keeping things on the QT. "We'll go through Current, if that's cool with you."

"You have the con."

We motored through the south cut and out into the Caribbean Sea, right through where Captain Augie had taken me the day before. We passed Meek's Patch and then Jimmy pointed the hull toward the southernmost of the two townships I had seen from a distance the day before.

"You grow up in Spanish Wells?"

"Yeah."

"You go to the school there?"

"Yeah."

"How old are you?"

"Fourteen."

"You going to work on a lobster boat?"

Jimmy scrunched his face. "Fishing's not really my thing."

"Me either. What do you want to do when you finish school?"

"I don't know. Something online."

"Like one of those kids who unwraps toys or does stupid stunts?"

"Nah. More like an online business or something."

"Fair enough."

We passed the town of Bluff off to our left, and I asked him why we wouldn't go via there.

"It's closer, all right, but I got wheels in Current, and the airport's inland either way."

I wasn't sure what kind of wheels a fourteen-year-old had, but I figured I was about to find out.

We headed to a point on the island where I saw a gap between North Eleuthera and the next island.

"You heard of Current Cut?" Jimmy asked.

"Heard of it, yes."

He nodded at the water in front of us. The placid turquoise

Caribbean Sea turned abruptly darker and lumpier, small white caps crashing into each other for no apparent reason.

"Hold on," said Jimmy with what I was sure was a glint in his eye.

We hit the narrow cut between the islands and suddenly took off, doubling our speed, the little boat tossed from crest to crest like a kayak on a river rapid. The aluminum hull slapped hard against the water, and for a moment I worried about its integrity. Then Jimmy angled the tiller, and the boat bounced toward a beach that had appeared on the far side of the point.

Then just as quickly as it started, it was done. We plopped down into more turquoise water as the deeper blue cut a path onward out to sea. Jimmy eased the little boat around beside a new-looking dock but didn't tie up there. Instead, he hit the gas with a twist of the wrist, and the dinghy shot up onto the sandy beach.

Jimmy levered the prop out of the water and then we pulled the boat up the beach above the high tide line. I followed Jimmy off the beach and up a street that led away from the dock.

Calling Current a small town was to redefine how tiny a town could be. In the Bahamas they referred to it as a *township*, as if that somehow declared it to be smaller than a plain old town. There were a handful of streets, and each held a handful of buildings, all randomly placed.

Jimmy led me three blocks inland. There wasn't a fourth block. The street perpendicular to us ran along the tree line, which marked the end of civilization. We stopped at a sun-bleached building with a dead lawn beside it. There was a small sign attached to the wall suggesting the building was a post office. We found an old motorcycle leaning on the rear wall of the building. It was a dirt bike with a keyless ignition and no chain securing it.

"You come here often?" I asked.

"Couple times a week, I s'pose."

"Don't take this the wrong way, but why?" I looked around and saw no stores or restaurants and no people.

"I use the post office," he said. "And I have a few friends here, so we, you know, hang out."

"Who owns the bike?"

"That's mine."

"You leave it unlocked?"

"Sure. No one here's going to take it. This isn't America. Besides, sometimes my friends use it."

"But gas is expensive."

"It is. And they can't afford it, so I don't mind who uses it, and they don't use much anyway. Where they gonna go?"

It was a common refrain.

Jimmy got on the bike and kick-started it. The bike's engine had a deeper growl than the boat. He nodded for me to get on the back, and at that moment I questioned my life choices. I was going without a helmet on the back of a dirt bike driven by a fourteen-year-old. But I didn't see a better option—or a worse one, for that matter—so I climbed on behind Jimmy. I thought about wrapping my arms around him, but he was so thin it was like holding onto a silk scarf, so I grabbed hold of the seat as Jimmy pulled out onto the road.

For a kid, he didn't ride like a lunatic, and the absence of traffic made the ride safer than walking in Miami. We rode along the coast past a collection of large vacation homes that didn't fit with anything in the township. Then we reached a place calling itself Lower Bogue, where the road turned inland.

Lower Bogue felt bigger—it had a smattering of storefronts and a decent-sized high school. But we rolled right on through, and ten minutes later we reached the wire fence surrounding the North Eleuthera Airport.

I hadn't paid much attention to the surroundings as I followed my driver on my arrival, and now I saw a handful of stores across the street from the small terminal building. Souvenirs and cold drinks and food, places to spend your last Bahamian dollars before flying away.

Jimmy stopped his bike right outside the terminal, where in the

US there would have been a white curb and a cop with a whistle and a bad attitude. Here no one cared. Jimmy told me to hold on, and he walked inside. The terminal doors were thrown wide open, perhaps to let any breeze through. Although there were no aircraft on the tarmac, there were a good few people loitering around, standing in the shade chatting or just waiting on life to happen around them. I noticed there were a few minivans parked along the fence by the tarmac, but not as many as when my flight had come in.

Within a couple of minutes Jimmy returned with a big black guy in an orange safety vest. He wore a wide smile and carried a good two hundred pounds well. He was broad across the shoulders and thick in the neck and had all the markings of a man not to be messed with.

"Mr. Jones," said Jimmy. "This is Carl."

Carl offered me a broad smile and his hand. I wiped the sweat from my brow with my left hand and shook with my right.

"Nice to meet you, Carl. Is there somewhere we can get a soda?"

Carl directed us across the street to a shop covered in blue siding the color of the water off Spanish Wells. I pushed in through the door and was hit by the frost of conditioned air. It had to be thirty degrees cooler than outside, but I didn't tense against it, rather letting out a long breath as the hairs on my arms stood to attention. The store was filled with all kinds of useless knickknacks and clothing and hats. I made a beeline for a fridge and bought three sodas.

When I handed Jimmy and Carl their drinks, they immediately took off for the outside. I wasn't keen to follow back into the humidity. But I had questions to ask and a Florida pedigree to protect, so I stepped out on the shaded patio and took a seat at a table where the others waited. I took a long gulp of my soda and then burped.

"So, Carl, I understand you rent cars on the side."

"That's right, man. You need something?"

"I need to know about a burgundy Camry that I got picked up in when I arrived a few days back."

"Yeah, I got a car like that."

"And it's currently rented?"

"Yeah, man. Rented it for a month, he did. Nice."

"Did you get a copy of a driver's license?"

"Nah. The boss wasn't so keen on paperwork, you know?"

"The boss? I thought you were the boss."

"No, him who hired the car."

"Oh. Did he pay with a credit card?"

"Cash in hand." He smiled at that.

"He paid cash, and you didn't see a driver's license."

"Nah. We pretty low-key here."

"Did he say where he was staying?"

"He did. Governor's Harbour. Pineapple Fields, I think he said."

"Pineapple Fields? What is that?"

"It's an apartment place. Vacation rentals."

"Okay. So you don't worry about him stealing your car?"

"Where he gonna take it? We are not that big an island."

"I assume there's no way to track it. No GPS or anything."

"No, I don't got that. People got that on their phones now, right?"

"I mean more for security, for tracking the car."

Carl smiled. "Nah, man."

I looked across at the terminal. Airports had security cameras, and although I couldn't see any, I suspected there was at least one. "Did you rent him the car here at the airport?"

"Nah. I left it with the key at the ferry dock."

"Gene's Bay?"

"Nah. The other one. Upper Bogue."

So there was an Upper Bogue. "Where's that?"

Carl pointed along the airport road in the opposite direction from where we had arrived. "About a mile."

"Does that go to Spanish Wells too?"

"Nah. It's on the other side, man. That one goes over to Harbour Island, mostly."

I thought about that as I finished my drink.

"Is there anything else you can tell me about this guy?"

"Just a guy."

"Black, white?"

"Black guy, yeah."

"Local?"

"Nah, man. This brother was Jamaican."

"Jamaican? I thought you didn't see any ID?"

"I didn't. But you can't hide that accent, man."

I couldn't always tell a Jamaican from a Bahamian accent, but I knew Lucas could pick an Australian accent from a New Zealand one from just the word *hey*, when I couldn't have told the difference after three weeks trapped on a life raft with a rugby player from each country. I suspected Carl had an ear for the local lilts that I didn't.

"Jamaican. Interesting."

I thanked Carl for his time, and he thanked me for the soda and said if I needed a car, to just call. He ambled back across the street and stopped in the shade for a chat with a guy who looked like he'd been waiting all day for just that thing.

Jimmy and I watched an American Eagle flight land, then we got back on his bike and headed toward Current. He stopped at a small joint with a solitary gas pump, filled the bike's little tank, and pulled a billfold from his pocket and paid the woman in cash. Then we motored back to the post office where he replaced the bike.

As we puttered back across the water toward Spanish Wells, I looked at Jimmy. He was certainly young of age, but as we crossed what was essentially an open stretch of ocean, I couldn't help but think he was older than his fourteen years. I tried to imagine a mother back in Florida allowing her teen to take to the ocean in a tiny dinghy, let alone demanding that he do it. Perhaps kids here grew up faster out of necessity. I didn't know, but as I looked at him squinting into the sunlight, I noticed the crow's feet forming on his otherwise smooth skin.

# CHAPTER TWENTY-FIVE

JIMMY TIED UP AT HIS PIER, AND I GAVE HIM SOME CASH, WHICH MADE him smile. Then I got into the cart and headed back to Mrs. Albury's. Lizzy and Mrs. Albury were both in their rooms, and when they appeared, they were wearing clothes that were a step up from their house clothes but not quite Sunday best.

"We're going to the bingo," Lizzy said in a way that made it sound like they had tickets to the Super Bowl.

"Awesome."

"You're invited."

"Thanks, I appreciate that, but I have things to do."

"How did you get on with young Jimmy?" asked Mrs. Albury.

"He's a smart kid. He'll go far."

"I think so. His mother doesn't like the idea, but some folks are too big for our little island."

"Did you find Carl?" Lizzy asked.

"I did. Nice guy. He doesn't have any kind of GPS theft protection on any of his cars though."

"Why would he?" said Mrs. Albury.

"I know, where would they go?"

"Yes, dear."

"Well, he said he delivered the car to the ferry dock that goes across to Harbour Island."

"Not here?" said Lizzy.

"No. And that's where all the tournament staff and competitors seem to be staying. So that car likely had nothing to do with Rusty. It looks linked to someone at the tournament though."

"Do you know who rented the car?"

"Not really. Carl isn't much for paperwork. He's more a handshake kind of guy."

"Takes one to know one."

"But he did say the renter wasn't local. He was Jamaican. And he claimed to be staying at some holiday rental place called Pineapple Fields. Governor's Harbour, apparently."

"There's a lot of pineapple fields down in Eleuthera," said Mrs. Albury. "Best pineapple in the world."

"I don't think this was a farm," I said.

"No, dear, I don't either. I heard some developers built a new place out near Tippy's. Called it after all them pineapple fields."

"You know it?"

"I haven't seen it, dear. I don't get down that way much anymore, but I've heard of it."

"From who?"

"Ladies at church."

"We'll see if we can put the word out on the wire," said Lizzy.

"I want to go down and have a look," I said.

"They'll see you coming a mile away, dear."

"Why's that, Mrs. Albury?"

"You might not stick out in Spanish Wells, but on Eleuthera you will, white boy."

"You're right," I said. "But I know someone who won't."

"Who?" asked Lizzy.

"You ladies enjoy your bingo. Take the cart, Lizzy. I'm going for a walk."

I considered taking the golf cart myself, but I wanted to stay off the main drag, or any other drag, for that matter. I walked out of the cluster of houses and straight across the island to the beach. The sun was falling, but the heat was still up, and people were bathing in the shallow waters and walking along the sand bars.

I headed up the beach past the bleachers, where a group of people was sitting wrapped in towels, enjoying a few beers. I passed the paddleboard woman's house and then finally reached the street with the trailer of kayaks.

I didn't take the street. Instead, I stepped up off the beach onto the grass at the rear of the Corrigan residence. There were no cars beside the house, but I figured that told me very little in a place where most things were within walking distance. I knocked on the back door and stepped back.

Kenrick Corrigan opened the door with a look that suggested he was already smiling before. He looked relaxed in a tank top that showed off his well-toned arms.

"Miami, come on in."

I came inside only because I didn't want to be seen outside. I wasn't sure what my presence might do to his career prospects if his superintendent decided to move forward with me as suspect number one.

"You know you can do your daily check-in at the station," he said with a wink.

"That's my next stop," I lied.

"Consider it done."

Elise was clearing dishes from the table, and the kids were watching TV. "Have you eaten, Miami?" Elise asked. They had, so I deferred.

"Would you like a beer?" asked Ken.

A beer would probably have gone down better than a Jimmy Buffett tour in Florida, but I got the sense that they were enjoying some family time, and I had no wish to intrude despite their hospitality.

"No," I said. "I can't stay. I just wanted to quickly pick your brain on something. Both your brains, actually."

"What is it?" asked Elise.

"I may have gotten a lead on the car that delivered me from the airport."

"How?"

"There's a pretty well-connected network of ladies in the churches around here."

"This is true," said Elise. "Old ladies with lots of time on their hands. They see everything, only they don't always care to share with the authorities."

"Why?"

"There's an independent streak that runs through the people here, Miami. The first group to settle came from Bermuda in the 1600s looking for religious freedom. They shipwrecked on the reef off North Eleuthera—"

"Devil's Backbone?"

"That's the one, and they lived in a cave now called Preacher's Cave. Many died, and they did it hard. Eventually they made their way over to Spanish Wells, supposedly because of the presence of fresh water. But for a century they were largely untouched and ignored, and that makes for a people both fiercely independent but also cautious of outsiders."

"And that's why I'm here. I need to get down to Eleuthera and see if I can track down this car. It's the only lead I have to clear my name."

"Is Jimmy not available?" she said with a grin.

"Does everybody know about that? No, I'm not going all the way down to Governor's Harbour on the back of Jimmy's dirt bike. But getting there is only part of the problem."

"Sticking out like an outsider is your problem," said Ken.

"Exactly."

"To be fair, Miami, you stick out here too," said Ken.

"I do?"

"It's the shirts."

"Yeah, that happens in Florida as well, so that's on me. But I need to find a way to sniff around down there without sticking out so much. I thought you guys might have some ideas."

Ken and Elise looked at each other and nodded. It was like watching some kind of telepathy thing happening. Or maybe that was just what happened when you were married for long enough.

"It's simple," said Ken.

"It is?"

"Ken will go with you," said Elise.

"What?"

"I can do all the parts that might involve you sticking out."

"And what would I do?"

"You'd stay in the car, mostly," said Elise.

"I don't have a car."

"We do," said Ken.

"Not a police car."

"Not a police car," said Elise.

"I don't want you guys to get into any kind of trouble."

"Don't worry," said Ken. "Tomorrow's my day off. We'll just go for a little drive."

I looked at them both smiling at me like they had all the answers. Maybe they did. They were two steps ahead of me, which put them twenty steps ahead of their boss. They were happily married with nice kids, and they lived on the beach in paradise. It occurred to me I had most of that, too, just not regularly enough of late.

"If you're sure."

"We are," said Elise. "Be here tomorrow at eight."

I thanked them and then left them to their family time. Elise demanded I take a go bag of dinner, and since I hadn't eaten and Lizzy and Mrs. Albury would probably get something at bingo, I took it gratefully. She filled a container with chicken and rice and tossed in a knife and fork like she was a takeout restaurant.

I didn't head straight back. Instead, I walked farther up the beach, picking at the chicken and rice as I went. There was a bit of spice in there, so once I was done eating, I stripped off my shirt, kicked off my shoes and left them with the remains of my dinner, and strode into the ocean.

The water was heavenly, and I dove under to cool myself and clear my head. I breaststroked out a ways but noticed that it hadn't gotten any deeper, so dropped to my knees and let the sand settle around me. Little fish edged toward me, then they darted away as if doing it on a dare. My eye caught movement to my left, and I watched a small stingray ghost across the sandy bottom so graceful it appeared to put no effort into moving. I watched it swim away into the turtle grass. In the grass I noticed a conch shell, so I floated over to take a look. It looked big under the water, but when I picked it up, it was smaller than I had thought. I turned it over to see if I was disturbing the resident snail, but there wasn't anything inside. It was as if the ocean was getting gentrified and the snails were having to move to cheaper digs. I placed the shell back in the grass and then drifted until there was sand underfoot.

I looked along the beach and across the water and up at the sky, and I wondered if paradise was truly paradise if you were alone there. It was one of those trees-falling-in-the-woods questions, and it lingered in a way that suggested it might stick around for a good while.

When I was suitably refreshed, I swam back to shore and then let the breeze dry me. Then I got dressed and picked up my dinner trash and headed up the street. I wasn't trying to hide my presence at the Corrigans' anymore, so I figured walking the main street would be the easier option on my calf muscles.

I walked along the edge of the road. There were no sidewalks, but so little traffic they seemed superfluous. A few golf carts whizzed by, and folks waved as they passed. I reached one of the streets that crossed the island and noticed a golf cart parked at some kind of streetside store.

It was Captain Augie and his family. He saw me and waved, so I crossed the road and wandered over to them. They were getting ice cream from an open stand calling itself Papa Scoops. Captain Augie introduced me to his wife and kids. They all looked happy and tanned, the way people often do when they stop off for ice cream. I could recall doing it with my parents back in Connecticut, stopping off at the Dairy Queen after a day at Woodmont Beach. They were some of my best memories.

"Hey, you know I heard your boat again," said Captain Augie.

"My boat? Oh, you mean the mystery dinghy?"

"Yep."

"Still not sleeping?"

"No, I heard it this afternoon."

"How do you know it was the right boat?"

"Every engine has its own sound. If I went along the docks and started every one, I'd probably find it."

"I don't think you need to do that, but thanks. You all have a good night."

I left them to their ice cream and returned to Mrs. Albury's. It was dark by the time I got back, and the cart was facing outward, suggesting that Lizzy had used it to shuttle Mrs. Albury to the church and that she expected to have to make a fast getaway at any time. I didn't go inside. Instead, I used the hose to wash the salt from my face and hair; then I went into the shed and turned on the fan. I lay on the cot and thought about Captain Augie's family, and Ken and Elise Corrigan and their kids, and long humid summers in New Haven, and dipped cones and frosty freeze and times when network television was all you had, one screen for the family to share, whether you liked it not.

# CHAPTER TWENTY-SIX

I met Ken Corrigan on the beach behind his house the next morning. The clouds had been torn to shreds to the point of looking like the bars on a cell. Maybe I was seeing things. Ken was in civvies —Bermuda shorts and pressed polo—looking like a model or even a New Age competitive angler. I was in my usual. I figured it wasn't the shirt that was going to make me stand out today.

A flatboat pulled into the beach near his house. It was as basic a vessel as there could be, and we didn't get in it but on it. The deck was just a flat top like someone had removed the sides from a pontoon boat, and the hull was built like a shallow kiddie pool. There was a console at the rear to control the thing, and a small platform built over the top of the outboard to gain elevation and search for fish, since the boat was so low it was like walking on water.

Ken gave a fist pump to the guy at the helm, a black dude with half his teeth missing as I discovered when he gave me his pearl-less smile and invited me on board. The guy pushed the boat back from the beach with a punting pole, and when we were deep enough, he started the engine, and we puttered across the flats toward Gene's Bay.

"This doesn't look like Rusty's boat," I said.

"I think you'd call Rusty's boat a bass boat. Isn't that what you guys fish for over there?"

"I don't fish for anything. That's Mick's job."

"Who's Mick?"

"My providore."

He nodded. "This is a flatboat. You can use the pole to get in where the fish are and never run aground, and it's almost all flat deck, which makes moving around with a fish on the line easy. Not a million miles away from a bass boat, but not as fast. Why do they need to go so quick for fishing anyway?"

"Apart from the macho component, I'm told some of the competitions have a Grand Prix start and the boats have to speed off to wherever they plan to fish. But it's mostly the macho thing."

The flatboat eased up to the dock at Gene's Bay, and we stepped off without a word. The flatboat floated away, and Ken led me to a long row of cars under the trees near the dock. He found a green minivan and pulled a key from under the front bumper.

"Excellent security," I said.

"Works a charm."

"We're not stealing a vehicle, are we, Corporal?"

"Nope. It's mine. But sometimes other people need to use it. Island life, you know?"

I did, and I liked it.

Again, I nearly got in the wrong side of the car, but once on our way, Ken pretty much drove up the middle of the road since there were no lane markings and no other cars to argue the point.

We took the Queen's Highway toward the airport and then kept going. Ken slowed as we reached Glass Window Bridge, where the island was only the width of the solitary traffic lane that crossed between the dark Atlantic on one side and the azure Caribbean on the other. Then on through Gregory Town and Alice Town and beach after beach with inviting water lapping at vacant sand.

As we drove, Ken cleared his throat like he had something to say along the lines of *I'm dating your sister.*

"Are you sure that you never got on board Rusty's boat?"

"Positive. I only ever saw it once when he was moving it, and I did nothing more than untie a line. Why?"

"We got fingerprint analysis back. Lots of prints on a working boat. Rusty's, the camera guy's, the producer's. And yours."

"That's not possible."

"And yet the boss says we have it. If you're going to change your story, you'll want to tread carefully. You're already on the record."

"I'm not going to change my story. It's not a question of evidence or what your boss knows or even what you think, Ken. This is about what I know, and I know I wasn't on that boat. If my prints are on board, I know someone put them there."

"Who?"

I didn't reply. My mind was spinning like a Hollywood agent's Rolodex. That thought made me wonder if anyone still used Rolodexes, which was replaced by the idea of the sins of the father. If one generation could fudge evidence, maybe another one could too. I wasn't ready to share that idea with Ken.

After about seventy-five minutes, we reached the capital, Governor's Harbour. It was a small town centered around a little harbor. There was more traffic here, which is to say I saw a car, but most people seemed to be getting around on foot. Ken told me it had been the original settlement after the Eleutheran Adventurers had left their cave to find a quiet harbor in which to starve and be miserable.

"Like the pilgrims in New England," I said.

"Very much. Their leader, William Sayles, ended up sailing west to settle what is now Nassau. The others stayed, but farming here was hard. The land is not that arable. Until they cultivated pineapples."

"And there it is," I said. "But I'm yet to see these pineapple fields."

Ken took a tight turn up the hill away from the harbor. "What's left are mostly to the south of here, but the pineapple trade died off once the US established pineapple farms in Hawaii."

"Commerce is a tough mistress."

"You say the strangest things."

"It has been noted."

We cut across the island—it was about three-quarters of a mile at this point—until we reached the Atlantic side, then we followed the road along the coast. For the most part we couldn't see the ocean for the properties and trees on the water side, but every now and then I was offered a glimpse, like a dealer offering me a taste of his wares.

We came upon a restaurant on the beach called Tippy's. It wasn't busy, but it did look like the kind of place that could get that way. Ken turned away from the restaurant into a parking lot on the other side of the road. He switched off the car and pointed up the hill. I had seen the sparkling new condos before I spotted the bar. Unlike the kind of apartments that dotted the landscape in Florida and had even started breeding on my Singer Island, these had at least considered their surroundings. They were sympathetic to the Caribbean style, yellow siding and wide verandahs tucked among the trees.

"So, this is the part where you don't fit in," said Ken.

"Thanks."

"I'll go up and talk to the office people."

"Okay."

"You stay here. You might want to roll down the window."

Ken got out and wandered off toward the condos. I sat in the car for about thirty seconds, then I decided I would go somewhere that I would fit in.

I walked across the road to Tippy's. It wasn't open yet. All the doors leading to the beach patio were locked up, but I could imagine them thrown open, so a cooling breeze flowed in off the ocean. Despite not yet being open, there were a couple of people sitting at tables fixed to the patio.

The view of the water and gathering clouds was spectacular, and I was reminded of my rule about restaurants with views. I had learned from hard experience in such places to enjoy the one but not expect too much of the other.

Ken found me about five minutes later. He slipped in opposite me and nodded.

"You ever come here?" I asked.

"Sure. It's a fun spot to bring the kids. They have music on the weekends, I believe."

"Do I fit in here?"

"I get the feeling you've fit in at every bar you've ever walked into."

"You'd be surprised. What did you learn?"

"Nothing. There's no mystery Jamaican staying there. The place is half full, and they're all Americans, except for one German couple."

It might have felt like a complete waste of time had I not been breathing in fresh salty air that invigorated both my body and my mind.

"Did you know that Eleuthera comes from the Greek word for free?" said Ken.

"Ironic that I got put in lockup then."

"That was on Spanish Wells, so . . ."

I smiled. "Now what?"

"I can take you to see some sights, but otherwise this day trip is a bust."

It felt like a crazy idea to play tourist while a murder charge hung over my head, but I couldn't think of anything better to do.

Then Ken's phone rang. He answered and listened. He gave a couple of affirmative "uh-huhs" and then finished by saying, "I know it. Thanks."

When he hung up, he shook his head with a smile and looked out at the ocean. "That was your girl Lizzy."

"Do yourself a favor and do not ever let her hear you referring to her as my girl?"

"Sorry, your associate."

"She could live with that. What's news?"

"It's the church grapevine."

"I think they were calling it a phone tree, but go on."

"They found the car."

Now it was my turn to shake my head. "Seriously?"

"They say it's at a house in James Cistern."

"Which is where?"

"Back the way we came."

It was twenty minutes back, past Governor's Harbour airport. A small township with a handful of restaurants and stores but an oversupply of churches. I counted seven, about one for every resident.

Ken seemed to know where he was going as he turned inland, then he drove along a sandy road that appeared to lead nowhere. The scrub grew thick on either side of the road, shading us from the sun, and I wondered how often it had to be hacked back and who did it and why, since the road was barely there at all.

Ken eased to a stop in the middle of the road. "If their intel is correct, the house is just up here on the right."

"It's a lonely place."

"Some people like it quiet. We'll go in on foot. This is the only road out."

"The other way?"

"Dead ends at the ocean."

We got out and walked another hundred yards. Ken didn't creep or crouch. He just walked as if he were on the way for a swim.

"How many do you think?" he asked.

"Mrs. Trout said two guys opened up Merrick's shack, so . . ."

"Okay."

"Do you have a gun?" I asked.

"No. Do you?"

"No."

"Good. That would be very illegal."

We reached a clearing in the scrub and found a single-family home with a lush lawn and killer views of the Atlantic Ocean. There was a sun-bleached burgundy Camry in the driveway.

"Let me do the talking," said Ken.

"You got it."

We crossed the sandy driveway, and Ken knocked on the mint-green door. It took longer than was necessary before someone answered. The man who did was a big black guy with a linebacker's build. He frowned at Ken as if he was disturbing a nap and then he glanced over Ken's shoulder and saw me, and his jaw dropped like he had just seen the tax collector.

He slammed the door shut before Ken could get a foot in the door. Ken banged on the door and called, "Police," but I got the sense that wasn't going to help.

"The back?" I asked.

Ken nodded and strode around the side of the house. I stopped as I reached the side, wondering if one of us should wait at the front. It was a rookie mistake. I didn't hear the front door open or the sound of footsteps on sand, but when my rusty instinct made me turn back, I saw the linebacker throw open the door of the Camry and start it before the door was even closed.

I didn't need to call Ken. He heard the car take off too. We ran out of the driveway after it, turning down the road toward the small town. The sandy road was no fun to run on, but years of training on City Beach paid dividends, and I powered across it like an athlete. I made a note to never tell Danielle about it, lest I end up running on the beach more often.

We didn't have to go too far. The Camry skidded to a stop when it reached the parked minivan. The thick scrub offered no room to pass, so the guy got out and ran. His linebacker build wasn't designed for long runs on sand, so I caught him quickly. I thought about diving for the tackle, but his lumbering motion gave me a better idea. I got right behind him and lengthened my stride, then I stuck my foot out and tripped him.

He hit the ground face first and took a good mouthful of sand, so when he rolled over, he wasn't trying to escape but rather spit it out. Ken dragged the guy up and pulled his hands behind him, then he took out a zip tie and cuffed him.

"Are you alone in the house?" he asked.

The guy was still spitting sand, but he didn't seem inclined to answer either way.

"I said, are you alone?"

"I got nothing to say."

"That wasn't a no," I said.

Ken pushed the guy back to the house, but I moved faster, so when I got there, I headed for the rear. There was a wood deck overlooking the ocean below, a great place to sit and take in the nature, except for the fact that there weren't any chairs or outdoor sofas or any other kind of furniture outside. It was as if the place had been vacated for the summer and then opened without permission. These guys had a definite MO.

I tried the sliding door to the house and found it open, so I slipped inside. The living room was orderly except for the beer bottles on the coffee table. The kitchen, however, was a mess. There were discarded plates and foodstuffs and empty corn chip bags. It looked like a college house share.

As I came back into the living area, I noticed the storm shutters from the sliding door had been stacked in the corner of the room. No homeowner would do that. I moved into the hallway and found a couple of empty bedrooms but two beds that had been slept in.

The door to the bathroom was closed. I eased the knob around and pushed the door open as quietly as I could. I wasn't sure it was the best tactic—if I were hiding in a bathroom, the chances were pretty good that I would be watching the door. I let the door fall open completely before getting into a crouch and poking my head inside.

No one was pointing a weapon at me. No one was watching the door. There was no one there at all. I stood and moved inside. There was a bathtub with a shell motif shower curtain pulled across it. It was a dumb place to hide, but I pulled the curtain anyway.

And came face-to-face with Rusty Reels.

# CHAPTER TWENTY-SEVEN

"FANCY MEETING YOU HERE," I SAID TO THE VERY ALIVE-AND-WELL Reels. He wasn't in his customary khaki. Instead, he wore a T-shirt with the Bahamas flag on it and a pair of fluorescent orange shorts.

He lost the little color he had in his face as I dragged him out of the bathtub and pushed him toward the living room.

"Don't hurt me."

"Sit. Don't move. If you move, you really will be dead."

He flopped onto the sofa. I strode down the hall, opened the front door, and saw the minivan pull into the driveway. I kept one eye on the living room and waited for Ken. He came across the driveway, and I saw the Jamaican sitting in the backseat.

"Anything?" asked Ken.

"He okay?" I asked, nodding at the minivan.

"He's tied in. He's not going anywhere."

"Then you best take a look."

Ken walked into the living room and looked at the sofa, then he frowned at me. "Is this who I think it is?"

"Rusty Reels, in the flesh."

"And very much alive," said Ken. "Mr. Reels, I am corporal Kenrick Corrigan of the Royal Bahamian Police Force." He showed Rusty his ID.

"Thank goodness," said Rusty. "This man assaulted me." He jinked his head in my general direction.

"Is that all?" said Ken. "You've got a lot of explaining to do."

"I can't explain anything."

"Oh, if you don't want to end up in jail, you'd better start trying."

"No, you don't understand. I hit my head, I think. I don't remember anything."

"You don't remember anything?"

"No."

"Your name?"

"No."

"How you came to be at this house?"

"Nothing."

"Who's the guy you're here with?"

"I don't know. He said he was a friend, but I really don't know."

"What's his name?"

"I don't know."

"He didn't tell you his name?"

"Maybe. I forget."

"You're still forgetting things."

"It would seem."

"Okay. You sit tight. I'm going sort this out, and we'll get you taken care of."

Ken directed me back to the front door.

"Amnesia? Seriously?" I said.

"It can happen, can't it?"

"Anything's possible, but if you had amnesia, would you sit around looking at the ocean view, or go find yourself a doctor?"

"Good point. But there was blood on the boat. Okay, I'm going to have to take these guys in. As you say, one might need a doctor."

"I'm not saying that. I'm saying it's all baloney."

"Well, the good news is you're not guilty of murder."

That thought had already flown through my mind like a BMW on the Autobahn. It had been replaced by the notion that if these guys were setting me up, Rusty's next move might be to claim I attempted to murder him. Unless he was also a victim.

"Someone set me up. Our Jamaican friend is in it up to his eyebrows, and Rusty might be too. They might not be done."

"I'm going to have a word with him," said Ken. He turned toward the minivan, and I followed. "You don't speak, okay?" he said.

I shrugged. I wasn't committing to any verbal contracts at this point.

Ken pulled the rear door open. The Jamaican's hands were zip-tied together where the seat belt was fixed to the car, so he looked like he was praying. He didn't have on his prayer face though.

"What's your name, sir?" said Ken.

"I got nothing to say."

"That's not going to help you. Who's your friend in the house?"

"There's nobody in the house. I was alone."

"You're saying that the man who has been sleeping in the room next to you was there without your knowledge."

"I got nothing to say."

"Where are you from?"

The Jamaican shook his head like a three-year-old refusing another mouthful.

"Not to worry. We'll print you at the station and mail the card to Nassau to find out who you are. You'll have to be kept in custody until then, but it should only take six to eight weeks."

"Huh?"

"You have a Jamaican accent."

"So?"

"What are you doing in the Bahamas?"

"Visiting."

"Who?"

He shrugged again.

"If you're just visiting, why did you pick me up at the airport?" I asked. Ken glanced at me, and I gave him an eyebrow raise.

"I don't know you."

"You drove me from the airport to Gene's Bay only a few days ago."

"You got me mistaken with somebody else."

"The guy inside says you kidnapped him."

"I never kidnapped nobody."

"I know the cops here," I said. "They like the simple explanations. And right now, the simple explanation is that he's been missing, and you've been caught with him. That sounds like kidnapping to me."

"I didn't kidnap nobody."

"So why was he tied up in the bathroom?"

"He wasn't tied up."

"How do you know if you didn't even know he was there at all?"

"I got nothing to say."

I didn't know if he'd seen it on a television show or if someone had told him to keep his mouth shut, but either way, he wasn't very good at it. Few people were. I had a lawyer working in my building in West Palm, and he said most people who got convicted were done on evidence they gave up before retaining an attorney. He said saying nothing was always the best policy, but people always felt the need to explain their way out of things, as if they were geniuses and the cops hadn't seen the likes of them a thousand times.

We left the guy to stew in the minivan for a while and returned to the house. Ken said he was going to search the place for evidence, and I should keep my eye on Rusty.

"I won't bother telling you not to talk to him, because you won't listen."

Ken asked Rusty to stand and then told him that he was going to search his person for identification. Rusty rose slowly, and Ken checked his pockets. There wasn't much to check, and he found nothing. Then he said he would take a look in the bedrooms.

I watched him go, and Rusty flopped back into the sofa.

"Hey, Rusty," I said.

"Huh?" he said, turning to me.

"You want a coffee?"

"Sure, I guess."

I went into the kitchen looking for a can of Folger's and discovered a Keurig machine. I found some pods in the cupboard and set the machine going, then I checked the fridge for milk. I poured a long dollop in the coffee and then returned to the living room.

"You want sugar?" I asked.

"No."

I handed him the mug, and he looked at it and his lip curled. He put the coffee on the table and sat back in the sofa.

"Something wrong?" I asked.

"No. Just don't feel like it, I guess."

"Right." I stepped over to him. He looked up at me. It was not the look of a man who didn't know me. I reached toward him, and he flinched.

"What are you doing?" he said.

"Checking you for a head wound."

"Don't come near me."

"Rusty, this goes one of two ways. The first way is I check you for the head knock you said you had, so I can make sure you are healthy enough to be moved across bumpy roads, or the second way is where I give you the head knock, and you travel unconscious."

Rusty didn't look convinced, but he let me feel his head. I was gentle despite every impulse to be otherwise. It wasn't conclusive one way or the other, but I didn't feel any bumps or abrasions.

I then grabbed him by the wrist and extended his arm. He fought it but not too hard as I slightly hyperextended his elbow. I looked at his veins and found no telltale signs of drug use. I repeated it on the other arm and got the same result. I had heard some users jabbed themselves in between their toes to hide the puncture marks, but I wasn't getting into Rusty's feet.

Stepping back, I saw him let out a breath. "I'm just going to check on the corporal."

I wandered down to the second bedroom, where Ken had opened the drawers to a tallboy.

"Anything?"

"Nothing. No ID for Mr. Reels."

"And the other guy?"

Ken had bagged a wallet. It was open in the bag to show the driver's license in the window slot.

"Michael Alexander. Jamaican," I said. "Carl was right."

"Uh-huh."

The address was in Ocho Rios, which meant nothing to me. "Anything else?"

"Nope. Most notably no passport. Which makes me wonder how he got into the country."

"You have a database of entry into the Bahamas?"

"What did you do when you arrived?"

"I filled out a card and collected my own luggage."

"Right. If he entered legitimately, there's probably a record on a piece of paper somewhere. But not very useful in the short term."

Ken pushed a drawer closed. "What about Mr. Reels?"

"Huh?"

"Don't even think about telling me you didn't talk to him."

"He's sticking with the amnesia thing, but it's complete hogwash."

"Can you prove that?"

"When I said his name he responded."

"He'll say it was to the sound, just reflex."

"Like I said, he's running with it, but it won't stand up under pressure. He said yes to a coffee, but when I gave it to him he suddenly changed his mind." The thought of that made me consider my own history with Rusty and coffee.

"Why?"

"I put milk in it. He's lactose intolerant."

"That's thin but okay. What if he's putting it on? What's the end game?"

"I need to think that through."

Ken finished his search and then told Rusty he would be taking him to get him checked out. Ken led us outside, then he closed up the house.

"You want me to take Rusty in the Camry?" I asked.

"No. If you did get picked up in that car, then your prints are probably in it, which will confirm part of your story. I'll get the local boys to come out. They'll need to inform the homeowner of the break-in anyway."

Ken told Rusty to get in the front, while I got in the back with the Jamaican. "We're all going to stay quiet," said Ken. "Anyone speaks, they'll be tied to the back of the van and will be running the rest of the way."

It was a silent trip back to Gene's Bay. No one wanted to run behind the van, most of all me. I spent the journey thinking that my prints in the Camry made me look like a co-conspirator in Rusty's kidnapping if that was the way that story was going to unfold. I was sure the amnesia was fake, but it didn't help answer the bigger question: namely, why Rusty was involved in setting me up when I didn't even know him.

Elise Corrigan was waiting for us at Gene's Bay. She was in a speed boat, and I helped the Jamaican get in, then I followed. I let Rusty take care of himself. Ken untied the line and pushed the boat away, then he jumped in, and Elise piloted us through the channel to the ferry dock on Spanish Wells.

We all clambered up a ladder to the dock. Elise took Michael Alexander's wrists and pushed him toward the station house on the other side of Main Street. Ken told Rusty to follow, and we dropped in behind. As we walked, he spoke quietly to me.

"You should make yourself scarce now," he said. "The superintendent isn't going to be happy, and his mood won't improve if he sees you."

"Roger that."

"I'll find you later."

# CHAPTER TWENTY-EIGHT

I LEFT THEM TO HEAD INTO THE STATION AND KEPT WALKING ACROSS THE island and past the baseball diamond. The tournament village was buzzing. I guessed the population of Spanish Wells had doubled since I had left that morning.

I walked out onto the sand and made my way to the bleachers. The tournament was underway, and the bleachers were half full. Some of the people seemed to be actually paying attention to the fishing going on in front of them. I stepped up between the spectators and found a seat about three-quarters of the way up. The wood boards were hot to the touch. I sat and looked out to the water. About eight or nine anglers were standing in the water about a hundred yards off the beach. They were flicking lines in and out of the water like they were fishing for trout on a Scottish river. Fly fishing. It hadn't occurred to me that this was how they caught bonefish. I had envisaged Rusty Reels dropping a line in and then sitting back, sucking on a beer until he got a nibble.

One guy got a bite, and he started the dance, the play between angler and fish. He reeled it in some but then let it run a little, before reeling in again. When he got the fish close, another guy swept in with a net and picked the fish out of the water. It was hard to see exactly how big the fish was until I realized that the person on the bench in front of me had an iPad streaming the video from the camera attached to the net guy's hat. The screen showed the vision of the guy using a phone to scan the fish and record its length, which was then automatically added to a leaderboard that took up the left side of the screen like the positions in a NASCAR race.

Once the fish hit the leaderboard, the angler removed the hook, and with the care of a child holding a puppy, he set the fish swimming away. Evidently everyone on the bleacher was watching the video because they gave it a golf clap, then they all started talking about it the way a crowd at Fenway chats about a base hit. I wondered how many times that same fish was going to get caught today. Perhaps they weren't as slippery as they thought.

Or as slippery as Rusty Reels. My mind drifted to his amnesia—which I was convinced was fake. I ran through every interaction I had with him, from meeting at the cemetery to chatting at the shack and then at the dock. The common element was that no one else was ever present. Then Rusty had given me an envelope of cash to pass on to Chase Hutchinson, which had subsequently been used as evidence against me.

It sure felt like Rusty was involved and not just an innocent pawn. But why? What had I ever done to the guy to make him want to set me up like that? And now he had been found with Michael Alexander, the only other part of the setup I could place. And why did Alexander have ID and Rusty none? Neither of them had passports, so how had they gotten into the country?

Rusty, I recalled from Danielle, had flown into Nassau from Atlanta, and Rusty's camera guy had confirmed as much. But what about Alexander? How had he arrived from Jamaica? And how had Rusty gotten from Nassau to the cemetery in Lake Worth—and back to Eleuthera—without a trace?

How did anyone get anywhere in the Bahamas? How did I get to Spanish Wells? How did Captain Augie get to Harbour Island? How had young Jimmy gotten to Current?

By boat. In a country made up of islands, most everyone had access to a boat. And people crossed to the Bahamas from Florida by boat all the time. Lucas didn't come any other way. Across the Gulf Stream to Bimini and then onto pretty much anywhere in the Bahamas. From Fort Lauderdale or Miami, a decent boat could be anywhere in Eleuthera in about eight hours. But not a flatboat or a bass boat or even a dinghy. A big boat. The kind of boat designed for the job.

My pontificating done, I headed back to Mrs. Albury's. I found Lizzy eating a sandwich alone at the kitchen table.

"Where's Mrs. A?"

"In the front room."

It was nice to know that her reception room was now more usable. I crept down the hall and stuck my head in and found her asleep in her chair, the AC turned off and the room as hot as ever.

Back in the kitchen I said, "It's hot in there."

"I know."

I held my hands out to ask why bother to install air conditioning if you don't turn it on, but Lizzy preempted me with a shrug.

Lizzy stood from the table as I sat, and she set about making another sandwich. "Did you find the car?"

"We did. Your intelligence is first class."

"And?"

"We found the guy who brought me from the airport."

"That's good." Lizzy made a ham and cheese and put the plate in front of me, then sat back down to her own lunch.

"Thank you," I said.

"You're welcome. So what else?"

"We found Rusty Reels."

Lizzy stopped with her sandwich halfway to her mouth. "Alive?"

"Very much. He's claiming amnesia."

"But?"

"He's faking it. I'm sure of it. So now I'm asking, why does Rusty Reels want to set me up for his murder?"

"You think that's what he did?"

"I was set up, no doubt. But now I find Rusty alive with the

Jamaican from the airport. Are they one thread intertwined, or are they two separate threads?"

"What do you want me to do?"

"Do you have access to a computer?"

"Of course. I brought my laptop."

"I assume Mrs. Albury doesn't have Wi-Fi?"

"No, but the church does," she said. "What do you need?"

"I need to know everything about Rusty Reels. Can you do a background on him?"

"I already did a little."

"You did?"

"I do that on every client. But you're asking for something much deeper."

"I'm talking proctology deep."

"Oh, Miami." She made a face like she'd just done a tequila shot and was sucking on the lime.

"Sorry."

"What will you do?"

"Rusty is one thread. I need to learn a little bit more about the other. Can I borrow your phone?"

"Of course. But there's something else. Another conch went missing."

"That doesn't seem all that important right now."

"Not to you, maybe. But these people don't see the crimes you do. And while I'm getting information on Mr. Reels, I thought you could earn your room and board."

"I thought that was the air conditioner."

"That was room; this is board."

"Okay. What do I need to know?"

She handed me what looked like a tourist brochure. "This is a map of the town. I've marked the locale of each known theft. And this is the name of the man who reported the last shell taken." She handed me a note.

Lizzy got up and took our plates to the sink, then she said she'd get started on the Reels file. She handed me her phone and walked back to her bedroom.

I sat back at the table and looked up a number online; then I dialed.

"Montego Bay Police," said the sing-song accent that answered.

"Can I speak to Lucia Tellis, please?" I said.

"I'm afraid she's no longer at this office. May I ask what it is regarding?"

"We worked together on a case once before, and I was just calling to catch up. Is she still with the force?"

"She is. She was promoted. She's in Kingston now."

"Do you have a number there?"

I was given a number and thanked the officer, then I dialed again. I got a generic switchboard and asked for Lucia Tellis again. This time I was put through.

"Sergeant Tellis."

"Sergeant, this is Miami Jones."

There was a pause. "Miami Jones, indeed. Long time, no hear. How are you?"

"I'm living in interesting times. And you're a sergeant now."

"Have been for a while. And you're calling through our switchboard. Did you lose my mobile number?"

"I don't currently have access to my own phone."

"Oh? Do tell."

I told her about the case and the alleged murder and about having my phone and passport taken by Bahamian authorities.

"What happened?" she asked.

"I found the guy. The alleged victim. It was faked to set me up."

"You really do have some fans, don't you?"

"It would seem."

"What can I do for you, Miami?"

"My client, Rusty, was in the company of a Jamaican. He was the same guy who collected me from the airport here. He's not saying much yet, but I thought maybe he was known to you."

"What's the name?"

"Michael Alexander." I gave her the address from his driver's license.

"Ocho Rios?"

"That's what it said. Isn't that near Montego Bay?"

"Along the coast a bit. I don't know the name, but then I haven't been in MoBay for a couple of years. Let me make a few calls and get back to you. Can I call this number?"

"Yes, it's my office manager's cell phone. Thanks, Lucia."

"I'll be in touch."

I left the phone on the table and was on my way out to the shed when it rang again. I picked it up and saw a local Bahamas number.

"Hello?"

"Miami, it's Ken. I just wanted to let you know, Rusty is currently sticking with the amnesia, but you're right, it's suspect."

"I know."

"There's more. Superintendent Bridges isn't giving up. He's talking about charging you with attempted murder."

"You really should stop telling me things like that. You could get in trouble."

"I don't care about trouble, but I know the boss. He's acting awfully strange."

"Okay, thanks, Ken."

I sat at the table and considered this new development. I didn't think finding Rusty would be the end of the case at hand, but I had thought it the end of my legal problems. That assumption now proved erroneous, and my mind was cast back to the sins of the father. What was Superintendent Bridges doing? Undertaking the same corrupt policing that his father was accused of or overreaching from a desire to prove those rumors wrong?

Either way didn't look that great for me. It seemed the likelihood of getting my passport back anytime soon was remote unless I could prove that someone else was behind whatever it was that had happened to Rusty. I had Lucia checking one end of the timeline, but I had a nagging feeling about the other end. About things that had happened forty years ago. About things that had been seen and then seen again.

I walked into the front room, and my movement roused Mrs. Albury from her doze.

"Sorry to wake you."

"That's all right, dear. I'm liable to drop off at a moment's notice these days."

"Can I ask you a question? Do you have Jimmy's mother's phone number?"

"She'll be at work, dear."

"Oh. She works nights?"

"Yes. As a cook at one of the restaurants."

"Do you know where she lives?"

# CHAPTER TWENTY-NINE

MRS. ALBURY KNEW THE ADDRESS IN THE WAY THAT PEOPLE KNEW ALL the addresses here—by description rather than street name and number. I dropped Lizzy's map on the cot in the shed and drove the cart out along the main street until I reached the house with the sign for filtered water by the gallon. Then I turned up the hill and realized I was about two streets along from Captain Augie's place. I kept going slowly until I found the house I was looking for. It was a wood siding place in need of a paint but with a neat yard. No conch shells.

I knocked and waited. When Jimmy opened the door, he was looking at his phone and not me. I could have been anyone, and I could have done anything. I just waited for him to look up. It took longer than was necessary.

"Miami?" he said.

"Yeah. If I needed to get to Bluff, could you take me?"

"Are you paying?"

"Yes."

"Then sure."

"Tomorrow?"

"Or now."

"You want to go now?"

"I don't want to go to Bluff at all, but I'm not doing anything else right now."

"Okay then. Let's do it."

He left the door open and wandered back into the house, so I stepped inside. I could see a living room with a big television on the wall and a kitchen at the back. Through the window I could see a small yard with a shed that reminded me of a smaller version of my current accommodations.

Jimmy appeared with a box wrapped in brown paper. Then we walked out, and he pulled the door closed.

"Do you know an old guy called Courtenay over there in Bluff?"

"Not personally."

"Enough to point me in his direction?"

"He might be working."

I hadn't considered that.

"I'll make a call. You need to stop at the liquor store."

"I'm not buying you alcohol, kid."

"Not for me. Trust me."

Jimmy directed me to a liquor store. I went in and bought a bottle of rum as directed, and when I came out, Jimmy was finishing a call.

"He's home. He worked the day shift today."

"I thought he didn't have a phone."

"No idea. I didn't call him. I don't generally call old-timers."

I wasn't going to ask if I fell into that category. I drove to Jimmy's pier, and we got in his little boat, and he pulled away. The sun was getting low, but there was still a good amount of daylight left. Despite the assurances of the locals, I wasn't keen on being on the water after dark.

We puttered out of the south channel and then cut south and east toward North Eleuthera. When we reached Bluff, I realized it was notable for its lack of a beach. I expected there to be some kind of ordinance about having a township without a sandy frontage. Jimmy pulled in behind a sea wall where a handful of small boats were moored.

Jimmy tied off to a rock and then walked me into the township. I saw a sign that read The Bluff Settlement with an arrow pointing in the direction we were walking as if we might miss the town. We might have. It wasn't a big place, but it was certainly more populated than Current.

We walked past a large home behind a high wall, and Jimmy stopped at a corner and pointed inland.

"Go to the Anglican church and turn right. Three houses down."

"What are you going to do?"

"Since I'm out, I'm going shoot down to Current and drop a parcel off. I'll be at the mooring when you're done, don't worry."

I wasn't worried until he said it. I walked up the street with my brown paper bag in my hand. There were a few people hanging around a house that seemed to do double duty as a grocery store. When I reached the church, I turned right and counted the houses. The one I apparently wanted was an old timber place with a small porch and a flower bed out front.

I knocked on the door and heard the floors creaking inside as someone came to answer. Courtenay opened the door and leaned against the jamb. He didn't give me any sense of recognition.

"Mr. Courtenay, I'm Miami Jones. We met a couple days ago over at the resort."

He nodded slowly. I wasn't sure if he was acknowledging that he had heard me or if he remembered.

"Do you remember me?"

"I'm not dead."

"I'm glad about that. I brought you something." I handed him the bag, and he slipped the neck of the bottle out. He was familiar with the brand because he slipped it back in and said, "You'd best come in."

I stepped inside, and he closed the door. The windows were open allowing a little breeze through, but the house smelled musty nevertheless. The house was simple. A main living room, a kitchen, and a door to another room I assumed to be a bedroom. The furniture looked like mid-century modern, and I considered telling him it was worth a fortune on the second-hand market in the US.

He picked two glasses from beside the sink and directed me toward two chairs that sat opposite each other over a low coffee table. He opened the bottle and poured us each a finger.

I held my glass up to him before I sipped the rum. I wasn't a huge rum drinker, but it was smoother than I had expected it to be.

"I just wanted to ask you something about the boat you found out there."

"I told you all I know."

"I don't mean *that* boat."

He didn't frown, but he didn't have to. Like mine, his brow was already wrinkled, so his frown was in the eyes. He reached for the bottle and poured another measure, then he sat back in his chair.

"I don't know what you mean."

"Sure you do. Let me tell you a story, and you can fill in the gaps. Forty years ago, there was a roaring drug trade flowing through the Bahamas. The place was awash in crooked cash. And into that sailed a little vessel—or maybe it was a big vessel, that I don't know. Two Americans sailing the Caribbean wander right through the main shipping route for the Medellin Cartel out of Norman Cay. Now, I don't know what happened to those men, apart from the fact that they ended up dead. But I do know two things: one, the murders were investigated and then covered up by a Sergeant Bridges, and two, you were on that boat."

Courtenay didn't sip his rum, instead sloshing it around in a whirlpool in his glass. I wasn't sure if he was concocting a story or reliving the past, but I was prepared to wait to find out. I wasn't sure why, but it felt like his answer had a bearing on my own situation.

"Let me ask you a question," he said. "How old do you think I am?"

My mother had raised me to never ask this question of a lady, and my father had taught me never to answer it if asked, but with an old man, I wasn't so sure on the etiquette.

"I'm not sure, but maybe seventy?" I felt reasonably confident I had undershot the mark by enough to make him feel good about himself.

"I'm fifty-five."

I nearly spat up my rum. The years hadn't been kind. I guess it went like that for some folks. I was probably one of them. I had spent most of my childhood and early adult life in the sun on baseball fields or in the wind and rain of a football field. My skin told the tale. But Courtenay had been through the wringer. The wrinkles, the salt-and-pepper hair, the stoop. They all conspired to tell a lie.

"I'm sorry, but it's not my area of expertise."

"I don't mind. It is what it is. I've lived in the sun, so there's that, and I got hurt once and never got fully better. It is what it is."

"Why did you ask me that?"

"So you could work out for yourself how wrong you are on all counts."

"How so?"

"When that boat was found, I was fifteen. Just a boy."

"The kid who brought me over here is fourteen, and I reckon he'd take his boat to Florida if there was a dollar in it."

"You think a fourteen-year-old took on some drug mules?"

"I didn't say you took them on. I said you were on the boat."

He shook his head. "No. And you're wrong about the sergeant too."

"How am I wrong? You sure know a lot for a guy who wasn't there."

He knocked back his rum and then leaned forward and poured us both another. "Why do you want to know about this? It's ancient history."

"But history is repeating itself, don't you think? Another boat, another man missing. And I'm wondering if for the second time the cops are looking at the wrong guy."

"They're looking at you, aren't they?"

"Yes, they are. And I know I didn't do it. What about you? You wouldn't touch the boat the other night come hell or high water. Because you've done it before and gotten burned."

He coughed and then sipped his rum. "Not sure what good it will do you."

"Me either. But I don't like secrets much."

He leaned back and took a long, gurgling breath. "So the first thing you're wrong about is me. I wasn't there. I wasn't on that boat."

"Who was?"

"My brother."

"How did he come to be there?"

"He found it, floating, as you said."

"Was he coming from the resort like you?"

"No, there was no resort back then, and this boat was a good few miles farther south."

"What was he doing out there?"

"Fishing."

"That sounds like a story."

"No, it's the truth. He and a friend used to go out and catch snapper and maki. Even the odd small tuna. They'd sell a few, and we'd eat the rest."

"They were out fishing and happened upon the boat?"

"Yeah."

"But unlike you, they didn't call it in."

"I wouldn't have this time, either, if Barnard hadn't been there. Not my business."

"Why didn't they call it in?"

"No one had phones back then."

"They could have towed it back."

"They were in a dinghy. This boat was a big thing, a yacht, fifty-footer."

"Why did they even go near it then?"

"My brother had heard stories about the cartels killing people on their boats for being in the wrong place at the wrong time. See, what you have to know is, back then, a lot of people got touched by the drug money."

"I've heard."

"Lots of people wanted their piece. My brother was one of those people. He wanted into that world. He was never content here."

"So what did he do?"

"He boarded the boat. He said they called out to see if anyone was on board, and when there was no response, he got on board."

"Why?"

"Why do you think? To steal. Drugs or money or whatever he could find."

"And what did he find?"

"He found a dead body."

Courtenay let that hang in the air and finished his rum. He didn't move for another pour, although I felt like it was perfectly warranted.

"What did he do?"

"He got out of there, that's what he did. He was a tough guy, but he'd never seen a dead man."

"What happened?"

"Eventually the boat was found. I don't know who found it. But it was brought up to Spanish Wells, I think. And the police checked it out."

I nodded. I finally got it. "And they found your brother's prints."

"Yes. Both of their prints."

"But how did they match them?"

"My brother had been in trouble with the police. I told you, he wanted his part of that life. His friend was never part of that, but once they matched my brother, it wasn't going to take much to link his friend too."

"The police thought your brother and his friend murdered these men?"

"Yes. The sergeant came to the house and said he could place my brother on the boat, and they wanted to know who the other prints belonged to. He wouldn't tell."

"So what happened? I thought the case went dead."

"The soldier came."

"What soldier?"

Courtenay poured himself another shot. I hadn't touched mine, so he left the bottle on the table.

"I'm not sure any good can come of talking about it."

"Except your brother got off somehow. I might not be so lucky."

"They promised never to tell."

"Promised who?"

"The soldier."

"It was forty years ago. I get the sense you've needed to get this off your chest for a long time."

"I've never spoken to a soul about it. Not even my brother." He sipped his drink. "The soldier came to our house. My family lived a couple of streets along back then. He told my brother and his friend that he knew they hadn't killed those men, and he said he had made a deal with the police. They were going to close the case down, but people might ask questions, so he said it was better if my brother and his friend weren't there to answer."

"Wouldn't that look suspicious?"

"People leave here all the time. There's not a lot of opportunity."

"So what did they do?"

"The soldier gave them fare. They went to Nassau."

"For how long?"

Courtenay swirled his drink again. "They never came back."

"Why? Didn't the whole thing die down?"

"I guess it did. But they got jobs there, and my brother's friend's parents moved out there a year or two later."

"Is your brother still there?"

"No." He sighed again. "No, my brother's dead."

I looked at my own drink but didn't swirl it. "I'm sorry. What happened?"

"He wanted his piece of that life. He died in a gunfight in Freeport about ten years later."

"I'm sorry," I said again. I downed my rum and poured myself another measure but held onto it. I wasn't sure how this helped me at all. The superintendent's father had killed a case. I didn't know if it was for money, and I wasn't sure it mattered.

"You wouldn't touch the boat the other night because of your brother."

Courtenay nodded.

"I don't blame you."

"What will you do now? About what I've told you."

"Nothing. It's between you and your brother and his friend, and the sergeant and this soldier, I suppose."

"It doesn't help you?"

"Not so much. You think the sergeant was paid off to forget what he knew?"

"I don't know. The soldier never said. A lot of people took money back then."

"Was he Bahamian, this soldier?"

"No. He was American."

"Huh."

"Why?"

"I don't know."

We sipped our drinks in silence for a while and then I asked him why he had never gone to Nassau.

"I wasn't my brother. This is my home. I like it here."

"I like it here too."

We drank and chatted for a while longer, then I remembered Jimmy was waiting. I thanked him for his time, and he offered me the half bottle to take, and I told him it was my gift. He walked me to the door, and we shook hands, then he put his hand on my shoulder and nodded gently.

As I moved to leave, I asked him, "By the way, what was your brother's name?"

"Leo."

"And his friend?"

"Philip. Philip Corrigan."

He closed the door and left me standing in the dim twilight taking in that little nugget. I walked back down the street toward the water. Jimmy was laid back on the grass.

"There's a waiting fee, you know."

"Don't worry, kid. I'll take care of you."

We got in the boat, and he headed for Spanish Wells.

"I assume you found him?" he asked.

"I did."

"Did it help?"

"I think so."

I did think so. I just wasn't sure who exactly it had helped.

# CHAPTER THIRTY

WHEN I WOKE THE NEXT MORNING, THE FAN WAS FLUTTERING THE bottom of Lizzy's map I had hung on a pegboard that once held a man's tools. It was the kind of hand-drawn map that one always found in tourist towns, designed to draw the eye to points of interest as well as local merchants, who had ponied up to be highlighted. It was rare the establishments on such a map were the best places in town, or the joints where the locals hung out. But money talked, and tourists took the easy route.

It was a little different in Spanish Wells due to the small number of establishments. It was like they had passed around a hat at a meeting of the chamber of commerce. Everyone was listed. The three bars I had seen, a lot of charter boat guys, and the cart rental place. There was a souvenir stand on a side street I hadn't seen, and the local museum. The churches and the Food Fair and Papa Scoops.

Then there were the little crosses Lizzy had made in black marker to show the locations of shell disappearances. There were enough for it to be more than one old lady losing her marbles, but not enough for it to be a gang of shell burglars.

I looked for a pattern. Humans liked regularity. People got up at the same time and took the same route to work. They told themselves they ate different things every night for dinner but went to the same steakhouse for special occasions, and they ate tacos on the same schedule, whether daily, monthly, or never.

I didn't find a pattern. I had noticed as I made my way around the small island that not every house had a yard with conch shells around its border. There were more of them at the east end and fewer at the west. There were more in the lower elevation blocks than the upper elevation blocks. I got the sense that collecting the shells had once been a thing—perhaps it was about status, but since few people seemed to buy them, perhaps people just liked the look of them.

But that was fifty years ago. As the town grew with the advent of artificial cooling and better access to the outside world, it grew west. First more houses on St. George's Cay itself and then when the bridge was built over to Russell Island, there too. Russell was still largely vegetation, but I could see the new houses dotting the coast, all bigger and better materials. But no conch shell borders.

The few yards with conch shells were largely east of the center line of the island. But there was a definite cluster at the east end, and I resolved to understand whether this was purely a function of opportunity or indeed some kind of pattern.

I took the golf cart for a little ride. I drove down the main drag past The Shipyard where a few people were having brunch on the verandah overlooking the water back toward the dock at Gene's Bay. The road continued around the eastern tip of the island, more small homes that were rented by the week or two, with nice front porches and views of low tide. I slowed to a walking pace, and the people enjoying coffee on the porches waved as I went by in the way that people on vacation often do but rarely do back in the big city.

None of the waterfront places had shells in their yards, so I started zigzagging the island, back and forth from north to south and north again. At the nose of the island, the streets were only a hundred yards long, but as the land mass widened, the streets got longer but never more than about five hundred yards.

I learned the island was cut into north-south slices, each about a quarter of the island wide. The westernmost slice had no conch borders and therefore no thefts. The next slice, which included Captain Augie's house as well as the yacht resort below it, had a smattering of yards with conch decorations but also no thefts.

The third quarter, where the bulk of the residences were, had the same number of yards with shells lining them. And the final quarter at the east end, where Mrs. Albury's house was, was the same. Although the last quarter had fewer houses, it was an older part of town and had a higher proportion of shell decorations, supporting my hypothesis the shells were an older affectation.

The notable thing about the final two quarters was they had the same number of opportunities for theft but not the same actual thefts. The east end had close to double. In my experience this was probably a function of proximity. When people stole things, they often did it in a specific locality based on their psychology. In more simple terms, some people stole things because they were close by, and some stole things because they were farther away. The first was about temptation—seeing something every day that they coveted but couldn't have. The second was about calculation—stealing but doing it away from their own patch to divert attention.

I drove back down the road, which I now knew to be imaginatively called South Road, until I got to the last known location of a theft. I drove one more street, then I cut up the hill. I stopped on top of it and looked down both sides. One view was the sand flats and the beach and the other way the piers on the channel and the view to Russell Island. I got back in the cart and drove around to the next street and stopped on the crest again, looking down both sides. I saw people walking way out on the sand bars on the north side and boats tied up at repose on the south.

I drove one more street farther, stopped on the hill, and looked around. I saw the people on sand bars on one side and a boat on the other, which caught my eye. A boat I recognized. And some thoughts clicked into place.

Back in the cart, I cruised down to Samuel Guy and then up the cross street Lizzy had noted. I pulled over just short of the crest of the hill outside a yellow house with a green golf cart parked in the driveway. There was a wire fence and a well-tended lawn. No border of shells. Instead a row of large shells guarded the front of the house like soldiers. There was an obvious gap in the line, as if one of the soldiers had gone AWOL.

I knocked on the door and waited. The man who opened the door had white hair and skin tanned like a leather handbag. He was old but indeterminately so—he might have been seventy, but after my poor guess with Courtenay, he could just as easily have been a hundred, he was so well preserved.

I introduced myself and told him I had gotten his address from the church ladies. He smiled. I wasn't sure if it was for the church ladies or the company.

"James Pinder," he said, inviting me in. His house was similar to Mrs. Albury's—all the space he needed and not a square foot more —but it was built from cinderblock and therefore felt cooler.

"Are you related to Augustus?" I asked as we reached his kitchen.

"Probably, somewhere way back. You'll find a lot of the same names on the island—Pinders, Sands, Alburys. A lot of the names go back to the Eleutheran Adventurers. Do you know about them?"

"I've heard the stories of Preacher's Cave."

"Right. Well, some of our people came then, and some came over the next couple hundred years, but even those people came two hundred years ago."

"And they didn't leave."

"Some did. It takes a certain kind of person to make it in a place like this, and those kinds of people don't tend to do well elsewhere."

"And you're one of those people?"

"I am. An islander. Would you like iced tea?"

"Please."

James poured two iced teas and led me back to the reception room at the front of the house. He had the windows open, and the higher elevation offered a breeze that Mrs. Albury's house didn't benefit from.

"How long have you been here, James?"

"I was born here. In the house I grew up in."

"Not this place."

"No, we had a house down on the east end. I lived there after my parents passed, but that place was destroyed by a hurricane about twenty years ago."

"Sorry to hear that."

He shrugged like that was life.

"So you moved here?"

He nodded slowly. "There weren't many houses up here when I was a kid, but by the time the old place was lost, people were living here, and the houses were solid, so my wife and I moved."

I looked around. I didn't see any evidence of a woman.

"Did you lobster? Is that a verb?"

"Sure, why not." He stood and removed a thick volume from a bookshelf, then he sat beside me. He opened the book to reveal old photographs. There were faded shots of people—young, old, and everything in between. He flicked the pages until he got to a spread with some shots clearly taken underwater. I saw what looked like a small wooden platform on the sea bed.

"What's that?"

"We call that a lobster condo. See, we put them on the ocean floor, and the lobsters find them and use them as shelter. Then we dive down and lift up the condo and pull the lobsters out."

"That's it?"

"That's it."

"Is that you?"

"That's me."

"You don't have a tank."

"No scuba. We free dive."

"As in, hold your breath?"

"That's right."

"Is that dangerous?"

"Depended on the depth and the weather. Bad days, yes, it was dangerous. I lost friends over the years."

He flipped the book closed and returned it back to the shelf. As he did, I noticed how orderly his home was.

"So, Mrs. Albury tells me you lost a conch shell."

He frowned as he stood by the bookshelf. "Yes. Let me show you."

I was pretty sure I had already seen it, but I followed him anyway. We walked out onto the lawn and stood looking at the row of upright shells with their tails stuck into the ground. As I saw them for the second time, I realized that they were less like soldiers and more like a chorus line. Each shell had bright pink lips like they were singers with their heads tilted in a jaunty fashion.

"These are conchs, huh?"

"These are more than conchs. These are all queen conchs."

"What's the difference?"

"Queens are bigger—not just the shell but the snail inside. They are the true Bahamian conch. Highly prized."

"You eat them?"

"I used to. We used to free dive for them. In some places there were conchs as far as the eye could see. You could take your pick. But that was a long time ago."

"So why would someone steal a shell they could dive for or find on the beach? I mean, I saw one in the grass when I went for a swim."

"Not like this, I'll wager."

"It was a conch."

"Queens at this size and condition are almost unheard of now. See, our rules for harvesting were very lax for a long time, and now the stocks have been depleted. As tourism grew, so did demand for this Bahamian delicacy, and the result was overfishing. The population might never recover. But even if it does, you'll never see queens get this large again. And commercial fishermen make a hole in the shell to detach the snail. These shells have no such hole because we collected them after the animal had died, so they're rare, and getting rarer."

I looked at the gap in the line of shells and then at James. He was looking at the shells like a farmer looks at a sick animal.

"Did these come from your old house?" I asked.

"They did. We had our entire yard ringed by shells we collected over the years. Me and my father before me, and his father before him. But the hurricane that took the house swept most of them out to sea." He shrugged. "Maybe the ocean was reclaiming its own. But these were all that were left. Three generations of my family."

I watched the years descend across his face. I had felt as if searching for stolen shells was a touch ridiculous, but I had done it to return Mrs. Albury's hospitality and to keep Lizzy off my back. I had been of a mind to wander into the water and find a few replacements and be done with it. I hadn't considered that a shell could be an heirloom, but here I was standing in an old man's yard looking at three generations of a family that had been here for many more, and the gap in the chorus line stuck out all the more for it.

"It would almost be better if they were all gone," he said. I got the sense he wasn't really talking to me.

"I'll see what I can find for you, but I'm not sure we'll get the exact shell back. But one looks like any other, right?"

"No." He stepped over to the line of shells and dug his hand into the dirt behind them like he was harvesting potatoes. He lifted a shell out of the ground and dusted off the bottom and turned it to me. The initials JP had been scrawled onto the outside of the shell in paint.

"J.P.? That's you?" I asked.

"Maybe. Me, my father, my grandfather. I'm the sixth James Pinder, that I know of."

"James Pinder the sixth. Sounds like a king."

"Not anymore. The others are all gone, so now I'm just plain old James Pinder. My daughter doesn't carry that burden."

"Does she live here too?"

"No. She married an American. You ever been to Idaho?"

"No."

"Me either."

He put the shell back in its place, and I shook his hand. I thanked him for his time, and he said I was welcome.

"I'll see what I find."

He gave me a melancholy smile and wandered inside, and I got in Mrs. Albury's cart and drove away.

# CHAPTER THIRTY-ONE

I drove back down Samuel Guy and stopped at the police station for my daily check-in. Ken Corrigan was standing outside like a man having a smoke, but there wasn't a cigarette in his hand.

"Reporting in, Corporal, as requested."

"Noted."

"How are your prisoners?"

"Technically, we have one prisoner and one medical case."

"He's still running with the amnesia thing?"

"He doesn't appear to have come up with anything better yet."

"This would be a hard place to forget."

"True enough."

"Did you grow up here?"

He looked puzzled. "No, I didn't. I was born in Nassau. I grew up there."

"And your dad knew Lucas?"

"He did."

"What's your dad's name?"

"What's with the Spanish Inquisition?"

"Just curious."

"Really. Well, my dad's name was Philip."

"Good name."

"As good as any. You're being very weird."

"Sorry, I was just interested in how he met Lucas."

"Through his friend."

"His friend?"

"Yes, Lucas had a buddy who my dad knew. They came fishing here."

"Your dad didn't know Lucas originally?"

"No. What's this about?"

"Nothing, really. Just coincidence. See, I met Lucas through a buddy of his too."

"That's often how people meet—through other people."

"What was his buddy's name? Do you know?"

"Of course I know. My dad always said the guy saved his life. His name was Lenny."

"Lenny Cox."

"That's right. How did you know that?"

"That's who introduced me to Lucas as well."

"Well, I suppose that's not that surprising. Lenny was like that."

"Yes, he was. I know how your dad feels. Lenny more or less saved my life too."

"Felt," said Ken. "How my dad felt. He passed away."

"I'm sorry. When was this?"

"Three years ago now. Cancer."

"Geez."

"Yeah. And Lenny's gone too."

"More than a decade now. He must have known your dad a long time ago."

"Before I was born. He said I was going to be named after him, but Lenny wouldn't let him. Said it was too much of a cross to bear."

"That's Lenny."

"They used it as my second name."

"Your second name is Lenny?"

He smiled and shrugged.

"I like that," I said. "I like that a lot."

"Listen, the super is waiting on a blood test for Mr. Reels. It's expected later today. If it matches and Reels keeps with his amnesia story, the super's probably going to come for you."

"Can I ask you a question?" I said. "You've lost your dad, and I've lost mine. What about the superintendent? Is his father dead?"

"No, he's retired and lives in Nassau. Why?"

"Just curious."

Ken frowned, and I told him I'd see him around.

Mrs. Albury was at the kitchen sink when I got back. Lizzy had her laptop open on the table beside a pile of notes.

"We're just debating lunch, dear. Ham or turkey?"

"Why don't I take you out for lunch?" I asked.

Mrs. Albury looked surprised. "Out? You mean a restaurant?"

"Yes. Why don't we wander down to The Shipyard? It's not too far."

"Restaurants are so expensive."

"It's on me, Mrs. Albury. I can assure you that putting me up is cheaper than a lunch out." I wasn't sure what the going rate was for a cot in a garden shed, but the idea suited my objective.

"I better get my face on." Mrs. Albury shuffled away, and Lizzy gave me a smile that made me feel like a decent human being.

"She'll be a while," said Lizzy. "You want to go through this?"

"Sure." I pulled up a chair.

"Okay, so I'll start with what you know. Mr. Reels was the all-American story. Humble beginnings, working class, all that. A politician's dream childhood."

"Such cynicism, Lizzy."

"You must be rubbing off. It started with him fishing with his father and ended with him being a big shot. He was one of the biggest reality stars on cable television before reality TV was a thing. He was worth a bundle. Big house, fancy cars, all the trappings. At one point he had four shows running at the same time, he bought a share of the channel, and he had endorsement deals with everyone from a worm producer to Chevrolet."

"I'm sensing a *but*."

"*But* then cable tanked. Within a decade his viewership went from its all-time high to fifteen percent of what it had once been. The big-money advertisers all moved on to the Kardashians or online into other sports."

"And the worm guys?"

"They probably stuck around because the only people left were older viewers who were of limited appeal to the mass-market advertisers. Now his channel's ads are for reverse mortgages and AARP, and even they aren't paying top dollar. But the short of it is, the lost viewers and ad revenue and endorsements cost Rusty millions."

"Poor guy."

"It gets worse. I've done some digging into his financials since. It seems he launched a new line of sportsman's clothing that failed badly."

"There's only so much khaki and camo the world needs."

"Then he bet the farm on an investment in a new electric boat."

"An electric boat?"

"In press releases he called it the Tesla of the sea."

"Catchy."

"No, not really."

"There seems an inherent risk in an electric motor around water."

"Actually, from what I've read, the technology is pretty sound, and getting better all the time. But just like with electric cars, they had to overcome some built-in fears. With cars it was about travel distance and what happened when the battery ran low and you were nowhere near a charging station. The car guys focused on city drivers who went ten or twenty miles a day, and they built their charging networks from there. But with the boats, well, you just showed a preconceived prejudice right there."

"I did?"

"Electricity and water, right? Not made for each other. Then there's salt and goodness knows what else. Plus, what if your battery does die on the water? It's not like you can carry a jerry can of emergency gas."

"Right."

"But most of these problems have largely been solved, so there's actually a fair bit of logic to electric boats now. At least enough for Mr. Reels to get investment in the project. But with his falling audience and lost revenue, he couldn't get money from what they seem to call *traditional lenders*."

"Which means?"

"Banks, venture capital, private equity."

"Which left?"

"Lenders of last resort."

"That sounds like payday lenders, loan sharks."

"Multiply the numbers into the millions, and you're onto something."

"Are you saying he got into deals with, what, the mafia?"

"I can't say that, but what I can say is that none of the companies involved are public companies or listed funds, and they sound a lot less friendly than Bank of America."

"He's got mob money on the line?"

"Something like that. One way to launder cash is to invest dark money in legitimate businesses. But that only works if the cash then gets out of the business and back to the organization or person laundering it."

"Let me guess, that didn't happen."

"No. The boat was a disaster. A lot of things that made no sense to me—flow issues, capacity problems—and some that did, like reliability and production hiccups. In short, the company produced a failed prototype and was sued by everyone and his dog who made a preorder. The business is in terrible shape, and from my reading of it, their only hope is a fire sale where they might get ten cents on the dollar."

"That wouldn't make for happy investors."

"I would think not." Lizzy picked up her phone. "Danielle texted me a police report from Atlanta PD. It seems there was some malicious damage done at the channel's headquarters."

"Such as?"

"The windows on Mr. Reels's SUV were smashed. All of them, apparently. He had them fixed, and it happened again. Three times in total."

"Ouch. They get video or anything?"

"Nothing. According to the police report, no one was talking, especially not Mr. Reels. So the police filed it and moved on."

"A warning for debts unpaid?"

"Or investments lost."

"You're saying that Rusty was going broke and losing money that belonged to less-than-reputable lenders, the kind that might break his kneecaps, or worse."

"That's what the paper trail suggests."

"So these mob guys might have had their fill and decided to off Rusty."

"They might have had it turned out he was dead. But he's not, is he?"

"No. So what gives?"

"Is it possible that Mr. Reels was attempting to fake his own death to get away from these people?"

"Anything's possible. But faking your death is one thing. Going on living with no money and no identity is another." I was hit by the thought that Rusty had no ID on him when we found him.

"But there might have been a solution to the money part," said Lizzy. "Maybe not all of it, but Danielle says the Georgia Bureau of Investigation had a whistleblower in the works who claimed that money beyond the known losses was disappearing from the cable channel."

"He was embezzling the channel?"

"It's just a theory. And then there's life insurance. I have no way of knowing what he had, but for someone so big back in the day, the policy might have been worth millions. His wife is probably the beneficiary, so she might be in on it. And you might not live like a prince, but you could certainly disappear and do okay with millions, couldn't you?"

"I dare say you could if you could claim it. So we're saying that

Rusty set it up to look like he was killed so he could escape the mob with a small load of cash."

"Like I say, it's a theory."

"Well, there's one part of your theory that still needs answering."

"Why you?"

"Right. Why set me up for it?"

"Assuming they did."

"If the rest of your theory holds, and it looks pretty solid, then my being set up fits. They could have done this whole lost at sea thing without me. Rusty lived on boats, and people fall off boats. It happens. They could have sold it. Introducing me only added a complication they didn't need. But they did it anyway, which suggests to me that someone wanted Rusty to disappear and for me to take the fall for it. A two for one. And that someone was either Rusty himself or someone else, and I don't know Rusty, and he doesn't seem to know me. I can't see why he would want me in jail."

"So someone else. Like the other man you caught?"

"Michael Alexander. But him I also don't know."

"But maybe he knows you. Or he's linked to someone who knows you."

"Maybe, but who?"

# CHAPTER THIRTY-TWO

I PUT MRS. ALBURY INTO THE PASSENGER SIDE OF THE GOLF CART AS Lizzy sat on the rear bench, and we puttered down the road to the restaurant at the end of the island. There was a line of carts parked out front, so I pulled into the steps and dropped off Lizzy and Mrs. Albury and then parked the cart farther down. I didn't have to go back around to get into the place—the side of the building was a verandah that looked across toward the dock at Gene's Bay, so I walked around the tables there to find the ladies.

We sat outside with a can of Sterno burning on the table to keep the bugs at bay. A young woman delivered menus and welcomed Mrs. Albury by name as if she was a regular. We ordered a round of iced teas and then a conch salad to share. After meeting with James Pinder, eating conch felt a little bit like dining on whale, so I left the salad to the ladies.

I was enjoying my lobster pasta when Lizzy's phone rang. She looked embarrassed by the social faux pas, but she glanced at the screen before killing the call, which she didn't do. She handed me the phone, and I saw the number, so I excused myself and left the table. As I walked across the wood decking toward the water, I answered.

"Sergeant Tellis," I said.

"Miami," she replied. "You move in interesting circles."

"Go on."

"I found your friend Michael Alexander in our database. You're right that he's out of Ocho Rios, but the database suggested he was associated with a crew in Montego Bay. I made a few calls to my old haunts, and guess who Alexander works for in MoBay?"

"I have no clue."

"Desmond Richmond."

I felt my guts churn. There was a signpost at the end of the island with wood markers showing how far various other Bahamian islands were from that location, and I leaned against it for support. There was no sign for anything as far as Jamaica, but I was instantly transported.

Danielle and I had been vacationing there years before when we ran into a young athlete who was caught in a power play between a local criminal and a corrupt athletics official. The criminal— Desmond Richmond—had kidnapped the young man when I had arranged for him to visit the University of Miami to try out for an athletics scholarship.

But Danielle and I, along with her Miami FBI contacts, had apprehended Richmond, and the last I heard he was in a medium-security federal facility in Marianna, Florida.

I stumbled away from the signpost to a nearby rotunda on the water's edge to escape the sun and ensure my brain didn't overheat.

"I thought he was in prison," I said.

"He was. He did a couple of years in Florida, and then his green card was revoked, and he was deported back to Jamaica, where he was tried and jailed for another couple of years for related crimes that had been committed here. Four years inside thanks to you, Miami."

"Gee, thanks, Lucia. I wasn't on any of those juries."

"I know that."

"What happened to him?"

"After he got out, it seems he became a model citizen."

"Really?"

"No, Miami. He returned to his local haunts in MoBay. Some of his so-called businesses had been taken over by others in his absence."

"Nature abhors a vacuum."

"Yes, but a criminal abhors someone taking his turf. Desmond took some of it back the hard way, and he recruited some new faces to build some new shady business."

"Faces like Michael Alexander?"

"One and the same. My contacts up there say Alexander is one of Desmond's chief enforcers."

"And now he's in the Bahamas."

"Which is interesting given that he doesn't appear to be the owner of a passport."

"Perhaps I'll pass that on to the locals."

"Do."

"But if we accept the idea that Desmond Richmond has been rotting in jail with a newspaper clipping of me up on his wall, how do we connect him to Rusty Reels? It's a long bow."

"Not so."

"Oh, good."

"I made a call to our immigration department. It turns out that Mr. Reels's production company applied for visas to come and film his show in and around Jamaica."

"When was this?"

"They applied five months ago, but they filmed here three months ago. Apparently his production company came to MoBay, filmed, and then left with a trail of unpaid bills in their wake."

"That sounds like par for the course. And it puts Reels in the same town as Richmond."

"I can do better than that. Mr. Reels's people chartered a local sports fishing boat to scout locations and take them around the place. The boat's name is *On the Loose*."

"Oh, goodness."

"Yeah, so you know who owns it."

"Desmond Richmond."

"The one and only."

"So we can put Rusty and Richmond on a boat together for the best part of a week."

"More or less."

"Do your contacts have eyes on Richmond now?"

"There's no active investigation, so no one is watching him 24/7."

"Then he might be here too?"

"Mr. Richmond has not been issued a valid passport since his release."

"Michael Alexander doesn't have one either, and he's here."

"Good point."

"How would they get here?"

"Not by air," she said.

"And not by road."

"True enough. Let me ask around and see if there are any decent-sized boats out from MoBay right now."

"Thanks, Lucia. I owe you one."

"We wouldn't have gotten Richmond in the first place if not for you, so let's call it even. Take care."

I took a long deep breath, in through my nose and out through my mouth. I was staggered by how small actions begat big results, both positive and negative. Acorns became oaks. I had no idea what poison oak came from, but it felt like I had planted it on a vacation years before.

I walked back to the table and returned Lizzy's phone, then I sat and finished my lunch. Mrs. Albury and Lizzy split a tiramisu for dessert. I couldn't stomach it. I sat and watched the placid water ripple before me as the churning in my guts became a tsunami.

# CHAPTER THIRTY-THREE

Mrs. Albury went and sat in the front room when we got home, and I wandered out to the shed, turned on the fan, and sat in front of it. I tried to picture Desmond Richmond in his cell. The image I came up with was the lockup at the police station where I had been a guest for a couple of nights. It was surely a more hospitable environment than either a federal pen in the US or anything in which one was likely to serve time in Jamaica, but it was the best my feeble imagination could do.

In my line of work, I had more than once been required to think like a criminal, to understand the person or persons I was up against. Some criminals and criminal acts were easy to understand. Sometimes people simply made mistakes. Sometimes they acted out of desperation, to stave off homelessness or hunger. Sometimes it was passion and a flash of anger in an otherwise cool head. I even understood greed, at least as a motive.

I didn't understand taking for taking's sake. The exertion of power simply because one could. To me, things always had a point. You didn't always get what you wanted in life, but you usually got what you earned. I had sat in the bullpen in a major league baseball stadium wearing the uniform of the home team after a lifetime of hard work and dedication to my craft. But I had never taken the mound. I had never thrown a pitch in anger. I was given a glimpse of the promised land and then was cast aside.

For the next years I had been certain I would get back there, that hard work would earn me another shot. A shot that never came. When my career ended in the minors I was adrift and confused, but I was also certain that there was a reason for it. I didn't share Lizzy's certainty of a higher power. I believed the reasons lay within—the reasons for success just as much as the reasons for failure, and the lessons I would go on to derive.

But I would never assume I had a right to anything. That something earned by another should be mine. I didn't understand Desmond Richmond back then, trying to control the life and career of a young athlete for no other reason than the exertion of power. I didn't understand him now, trying to set me up for something in retribution for his own shortcomings.

But my friend and mentor, Lenny Cox, had taught me everything important that made me who I had become, and if I had pitched the perfect game in Oakland, I might never have gotten to know him the way I had. I would never have learned his lessons, known his truth.

Lenny always said that a tuxedo would get you into any room, and he had bought my first tuxedo to prove the point. He also told me that I should never start a fight, never throw the first punch. Always give someone the chance to explain, to stand down, for better angels to prevail. But if you ever did find yourself in a fight, you fight to win, and you don't stop until you do. The knock at the door pulled me back into the room. "Yeah?"

Lizzy pushed her way into the shed. "You want to tell me?"

She sat on the cot, and I told her. She knew most of what had happened years ago with Richmond, so I cut to the chase. Lizzy took it in silence until I was done.

"It's him, isn't it?"

"I don't have definitive proof, but it smells that way."

"Think about it. Rusty's company was hemorrhaging money—leaving a trail of unpaid bills in Jamaica is what you said. It's not hard to imagine him balking at paying Richmond, a man who would not take kindly to getting bilked. They negotiate a plan. Maybe Mr. Reels has mentioned something on the boat about his lenders, the stress he's under. When Richmond applies his own pressure, the truth comes out. Rusty has no cash and has people worse than Richmond wanting their money. It's not hard to see Richmond coming up with a plan. To fake Mr. Reels's death to escape these guys. Like you say, maybe there's insurance money that can keep Mr. Reels going, but anything's got to be better than being dead. And all Richmond wants in return is for Mr. Reels to set you up for his murder."

"That and probably a bit of the insurance payout action. He's no one's idea of altruistic. But I can't get my head around it, Lizzy. I wasn't on the jury, and I didn't put the guy in jail. The evidence did that."

"You know as well as anyone he wouldn't see it like that. People like him don't see their demise as a consequence of their actions; all they see is yours."

"It makes me reconsider a lot of my life choices."

"Self-reflection is a good thing. I'd tell you to pray on it, but I know I'll have to do that for you. But right now, we need proof. You won't get your passport back with nothing but a story."

"I know." I drifted away for a minute. My brain started whirring. Perhaps Lizzy knew the look in my eyes because she remained silent until I came back.

"Can you send a text to Sergeant Tellis and ask her for the most recent mugshot she has of Desmond Richmond?"

"Consider it done. What about you?"

I smiled.

"You've got a plan, don't you?"

"Better than that, Lizzy. I've got half a plan."

# CHAPTER THIRTY-FOUR

I sat on my cot staring at Lizzy's tourist map until all the tumblers clicked into place in my brain, then I got into the golf cart and zoomed back down Samuel Guy. I reached the street I wanted and again headed up the hill, then I stopped outside the house with the wood siding in need of a paint.

I knocked on the door and waited until young Jimmy opened it and eventually looked up from his phone.

"You need a ride to Nassau now?"

"Give it time. Is your mother home?"

"No, she's at work."

"Do you have your boat key with you?"

He reached into his pocket and pulled out a keyring and spun it around his finger. I snatched the keys from him, and he was about to protest when I barged past him and strode into his house, giving him something completely different to complain about.

"Hey, man, what are you doing?"

I didn't stop for a chat. I walked straight through the kitchen and out the back door and across the lawn. I flicked the keys around the ring until I got the small one I was looking for, and when I reached the garden shed, I put it straight into the padlock securing the door.

"You can't do that," said Jimmy.

"Just did."

"You can't go in there."

"Beg to differ."

I slipped the lock out and grabbed the door handle, and Jimmy put his palm on it to stop me. I grabbed his wrist with one hand and twisted it around and down, and he howled as his whole arm was forced to follow suit lest it break. As he went to ground, I opened the door with my other hand.

I make a lot of bold pronouncements. I figure it's a product of my sporting upbringing. I never did point at the bleachers like Babe Ruth, but then I was also a big believer in making sure I could back up my big pronouncements, and I wasn't much of a slugger. And I had to admit I got my fair share of them wrong—as I had in thinking Mr. Courtenay had been on the boat all those years ago. But it was amazing how often those incorrect conclusions turned into something good. It reminded me of the saying about fortune favoring the brave. Despite that, I did enjoy it when I got one right on the money.

I pulled the door fully open and let go of Jimmy's wrist and stood back to look at the shed full of conch shells. There were all kinds, colors, and sizes. Some looked pristine, like they had been cleaned for display at the American Museum of Natural History, and others were covered in dirt as if they had been mined from the ground, not the sea. It was a hell of an impressive display, if one could call a bunch of stolen loot such a thing.

I pushed the door closed and replaced the lock and then walked back inside the house. I was sitting at the kitchen table when Jimmy shuffled in, ashen faced. He took my lead and sat at the table but didn't make eye contact, and he said nothing at all. I figured that was a good policy to have if he was going to embark on a life of crime.

"You're the talk of the town," I said.

"Me?"

"The Conch Thief, I think, is the most popular moniker."

"Look, you've got it wrong. I didn't—"

"Don't embarrass yourself or insult me by denying it, kid. You've been stealing conch shells from people's yards."

"Please don't tell my mom."

"Your mom? Jimmy, your mom is the least of your problems. People have complained to the police. It's theft, and you could go to jail."

"Jail? I'm fourteen."

"Well, you could go to a home or something. I don't know what you guys do in the Bahamas, but a police record is a police record. And it's not a good thing."

"But it's just a few conchs."

"That other people own."

Jimmy's jaw dropped, and even more telling, he stopped looking at his phone.

"May I ask why?"

He sighed. "You asked me about it yourself. I'm not a fishing kind of guy, and honestly, that's what a lot of boys here aspire to. Unless I'm looking to tend bar at a hotel on Harbour Island, I'm not exactly flush with options."

"So we go from fishing to crime?"

"No. I'm looking online one day, and I see this guy who's flipping stuff on eBay."

"Flipping?"

"Yeah, you know, arbitrage."

"Yes, I know arbitrage, but I have a college education. How do you know arbitrage? You're fourteen."

"I saw it online. Buy things at a discount in one market and sell them in another market at a profit. I saw people going to garage sales and buying people's old stuff and flipping it for profit, right?"

"Why wouldn't people just go to the garage sale for themselves?"

"Because they can't or won't. They're time poor, or they're not in the same market. You could buy something in New York and sell it online in California, but no one's traveling that far to go to a garage sale, are they?"

"I'm not crossing the street to buy someone's junk, but that's by the by. And it doesn't explain the conchs."

"You see a lot of garage sales in Spanish Wells?"

"No."

"Exactly. There's nothing to flip. So I'm online one day, and I come across conch shells. We have them lying in the ocean, right?"

"Yes, I've seen them. But not as many as there used to be, so I'm told."

"That's true. Boomers overfished everything, conchs included. But here's the thing. I see online that the big conchs, the queens, they get top dollar. Especially the ones with no holes in them. And lots of people have them lying around their yards."

"A decorative border is not lying around."

"It's not that great a look, though, is it? Let's be honest."

"I might not do it myself, but that's not my decision to make, and it's sure as hell not yours either. Some of these people have been collecting the shells for generations, Jimmy. The conchs mean something to these people."

"Really?"

"Yes, really."

"They're just shells."

"Some of them are, but some of them aren't. Some of them are important to the people who own them. And you're stealing them."

"I'm sorry."

"Are you? Or are you saying that to get out of trouble?"

"I didn't think it was that big a deal."

"What did you do with them?"

"Like I say, I saw them online. In the US people want to buy them for decorations or whatever, and they love the big old ones because you can't really get them in the US anymore. I saw one in this old yard, and I figured no one would miss it. The place was a bit of a dump anyway. And guess what? They didn't miss it. So I cleaned it and sold it online. When no one said anything, I figured I'd do it again. And then I hit the jackpot."

"Jackpot?"

"I found one where the snail critter had died inside and the shell had become clogged with sand and whatever, so when I cleaned it, I found a conch pearl."

"What's a conch pearl?"

"What do you think it is? It's a pearl, like from an oyster, but not white. They're pink and usually much bigger than an oyster pearl."

"You sold the pearl online?"

"Yeah."

"How much do you get for these shells?"

"About a hundred bucks, plus shipping."

"It's not exactly a king's ransom."

"I'm fourteen. It's better than nothing."

"How many do you sell?"

"Maybe one a week, sometimes two."

"And what about this pearl?"

"I got two grand for that."

"Two thousand dollars?"

"Yep."

Maybe crime did pay. "What happens when you've taken all the shells on the island? Are you gonna start boosting people's televisions? Maybe a golf cart or two?"

"No."

"This is how it starts, Jimmy. Cutting corners, looking for the easy money."

"I'm not looking for easy money, Mr. Jones, honest. I'm looking for any money. You see another option round here?"

"There's always another option to crime." I was starting to sound like my father, or worse, Detective Ronzoni.

He picked at his fingers. "How did you know it was me?"

"You looking to refine your plan?"

"No."

"Well, don't, because it won't work. In the course of my own troubles, I learned a small dinghy was coming into the docks just down from here late at night. And your mother often works late, right? Then when you took me over to Current, you left your dirt bike at the post office, and when you took me to see Mr. Courtenay in Bluff, you brought a parcel and said you were going to nip down to Current while I was talking to him. I didn't think anything of it until I learned a little history about this area. The drug runners back in the seventies and eighties used Spanish Wells and other Bahamian islands as stopping points for the drug trade. They moved their nasty product through by aircraft and boat, and even tried sending it through the mail. So then something clicked. Where were the stolen conchs going? Perhaps away from here. And how? Perhaps through the mail. And who went to the post office more than most? You did. Then I realized there was a post office here in Spanish Wells. So why go all the way to Current? Eventually people around here would start talking, wouldn't they? Those ladies at the church know everything that goes on here. But Current is just far enough away to keep it quiet, at least for a little while."

"Damn."

"Yeah, damn. You know it's illegal to import conchs into the US."

"That's for the buyer to worry about. It's not illegal to send them. I always keep a close watch, make sure people get what they paid for. I was ready to refund anyone whose shell got confiscated."

"Did that happen?"

"Not once."

I shook my head. "Are you getting any of this? Do you see how serious this is? Not the shells themselves, but the idea of taking something that isn't yours."

"I guess."

"Don't guess, Jimmy. Know."

"You sound like Yoda."

"And you sound like a kid a few years ahead of a stretch in prison."

His expression soured.

"Look, you're an entrepreneurial guy. You're going to go places. But if learning about the old drug trade reminded me of anything, it was that the easy street always comes to a dead end. All those guys living like kings at other people's expense, they all ended up in jail or dead."

The corners of his mouth turned down, and I thought he might cry, and I was reminded that he was only a kid.

"What's going to happen now? You going to use me to plea your way out of your situation?"

"It doesn't work that way, kid. You don't get to plea down a murder charge with a conch thief. No, I'm getting off my thing because I did the work, and I found the guy. He's not dead."

"He fell off his boat himself?"

"Not exactly."

"What about me?"

"Let me tell you what's going to happen. I'm going to keep this thing quiet. You're going to learn a lesson and take your licks, and I'm going to know if you don't and then I might change my mind and sing like a canary."

"Really?"

"Really. But I have four conditions, and they are non-negotiable and not up for discussion. No buts and no bargains. One, stop stealing other people's conchs."

"I don't want to do that anymore anyway."

"Well, let me amend that to stop stealing anything. Two, you're going to return or replace the shells you've taken. If you've sold them, you will replace them with something as close as possible. On that, did you sell the one from Mr. Pinder around the corner?"

"Not yet."

"Good. It's got his initials on it. Take it back. The others, just replace with something similar, okay?"

He frowned. "Yep. And the money?"

"I should confiscate it and give it to the save the coconut trees or whatever charities you have around here. But I'm not. The good people of Spanish Wells are going to spot you."

"Huh?"

"You're going to use what you've got as seed money. You said you learned how people flipped stuff, so you're going to do that."

"But there's nothing else good here."

"Have you heard of drop shipping?"

"No."

"It's where you buy a whole shipment of some product, and you send it to a warehouse who then sends it to your customers as and when you sell each item. They take a cut for storage and packing, but you never have to even see the product."

"That's a thing?"

"Not a thing I know much about, but I'm willing to bet by the week's end, you will."

His expression picked up.

"Which brings me to my third condition. You are going to pay back each and every person you stole from."

He didn't look happy about it, but I was encouraged by the fact that he didn't protest. "You're not going to take the money, but I'm going to give it back?"

"You're not giving back money. You're giving back time. A lot of the people you took stuff from are older folks who don't have much family around them. You're going to drop by and have a cup of tea with them."

"I don't drink tea."

"The tea is not important, kid. I know you don't get this, but you're going to do it anyway. Give them an hour of your time. Stay awhile and listen to their boring stories. You'll be surprised by how many of those stories end up being better than any Hollywood movie."

He didn't look convinced, but he nodded.

"And trust me," I said. "This will put you in the serious good books with your mother as well."

"Okay. I guess I can do that. You said there were four conditions."

"I did. The fourth one is for me. I need you to help me with a little job."

# CHAPTER THIRTY-FIVE

I LEFT JIMMY TO CONTEMPLATE HIS LIFE, HOWEVER A FOURTEEN-YEAR-old boy did that, and then I drove back down island. I had told Lizzy I had half a plan, but even running those plays was dependent on recruiting a few players to my team.

I stopped outside the fence around the baseball diamond and walked in through the sponsor's village. There were a lot more people milling around now, and the mood was easy. I carved my way through the throng to the organizer's office. The inside felt like a restaurant cold store.

Chase Hutchinson didn't look happy to see me.

"No," he said, standing from his desk.

"Hutch, buddy."

"No. Get out."

"Hutch, you owe me one."

"I owe you one? Ha! That's a laugh. I ended up in jail because of you."

"For a couple hours. I ended up there for two nights, thanks to you."

"Nothing to do with me, killer."

"I'm not a killer, although I have beaten a few people to a pulp in my time. But I'm not here about that. I'm here to discuss what I can do for your little tournament."

"Little?"

"But about to get much bigger. You're about to get more buzz than you can handle."

"I can handle a lot of buzz, pal."

"Well, this is more than you ever dreamed."

"Is that so? And how is this little miracle going to happen?"

"Rusty Reels is alive."

Hutchinson's eyes narrowed. "Get out."

"I'm serious."

"How?"

"I found him. He's at the police station up the street right now."

His eyes were darting around in their sockets as if they were attached to the cogs in his brain that were clearly whirring at top speed.

"There's a plan to hurt your tournament, but I'm about to bust it wide open. I just need a little help to do it."

"What help?"

"I need the number for one of your competitors. Molly. She's staying over on Harbour Island."

"Is this some stalker thing?"

"No. I met her the other day, and she seemed like one of the brighter bulbs. I need her help, too. And trust me, she's going to want to help me, and she's going to be awfully miffed if she finds out she had first dibs on this and I went elsewhere because you blocked me."

Hutchinson thought about it for a moment and clearly decided Molly was not the kind of person he wanted to upset. But he was also considerate of the whole potential stalker thing.

"I'm not giving you her number, but I will call her from my phone and let you talk to her if she wants to. And you'll do it in here."

"Deal."

He didn't dial the number. No one did that anymore. He just

looked up her contact record and hit the little phone icon. He put the call on speaker.

"Hey, Molly, it's Hutch from the promoter's office."

"Yeah, Hutch, I can see your name on my screen. What's up? I got gear to prep."

"Do you know a guy called Miami Jones?"

"The guy who killed Rusty, allegedly?"

"That's him. He's here, and he wants to speak with you."

"About what?"

"About the biggest online audience you've ever had," I said.

Hutchinson frowned.

"You got sixty seconds, Jones," said Molly.

"Okay, well first I wanted to thank you for your tip."

"I don't know what tip you're talking about. And that's ten seconds you won't get back."

"Gratitude is its own reward," I said. "And you told me to find whoever was setting me up rather than Rusty's murderer."

"Oh, that. How'd that work out for you?"

"It changed everything."

"Are you still on the hook for murder?"

"There was no murder. Rusty faked his own death."

"Seriously?"

"Oh yeah. And tomorrow I'm going to break the whole thing open."

"Good luck with that."

"What would it do for your livestream numbers if you caught Rusty Reels escaping on video? And let me add, there are gangsters involved. It's an international conspiracy. There's a pretty good chance of a boat chase."

"A boat chase?"

"No one escapes the Bahamas by road. And you could stream the whole enchilada. It's got to be more exciting than landing a few fish full of bones."

"Will there be gunplay?"

"Anything's possible."

"Fans would go ballistic for gunplay."

I wasn't too sure about the phrase *gunplay*. I really didn't care for those two words in the same sentence.

"If Rusty's going to make a break for it, does that mean you don't have him yet?"

"We have him. He's with the police. But he's going with an amnesia story right now."

"Geez, that old trope."

Everyone was a critic.

"Yeah. But I happen to know he's still got a reason to run, and I'm going to shove that reason in his face tomorrow. He's going spook like a herd of cattle in a lightning storm."

"Pretty much anyone and anything would spook in a lightning storm."

"I'm working on the fly here. So what do you say?"

"What do you need?"

"I need you to round up your posse, video cameras at the ready."

"All right, I will. But you jerk me around, Jones, you'll wish you had been sent up for murder."

"Roger that."

I told her I would be in touch in the morning, and Hutchinson said he would assess the competition schedule and let her know. When he ended the call, he looked at me.

"Is all that true?"

"Most of it."

"I can redo the schedule for tomorrow so we can stream the wading event in the morning and leave the boats open to capture this thing. If it is what you say, it could be pretty great footage."

"Even if it's one of your competitors?"

"It's one of our competitors, sure, but not one the sponsors care about. No one's hitching their wagon to an old guy in khaki. He's thoroughly expendable."

I said nothing. It was a cold way to look at people, but I

supposed my silence made me complicit—my silence and the fact I was orchestrating the whole thing.

"It would be better if this all happened over in the sound, 'cause that's where I've got the most camera positions."

"I'll keep that in mind." I didn't say I had no control over where Rusty might go or what he might do. The whole thing might end up being pointless. The cops hadn't even released him, and when they did, they might send him to a hospital in Nassau. Or they might charge him with something, like faking his death, if that was a crime, which I didn't think it was. And if they did release him, he might decide to go home and face the music, in which case our cameras would get nothing.

All the evidence I had that Desmond Richmond was aiding Rusty was circumstantial, a Jamaican in custody and a gut feel. But the fact was I didn't need video, and I didn't really care if they hit streaming records or not. What I needed were eyes. If Rusty was going to flee, he could do it in any direction and in any number of ways, and I couldn't keep my eye on all of them. If it came to nothing, I would have to deal with the wrath of Molly. But I needed her and her fellow anglers out there, just in case.

But the twitching in my pitching shoulder was kicking into overdrive, and it was telling me I was onto something.

But I needed Rusty Reels out of jail.

# CHAPTER THIRTY-SIX

I DIDN'T GET BACK INTO THE GOLF CART. I WAS PERFECTLY HAPPY walking the short distance to the police station. I stepped in the door and found Ken Corrigan standing at the duty desk. He saw me and glanced back into the station house, then he waved his hands for me to get the hell out.

So I did. I leaned against the wall in the shade, but the wall had retained the day's heat, and I felt like a flatbread in a tandoor. A couple of minutes later, Corporal Corrigan stepped outside and looked along the street and then back and seemed disappointed to find me waiting right outside the entrance.

"You need to not be here," he said.

"Why?"

"The boss is on the warpath. He's got evidence that places you on Rusty's boat, and the blood test matches Rusty's blood type."

"I could have told him that."

"But it adds to the fingerprints."

"Which you found where, exactly?"

"On a coffee cup in the console. He wants to bring you in for attempted murder."

"He's really getting on my nerves, you know?"

"I've never seen him like this. He's such a straight shooter I sometimes think he's made of wood, but something about you got to him."

"It's not me. I almost wish it was."

"What does that mean?"

"What's going to happen with Rusty?"

"The superintendent doesn't see any crime there."

"He's going for Rusty's amnesia story?"

"He's worried about it more than anything. We had a medic come over from the clinic earlier, and she said it wasn't definitive and he needed an MRI or a CAT scan or something we don't have here and a proper psych evaluation, which we also don't have."

"So what happens now?"

"The boss wants to ship him to Nassau and get him checked out."

"That's not going to work."

"What's not going to work?"

"Nothing. He's faking it. I know it."

"But we need to prove it."

"And what about the Jamaican?"

"He's another thing. He doesn't have a passport, so can't prove he's in the country legally. He'll probably be shipped to Nassau, too, and then deported, I guess."

"And that's it."

"No, that's not it. There's you, remember? Attempted murder?"

"Yeah. I need to bonk that on the head. Everything else depends on it."

"Everything else? What are you talking about?"

"Listen, I have a line on our Jamaican friend. He's muscle for a bad news operator out of Montego Bay—a guy called Richmond."

"How do you know that?"

"I have a friend in the Jamaican police. She looked him up. The long and the short of it is we can link Rusty to this Richmond. And my office manager did some digging on Rusty. Turns out he's in debt up to his eyeballs to some bad dudes in the states."

"Bad dudes?"

"The kinds of people that prefer to break bones than send late notices. Thing is, if Michael Alexander is here, then there's a chance Richmond is here, and he's not the kind of guy you want hanging in your neighborhood."

"What are you saying?"

"We need to flush him out, and to do that we need to set Rusty loose tomorrow."

"Even if we did, there's no guarantee that he'll go to this Richmond guy."

"No, so we have to give him an incentive. You need to give him something to think about overnight in his little cell."

"The boss is saying we should move Rusty to the medical clinic."

"Is it twenty-four-hour?"

"Nothing in Spanish Wells is twenty-four-hour."

"Then you can't leave him there alone, and it's too late to ship him to Nassau today. You need to keep him in the cells for his own good and because he'll do a lot more thinking in a cell. Trust me on that."

"I might be able to do that, but I don't see the boss just setting him loose tomorrow."

"It's time the superintendent and I had a little talk. Do you know the little rotunda on the water near The Shipyard? Tell him to meet me there. We need a private chat. If he still wants to bring me in after, I'll come quietly and of my own accord."

# CHAPTER THIRTY-SEVEN

I WALKED BACK TO THE GOLF CART AND THEN TOOK OFF DOWN SAMUEL Guy to the end of the island, passing churches and Mrs. Albury's house and yards with conch shells missing like teeth. It was the mid-afternoon lull at The Shipyard, and even the hardiest tourists escaped the humidity by hiding in their air-conditioned rooms or being on the water. I parked at the building and walked to the rotunda on the water. It was a pleasant enough place for people to sit and eat a snack or enjoy an evening drink, but now it was empty.

I sat watching the little blue fish swimming around the base of the rotunda for about ten minutes. Superintendent Bridges didn't arrive with lights and sirens. He arrived in a golf cart driven by Corporal Ken Corrigan. Ken parked near the restaurant about fifty yards away, and the superintendent got out and walked over to me.

He was still in his khaki uniform, and he still looked like the heat of it didn't bother him. He stepped up into the rotunda and walked over to me. I didn't get up.

"This would have been easier at the station, Mr. Jones."

"I thought it would be better if we had a private conversation."

"Everything you say is a matter for the record and admissible in court."

"Not for my sake."

He frowned and removed his hat, then he sat so we were at an obtuse angle from each other.

"What is it you wish to say before I take you in, Mr. Jones?"

I took a long, slow, hot breath. I figured when time wasn't on my side, I might as well start at the end.

"Your father wasn't corrupt."

Bridges' expression didn't change from its standard frown.

"I don't know what you think you know, but I don't need you to tell me that."

"With all due respect, sir, yes, you do. Because you've been living with the idea that the opposite might be true for too long."

"Mr. Jones, if you have nothing pertinent to say about your case, then I believe you promised to come quietly."

"I did, and I will. But first I want you to know some of what I know. Several nights ago, a boat was found floating off Royal Island with a blood-stained deck and no crew."

"I wrote the report, so I know what was out there."

"I discovered another boat was found out there, also with blood stains and missing crew. Only this one was forty years ago."

"I hope you spent your time more wisely than that, Mr. Jones."

"I think so. See, I learned a few things. I learned how the blood got on the deck in our recent case, and it wasn't from a bang on Rusty's head. His cameraman told me he thought Rusty had a drug problem because he found syringes and needles in his room. But Rusty didn't have the markings of a regular drug user. That's because he used the syringes to collect his own blood, probably into an IV bag that he tossed into the ocean after he splattered it across the deck of his boat and then 'disappeared.' I'm willing to bet it would take an expert two seconds to prove the blood splatter doesn't match any kind of head knock, which would make sense since Rusty has no cuts or abrasions on his head or anywhere else."

"I also learned how my fingerprints got onto the boat—and it's worth noting they were not actually on the boat. They were on a coffee cup that could have come from anywhere but was handed to me by Rusty Reels at the shack the morning before he disappeared. I also learned something else about fingerprints—the man in your cells, Michael Alexander, his will be on the storm shutters at the beach shack. Not mine though. So, you see, I learned plenty that will ensure a magistrate will throw my case in the garbage."

"We'll let the magistrate decide that."

"And end up with a cloud hanging over another Bridges?"

I saw the superintendent stiffen and knew I was walking a razor-thin line. "But like I said, I know your father wasn't corrupt, and what's more, I can prove it."

"You think you can prove something from forty years ago."

"I do. Maybe not to the satisfaction of a court of law, but this is not for a jury."

"Who is it for?"

"It's for you. We both know this thing has hung over your family for a long time. I'm willing to bet that your father has never spoken about it, so you've had to live with people's assumptions about you your entire life."

"What you think will make no difference."

"I agree. But what I know will. It will make a difference to your father. It will make a difference to you."

The superintendent looked out toward the water for a moment, then back to me. "What do you think this is going to get you?"

"Your help. You get your father on the line, and we can talk to him, and you'll see what I know. And I think it will make a difference to you. A big difference. And if it does, you're going to help me prove the truth and clear my name. Or you can take me in now, send me to the magistrate in Nassau, waste more of my time and make me spend more time in jail for no reason and let the actual criminals get away. Of course, eventually I'll get out because I can poke so many holes in your case now it's practically a voodoo doll. But then you'll never learn what I learned because the people who spoke to me will never speak to you. Not about this. You'll never know the truth. And it will continue to eat you alive."

Superintendent Bridges looked like he'd just lost big at the poker tables. But he glanced out at the water again like a man with plenty on his mind.

I waited for him to say something. I was happy to wait as long as it took. And it only took about a minute and then rather than speak, he stood. He pulled his coat taut and then almost snapped to attention.

"All right, Mr. Jones, we'll do it your way. But if you are wasting my time, I will make it my mission in life to see you rot in a cell on an abandoned atoll."

"Fair enough."

I didn't stand. I didn't need to get up to hear a phone call. But the superintendent stepped out of the shade of the rotunda and down the steps.

"We can't make the call from here?"

"I don't wish to do this over the phone," he said.

He walked back to Corporal Corrigan, and for a moment I wondered if a double cross was in play, but then Ken pulled on the wheel, made a wide U-turn, and drove his cart away. Superintendent Bridges stood outside the restaurant and waited for me to walk out to the gravel strip.

"You have a cart?"

I nodded.

"Let's go."

We got into Mrs. Albury's cart, and the superintendent directed me around to the ferry terminal. We parked and waited, and everyone around eyed us like a teenage couple looks at a parent who just wandered down to the basement.

Within a few minutes the government ferry arrived. There was nothing special about it—it was an old boat with seats along the sides and space in the middle for luggage and cargo. When all the people and goods were loaded, we chugged the short way across to Gene's Bay.

"You want to give me a hint?" I asked.

If I wasn't sure he was incapable of it, I would have said Superintendent Bridges smirked at me. He seemed to be enjoying my uncertainty.

When we reached the dock, we disembarked, and the superintendent walked to a minivan waiting in the middle of the dock like we were some kind of A-listers. Bridges got in the front beside the driver, and I slid the door open in the back and sat beside a box of potatoes.

Fifteen minutes later we were at the North Eleuthera airport. It looked like an afternoon flight to the US had recently departed, as the line of minivans by the fence was thin, and most of the people around seemed to be making their way home rather than hanging around.

Our minivan pulled up out front of the terminal building, and Superintendent Bridges got out. I assumed I was supposed to do the same, but I hesitated. I had no earthly idea what I was doing back at the airport. Was he deporting me? Did he have the authority to do that? I was trying to think through the options as fast as possible, but I ran out of time. Bridges opened the sliding door and gestured for me to get out.

A few people glanced our way, but no one paid us any mind. Or perhaps they paid the superintendent no mind. I might have been tackled had I been alone as I strode out onto the airport tarmac.

"You care to share what we're doing here?" I asked.

"As requested, talking to my father," he replied.

"He works at the airport?"

"Mr. Jones, I don't know if the purposefully dullard thing is an act, but it grows tiresome."

I said nothing. I got the sense I should be offended, but I wasn't sure.

We strode along the side of the compound on the opposite side of the fence from where the minivans lined up. On this side there was a line of small aircraft parked tail in against the fence. The superintendent strode along until he reached one he liked the look of, and he started doing what appeared to my untrained eye to be preflight checks.

"I'm going to jump right ahead and assume you think I'm getting in this thing," I said.

"Option B is a lonely atoll."

A guy appeared from the rear of the plane, and he spoke to Bridges, who signed a form on a clipboard, then he slapped the guy on the back and got in the aircraft. The guy ambled around to me and opened the door. I gave him the once-over, then I did the same to the aircraft.

But I got inside. The guy slammed the door home and then walked around the front and removed a tie from the prop.

"You fly?" I asked Bridges.

"I do. Surprised?"

"Constantly."

I was always surprised when I met people who flew. And I don't mean folks who get on a jet to Aruba, but the ones who took the controls and got the damned thing off the ground. They always seemed so normal when you met them, but then you learned they were pilots, and it changed your view of them forever. Flying was such an unnatural act. I didn't necessarily belong in the ocean, but in a pinch I could swim. But there were no circumstances where I could replicate the efforts of a bird.

The thing about small aircraft is that they don't feel like commercial airliners. Even budget airlines have planes that feel finished, with interiors and carpets and these days even mood lighting. But small aircraft had the feel of a French rally car. All function, no form. The doors rattled and the windows slapped, and the seats were like something from a 1950s school bus. The dashboard was sparse and dirty. Back in the eighties we had a neighbor who was always out of work and never had any money, and they drove an ancient, beat-up Buick that looked better on the inside than a small aircraft. If this thing were a car, you'd probably still get in it, but you wouldn't be at all surprised if it broke down en route. That thought was a problem when you translated it into being a few thousand feet in the air.

The superintendent put on headphones and gestured for me to

do the same. Then he spoke to someone somewhere and was cleared to pull out. He turned on the engine, and the prop started spinning, and before I had time to consider whether my will was up to date, Bridges hit the gas, and we lurched away from the fence and out onto the tarmac. He puttered along a road out to the main runway, then he zoomed down to the end and spun the aircraft around. Bridges again spoke to someone using terms like *alpha* and *niner*, and a crackled response came back that meant nothing to me but caused the superintendent to send us hurtling down the runway.

We bounced and rattled and hummed along the strip of asphalt, getting faster and faster and closer and closer to the thick trees at the other end. But we only got about halfway before the nose lifted and the bumping stopped, and we pointed at the sky like Icarus.

We weren't five hundred feet up before the superintendent banked, and I got an eyeful of green vegetation as my face hit the side window. Then the green was replaced by blue, and the island of Eleuthera was behind us, and Bridges righted the aircraft, and we shot above paradise. I saw Spanish Wells out there, the sandbars weaving their way through the water, and I saw Royal Island with its hidden harbor and tiny resort and then I saw nothing but water.

I had a microphone attached to my headphones, but I didn't use it. I just watched the water get darker and deeper, and I wondered how far it was to Florida. I turned and looked at the superintendent. He was checking dials and readouts but held the yoke with a single hand like how my dad used to drive on family vacations. He looked at ease and a little less stuck up than he had on the ground, and the uniform served to give me more confidence that we would arrive in one piece.

About twenty minutes later the superintendent spoke into his headset and got another garbled response. I hadn't realized that training to fly also involved learning a new language. He banked slightly and kept the heading for a few minutes, then he banked the other way, and to my horror, we started to fall from the sky.

# CHAPTER THIRTY-EIGHT

I GRIPPED THE BASE OF MY SEAT AND TURNED TO BRIDGES, BUT HE STILL looked unhurried and unfussed. He spoke to someone as our nose headed for the water, and I waited for him to give me instructions on what to do. I figured there wasn't going to be an oxygen mask falling, there were no babies to take care of, and the emergency exit was beside me. Perhaps getting out was self-explanatory.

We kept falling but not fast, sometimes a gradual glide and occasionally the odd drop that sent my guys into my throat. I noticed then that the prop was still spinning, so I questioned my crash analysis.

"All good?" I asked.

Bridges nodded and held up a thumb. Then he pushed the yoke, and we dipped again, and I wondered if he was doing that on purpose just to put me off my game. Then I saw the water coming up fast from below. A couple of hundred feet, then a hundred. I gripped the seat again and then a beach flashed by, and we were over foliage. Then suddenly the world went wide and open, and the black tarmac swallowed us up, and with a bump and a shudder, the landing gear hit the ground. Bridges played with the controls, and the noise of the engine engulfed us as we slowed down.

"Where the hell are we?" I asked.

"Welcome to Nassau," he said.

The whole flight had taken less time than it took to drive from Singer Island to West Palm. Nassau airport was a bigger place than North Eleuthera, that was for sure. It looked like a decent-sized airport, roughly the size of Palm Beach International. We bounced along the runway at a good speed as if in a hurry to get out of the way of an incoming jet. Bridges left the terminal gates behind and continued as if we were going to drive downtown in our Cessna, but eventually he pulled off to the side. At the far end of the complex was a small collection of hangars and an area that looked like the parking lot at Walmart, if everyone flew to Walmart.

We were directed into a slot by a guy in a fluorescent orange vest, then Bridges shut down the engine and the aircraft came to a shuddering stop. I hung up my headphones and clambered out of the aircraft, then I met the superintendent at the front of the plane. He asked the guy to have it fueled, and he strode away toward a building marked as the General Aviation Centre.

We walked straight through to a taxi waiting outside. The superintendent got in curbside and didn't slide over, so I ran around and got in the other side. We drove for about twenty minutes, then the taxi cut into a subdivision that had a front gate but no guard. There were single family homes and an apartment block and a few good empty lots. I saw a pool in the center of the complex, and the trees surrounding the entire place gave it a peaceful feel. I couldn't help thinking the same place in Florida would have chopped down some of that peace to create golf course lots.

We stopped outside a yellow stucco home with a terracotta roof. The superintendent paid the driver, and we got out and walked to the front door. When it opened, I saw an off-duty version of the superintendent standing in the hallway. Bridges was a chip off the block, or maybe a clone. The man was a little further along with the gray in his hair but otherwise a casual replica in his polo and Bermuda shorts.

"Son," he said, offering his hand to the superintendent. He

didn't seem shocked to see Bridges, and I wondered if Ken Corrigan had called ahead. They shook hands, and Bridges gestured to me.

"Father, this is Miami Jones. Mr. Jones, this is retired Chief Superintendent Theophilus Bridges."

I shook the man's hand and marveled at the names these folks managed to give each other. It was no kind of criticism. I had a bit of an old-fashioned doozy myself, so maybe if I retired to the Bahamas, I'd have to drop the whole Miami thing.

"Theo," he said, and I saw the logic in that. Grand names are grand, but they can be a bit of a mouthful.

Theo led us back into the house to a great room not unlike something you might find in Florida. A couple of sofas, rarely used armchairs for those times when you had extra guests, a flat-screen television, and an antique rolltop desk.

"I was surprised to get a call from Corporal Corrigan," he said.

"It was a last-minute decision," said the junior Bridges.

"Won't you sit. What is it I can do for you, gentlemen?"

For the grand name and the upright manner and formality of shaking hands with his own kin, there was a gentleness in Theo that I didn't see in his son. Perhaps if I ever met the superintendent in his Bermuda shorts, he might come across differently.

"We have an unusual situation," said the superintendent. I knew his name was Archer, but not in that uniform. "We found a boat at sea a few days back."

"Nothing unusual about that, in and of itself."

"No, but this one was . . ."

For the first time I saw Superintendent Bridges look uneasy. Fathers can have that effect on their boys. I've seen it in action with guys from litigators to gardeners to priests. But there was an added wrinkle here: me. Bridges had brought me to his father's home against all protocol and logic. It was true what I said that we could have done this on the phone from the rotunda in Spanish Wells. But he had chosen to fly me to see his father.

He wasn't looking for help or vindication with his case. He was a smart guy, and he had to know that pigheadedness was only going to take his case so far, and that was as far as a magistrate, who would probably scold him for bringing such a flimsy case before the court. This was about something bigger than this case and a whole lot bigger than me.

This was about the relationship between a father and a son, about some words that had been said and some others that had never been shared. About perceptions and expectations. About things that I would never have to live through.

Having a father who dies on you during college negates all expectation, and whatever expectations I had would have been low by that point. Dad effectively checked out of life after the cancer took Mom, and in some ways, the car accident that killed him was a mercy. It meant there were no uncomfortable silences or hidden secrets, no looks of disappointment on either side.

But that didn't mean there was nothing. As I told Lucia, nature abhors a vacuum. In the place of expectations there were what-ifs. There was no disappointment, but no pride, no joy to balance the sadness. My father was a janitor at an Ivy League college, enough irony for anyone. But he was also my hero and the greatest man I ever knew, until one day he wasn't, when hero became zero and greatness was replaced by the disgust of a teenager looking at his drunk of a father passed out on the living room floor.

And then, while I played baseball and partied in the sun at Miami, the chance for a conversation to be had decades later was stolen away in a sickening mess of plastic and Detroit steel.

"Picture, if you will, Theo, a boat found floating," I said, taking the baton the superintendent was about to drop. "In the Caribbean east of here, just off Royal Island. A boat that didn't belong there. Whatever crew had been on board was lost. Blood stains on the deck."

Theo sat, stern faced, as if taking in the information accurately were of vital importance. I saw no recognition in his eyes.

"The local people are watching the investigation as you would expect. These are not people accustomed to such crimes. There is pressure on the local police force to do the right thing, to find the perpetrators, to close the case."

"Always," said Theo.

"But there is also pressure to make the case go away."

Theo glanced at the superintendent. "Go away?"

"Disappear," I said. "Be forgotten. Not exist anymore."

"I don't care for the sound of that, Archer."

"But there are many ways to end a case, right, Theo? You could solve it, of course. I'm sure that's always the preference. But when the pressure comes from the highest office, there can be temptation. Temptation to close a case by charging a scapegoat, or to close it by finding no suspect at all."

He looked at his son. "Where is this going, Archer? What has happened?"

"The right thing must be done," I said.

"Of course."

"Even under pressure."

"Especially under pressure."

"Even the kind of pressure applied by something like the Medellin drug cartel."

Theo's head snapped back to me. "The cartels are gone, dismantled."

"Now they are. Not in the 1980s."

"1980s? What are you talking about, Mr. Jones? I thought you were referring to a current case."

"Did I not make that clear? No, I was talking about the killing of two US citizens in the waters north of Norman's Cay."

"Archer, what is this man talking about?"

"You know what I'm talking about, Theo."

"I surely do not."

"Sure you do. You were the investigating officer."

Theo stood. "I do not talk about closed cases. Perhaps it is time for you to leave."

"I can't, Theo. Because if I do that, your son may well cross a line he can't cross back."

"That's preposterous."

"It's really not. Imagine now, if you will, another boat found floating in the same waters, no crew, blood-splattered deck. Only this time it's a smaller boat and a different time. No drug cartels but certainly an entire island watching to see what the son will do with a case that so closely mirrors one handled by his father forty years ago. An island where the prevailing wisdom is that the father covered up cartel murders by order of the prime minister's office."

"I don't know what you think you know, young man."

"I know two things: one, your son was never going to cover up this case, but under the heat of the magnifying glass, he might have gone a little too far the other way to find a suspect. And the second thing is, I know that sometimes covering up the case is exactly the right thing to do."

"Never, the law must be adhered to."

"This is not a question of law. It's a question of perception, and how perception can affect evidence."

"Evidence is evidence," said Theo.

"Not according to my mentor."

"Your mentor? Who is . . . ?"

"Lenny Cox."

I watched Theo's jaw drop open. He regained his composure like a pro, but the truth had split open like a poorly sutured wound.

Theo sat back down and clasped his hands together. "How do you know this name?"

"I told you."

"Your mentor? So what does that make you?"

"Very lucky. But if you're asking if I'm in a similar line of work, then, no. I met him later."

Theo lifted his chin and looked at me as if studying the ingredients list on a microwave dinner.

"Mr. Jones, I'm not inclined to believe you."

"I get that, sir, I really do. Because this is not something you have spoken of for forty years, and you have every expectation that he held the same vow."

"Correct."

"And you'd be right. He didn't. At least not to me, and I expect, as you do, not to anyone."

"So why do you raise this now?"

"Because several days ago I was arrested for murder."

Theo's expression grew serious, and it was pretty stern to begin with. His eyes were on mine, reading me. Then he turned to his son.

"Does the evidence support conviction, Archer?"

"The case is fluid," said the superintendent.

"That sounds like a politician."

"This is the job of a politician. You know that."

"Our job is justice, not politics."

"Dad, please. You know as well as I do, sometimes politics *is* justice."

"So why have you brought a murder suspect to my home?"

Again, the superintendent looked uncertain, and for a moment I was going to butt in, but I saw his shoulders roll back and his chest lift.

"Because he holds the answers to the most important case of my life."

"Then uncover the evidence, Son."

"That's why I'm here."

Now, Theo looked confused.

"You hold the evidence, Theo," I said. "You have done for forty years."

"I don't speak of that," he said. "I thought you understood that, Archer."

"I thought I did also. But then I found a blood-stained boat out on the water, and I realized that I had lived my life in the shadow of something I never understood."

"What's to understand?"

"Your silence. Everyone thinks you covered up a case, for the cartel, for the prime minister, who knows? And I've spent my life living with that. Because you could have cleared your name by speaking out, but you never did. Rumor was all the evidence people had."

"Do you think I took bribes? Is that what you think?"

"It doesn't matter what I think—"

"To hell it doesn't!" Theo's voice broke like a sonic boom. He took a deep breath and licked his lips. "What the world thinks was never my concern. But what you think, Son, that is the reason I kept my silence."

"I don't understand."

"I don't have an explanation on hand."

"Let's let the evidence do the talking," I said. "I'll tell you what I've learned, and you can fill in the gaps, Theo, as you wish."

Neither man said yes, but both stayed mute and kept their eyes on me.

"The early 1980s. The height of the Colombian drug cartels. Carlos Lehder. Norman's Cay. Authorities turn a blind eye because Lehder has lined their pockets all the way up to the prime minister," I said. "Eventually, the massive quantities of drugs on American streets become a political nightmare, and the US government is forced to crack down. They tell the Bahamian government that being a waylay point for the drug traffickers is not acceptable. But the Bahamian government is slow to move. Of course they are: they're getting huge cash payments from Lehder and Co."

The two men shifted uncomfortably and kept their eyes on me.

"Now, the facts tell us that an American-registered boat ventures into the waters between Norman's Cay and North Eleuthera. The boat is found drifting south of Royal Island with a dead man on board, another missing, presumed drowned. The boys who find the boat are locals. One of them has had some trouble with authorities in the past, petty theft, minor drugs, but the other boy has no record and by all reports is a good kid."

I noticed Theo sit up straighter as I continued. "The officer in charge of the investigation is you, Theo. You have the boat towed back to Spanish Wells, and you print it, and you find prints that match the victims, but you also find two other sets of prints."

"You have a lot of hypotheses there," said Theo.

"No, I don't. That's coming, but so far everything I've said is fact."

"And you can prove this in a courtroom?"

"Facts don't begin in the courtroom, Theo. They are what they are. Courts just establish rules for presenting them. But I've established my own rules because I have no need or desire to go anywhere near a court. But they're facts, and I can still prove them."

"Go on."

"The unknown prints on the boat belong to these local boys. You establish this for a fact with one and supposition with the other. You go and visit this young man and discover his friend with him. I don't think you ever actually matched prints to the second boy, but I can't prove that one way or the other."

"Why would I not do that? That would be improper procedure."

"I'm sure it's not what's written in the manual, but sometimes procedure has to be more flexible than the handbook allows. Where I come from, it's illegal to drive on the wrong side of the road, but I'd do it to avoid hitting a bear, despite what the book might say."

Theo raised an eyebrow.

"So at this point the scuttlebutt around town is that local boys are keen for their taste of the drug money and have attacked a boat they think is a drug boat but turns out to be a pleasure cruiser. In the mêlée, the two innocent men on the boat are killed. And you can place those two local boys on the boat with prints."

Theo clenched his jaw, and I noted that the superintendent wasn't taking his eyes off his father.

"This is where things get funky, and also where they link to our current case. You had the evidence, and the rumor around town was one possible explanation. But there was another: that the boys had found the boat with the men already dead as they claimed and had left their prints onboard while checking the boat for signs of life. But this version created a problem. Version one, that the boys attacked the boat, was already the rumor, and you know as well as I do, that sort of talk is hard to quell once it gets momentum. So all you would have to do is present the prints, place the boys on the boat, and case closed. They'll probably go to prison. Justice is seen to be served. But the second version, that the sailors were already dead, is less palatable. If the boys didn't do it, then who did? You don't know. You can't prove any alternate theory. Maybe the cartel? But that version means you don't solve the case; no justice is seen to be done. And the prints prove the boys were there, so regardless, they will wear a mark on their backs for the rest of their lives."

"How does that relate to today's case?"

"I spoke to the two men who found Rusty's boat. One of them told me the other was reluctant to touch the boat in any way, suggesting they would get blamed for whatever happened. That felt unnecessarily panicky to me. So I spoke to him."

"I don't know who found your boat," said Theo. "But they weren't there for mine."

"They weren't a suspect, Theo, but they were there. That's how I learned about your visit, and more importantly, I learned about somebody else's visit."

"Who?" said the superintendent.

"An American soldier. That's what they called him. There was no name. Just the *American soldier*."

I looked at Theo. He was a tough old guy. He looked more defiant than he had before. I knew the look. The set jaw of a man about to dig his heels in despite himself.

"I had no idea what all this meant," I said. "Until I later put two and two together and came up with aha. The soldier wasn't technically a soldier. He was a marine. A marine who spent a good deal of his career outsourced to one of the three-letter acronym agencies we have in the US. It was my friend, Lenny Cox, which changed everything. Because I knew this man. He didn't care about any handbook or the rules that some bureaucrat wrote down to keep us all in line. He only cared about right and wrong."

I looked at both men, who were watching me now. "So I started thinking about what happened, the timing of it all. Reagan was under pressure to solve the drug problem, but the cartels were well hidden by Colombian forests and a veil of bribes. Your government was swimming in drug money, and no one wanted to end the party. Then I looked at what happened later. The drug kings, Lehder and Escobar, fled to Central America—Panama and Nicaragua. The US got involved down there in both official and unofficial capacities as we learned from the Iran-Contra hearings. So if the administration was happy to send select troops then, why not before, to close down the drug shipments?"

I paused.

"Lenny was here. I can't prove it. No one will even recognize a photo after forty years, but he was here."

"What does that mean?" asked the superintendent.

"It means between two hard choices, your father chose the tougher of the two. But also, the right one."

"I don't understand."

"I can explain it," I said to Theo. "At least what I've put together in my head. But I think it's time your son heard it from you."

Theo blinked several times. "What I am about to say stays in this room. Am I clear?"

"Yes, sir," said Superintendent Bridges.

"Crystal," I said.

"Mr. Jones is right. Lenny Cox was here. So were people from the US embassy and the FBI. They were all concerned with the deaths of US citizens in Bahamian waters, as they should have been. And, yes, I found prints on the boat. One set belonged to a local miscreant, and the other I couldn't place in our records, but after speaking with the boy, I came to believe it was his friend. So, yes, the evidence would place them on the boat, but he claimed he boarded to check if everyone was okay and found the dead man. They panicked and fled."

"But?"

"As you say, there were many local rumors. And one of these boys was trouble. He had stolen before, and it wasn't outside the realms of possibility that he would escalate to kill during a robbery. They all start somewhere."

Theo took a deep breath, long and slow like he was trying to hide it.

"There were no other suspects but plenty of theories, and I discussed them with the US embassy liaison, but in the end, the boys looked good for it. All I needed was to find any property from the boat in their possession, and I knew I would have a solid case."

"But?"

"The second boy was a good kid. He had solid grades and was finishing up school. He hadn't gone into fishing, and there was hope that he might even become a police officer. I had spoken to him about it. He had never been in trouble. But sometimes good people get mixed up in bad things that cannot be excused."

"What happened?" asked the superintendent.

"I was going to go and search their premises and then arrest them, but I hesitated. Something didn't smell right."

"I don't think that's in the handbook," I said.

Theo glared at me.

"Sorry. Go on."

"Then I got a visit. From your Lenny Cox. He told me he knew what happened on the boat and that the boys had nothing to do with it."

"Did he provide any evidence?" asked the superintendent.

"All he provided was eyewitness testimony. See, I told him I had evidence, and he suggested that I destroy it. I told him that was not possible. I told him that people lie, but evidence does not. He said that if the evidence sent those boys away, or even tagged them as killers for the rest of their lives, then the evidence did lie. I asked him how he was so sure they hadn't done it, and he told me he would give me the unpolished truth, and in return he asked that I forget the rules and do what felt right."

Theo sighed, then continued.

"Mr. Jones is right about the US government trying to stop the cartels. It still affects them today, as it does us. But the politicians in the US wanted to close it down fast, and the politicians here wanted to close it down slow. Even Prime Minister Pindling was accused of taking tens of millions from the cartel. There was no mood to stop the flow of money. So the Americans quietly sent in their own people.

"They tracked the sailboat from Key Largo, around the south of Andros, to Exuma. Lenny said they could place it on Norman's Cay. He said it was loaded with drugs to return to the US and sailed north in our direction. They decided to intercept it in Bahamian waters to send a message to the cartel."

"Our government would not have been pleased with a foreign state interfering in our territory," said the superintendent.

"No, they would not. But the Americans weren't planning on claiming responsibility."

"They killed their own people?"

"He said the plan was to capture the men, destroy the cargo, and leave the boat."

"But they didn't capture the men on board."

"He told me that he led the team. He said when they attempted to board, one man fired upon them, and Lenny shot him, and he fell overboard. Lenny then boarded and found the second man in the galley. He said it was filled with packages of drugs, barely room to move. He said the second man told him that the cartel would kill them all, and their families, and that he was going to tell the cartel that the Americans were here."

"And what happened?" the superintendent asked his father.

"Lenny said he shot the man in the head."

"Just like that?"

"He said they were at war, a war on drugs as their president had called it. He told me that the two men were wanted in the US for drug and prostitution crimes."

"But they ordered their own people killed?"

"No. He said it was his call. He said bad men meet bad endings, and his team's mission was to save tens of thousands of people from drug overdoses. He said they decided to cut the bags open and throw them overboard but leave the man on board, floating out there for the cartel to find."

"And you believed him, Father?"

"Yes, Son, I did. He could have made up a story where he wasn't even there. But he admitted to a police officer he had killed two men. I believed him."

"But you didn't arrest him?"

"That was not on the cards, Son. He was armed, and I was not. It was never up for debate. His objective was to clear two boys that he didn't even know. It was a risk he didn't need to take, but he did."

"So what did you do?"

"I had to honor that. He reminded me that if the record showed the boys were involved, that the cartel might come looking for retribution. I did what I had to do."

"You destroyed the evidence."

"The one and only time. Lenny said I would never see him again, and I never did. He said he would never speak of it to anyone, and I did the same."

"And the boys?"

"I went to Bluff to tell them there was no case to answer. They were gone. Looking for work, I was told."

"I wonder what happened to them?" asked the superintendent.

"The bad one, I don't know."

"He died," I said.

Theo nodded softly, as if this was no great surprise.

"And the other?" asked the superintendent.

"He popped up in Nassau. He joined the police force."

"Is he still in?"

Theo shook his head. "No, we lost him not long ago."

We sat in silence for a while. I didn't know what the other men were thinking, but I was thinking of Lenny. I suspected it wasn't the first time he had gone outside the lines, and I knew it wasn't the last, but I learned that the man had been just as true to his beliefs before I met him as he had been after.

Theo turned his keen eye on me. "May I ask you a question?"

"Yes."

"You spoke of this man, Lenny, in the past tense."

"He died ten years or so ago."

"How did he die?"

"Saving me."

Theo nodded and processed this before speaking again.

"Why are you here?" he asked. "Not to hear that story. To clear your name?"

"A little of both. To confirm that my memory of a man was consistent with who he was. And, yes, the other. But the thing is, I don't have a father. He died a long time ago, and we never got to talk about the things we should have talked about. Lenny Cox kind of became my father figure, so when I learned he had been here, it kind of made me think about your son."

Theo glanced at the superintendent and then back at me.

"How so?"

"He's lived his whole professional life—maybe even more—with a cloud over him. The idea that his father, such a proponent of the rule of law, might have bent it or even broken it, and he might have done that in return for a little cash."

Theo spun to his son. "You think that?"

"No, I never believed that."

"It doesn't matter what he believed," I said. "It only matters what lay down in his guts. And what lay down was that you had not followed protocol. You had defied the evidence at hand. People lie, but evidence never does. Except we can see that this isn't true. My guess is his faith in evidence has made him a pretty good cop but a pain in the backside to work with."

I smiled, but neither of the other men did.

"That cloud made him a zealot to the rules, to the evidence, even when, in my case, the evidence lied. Someone set me up, a criminal with an ax to grind. You used your instinct back with Lenny, and the silence around that decision has caused your son to believe that instinct is a failing rather than a tool to back up what the evidence might be saying out of the side of its mouth."

"You think he's going to change his mind?"

"I don't know. I hope so because the evidence won't stack up once I'm done with it anyway. And there's a bad guy out there, and I want to get him." I turned to the superintendent. "And like Lenny, I can't do that without your help."

I stood. I wanted to leave them alone and sit in silence together or talk it out. I never had the chance to do either, and I had no way to know which way it might have gone, but this was their relationship. Here I was just a billboard on the way to somewhere. I wasn't the highway.

The problem was that the superintendent had flown me to another island, and I had no way to get back. And I needed to get back.

Theo Bridges pressed on his thighs and stood slowly, then the superintendent followed. I walked to the door and shook Theo's hand, and he simply nodded. Then father and son shook hands.

"Good to see you, Son."

"You too. Tell Mother I'll be back weekend after next."

"Will do."

We walked out to the curb, and the superintendent called a cab. We waited for fifteen minutes in silence, then we got in and drove back to the airport, where the small plane was waiting.

The superintendent did his preflight checks around the aircraft and then we got in. Within ten minutes, we were in the air. The sun was low, and the waves played shadows across the water. I wore a headset to muffle the sound but said nothing on the flight. I hoped the superintendent was concentrating on flying, but I suspected his mind was elsewhere.

We landed as sunset burst across the sky, and taxied back to the fence, then I followed the superintendent out to a waiting minivan. How these people knew he was arriving places, I had no idea.

We drove through the scrub to the dock and got out, and the minivan drove away. The superintendent walked over to the small shelter by the ferry dock. No one else was waiting.

"Ferries run this late?" I asked.

"No. The *Knight Rider* will be along soon enough."

I was excited by that prospect. We stood at the empty dock

looking across the water at Spanish Wells in silhouette as the last of the day shot purple and blue spears across the sky.

"How did you know?" asked the superintendent.

"Know what?"

"This friend of yours, Lenny. How did you know it was him if he never spoke of it with you and no one here knew his name?"

"Except your dad."

"And you certainly didn't get it from him."

"Sideways, as usual. I met someone on the island who had a mutual friend. He told me that his father claimed that Lenny had saved his life. Then I found out that the boy from the boat, the one with the bright future, turned out to be this guy's father. I put two and two together."

"The man who became a policeman in Nassau has a son in Spanish Wells?"

"He does. And the son followed the father into the family trade."

Superintendent Bridges thought about this for a moment, then looked at me.

"Corporal Corrigan? The boy Lenny saved was Philip Corrigan."

"It wasn't just Lenny who saved him, you know. Your dad was equally responsible."

The superintendent nodded. "He also let a killer go free."

"To be fair, Lenny was a soldier, and it's kind of what they do. And if it makes any difference, he didn't let him go free. He was going to leave regardless. Trust me on that."

"Does Corporal Corrigan know that my father nearly locked his father away?"

"No, I'm not sure Ken knows his parents even came from Bluff, or if they did, maybe distantly. His father was already a police officer in Nassau when he was born, so that's all he knows. His dad never even explained how Lenny had saved him. It was treated as a throwaway line in their family."

"Do you think he should know?"

"My gut says he seems pretty happy with his lot. I don't think it's necessary."

The superintendent turned to the sound of an approaching speedboat. "Fathers do tend to keep things from their sons."

"Star Wars ain't for nothing."

The superintendent frowned at me as the *Knight Rider* pulled up to the dock. I was disappointed to see it was nothing more than a speedboat, but we clambered in, and I paid the guy and then sat beside the superintendent at the stern, and the driver turned up the tunes on his radio and headed back from whence he had come.

"The evidence pointed to you," said the superintendent.

"I know. They almost did a good job."

"But you say the man behind it is a bad sort?"

"Very. He's done time—in two countries if you can believe that."

"I don't like bad men in my town."

"That's a good quality in a policeman."

"If I return your passport tonight, what will you do?"

"I'm not available to receive it tonight. I have some business to take care of tomorrow."

"In that case, what do you need?"

# CHAPTER THIRTY-NINE

THAT NIGHT I LAY ON MY COT IN THE GARDEN SHED AND DREAMED about being at the World Series with my father. It was the San Francisco Giants versus the New York Yankees. I had never played for either organization, but I had played in the organizations of both of their crosstown rivals. I wasn't sure what to make of that, or the fact that my father and I had both been Red Sox fans. Or the fact that I had never attended a World Series game with my dad.

In the morning, I used the hose in the backyard to wash my face, but I didn't want to wake Lizzy or Mrs. Albury, so I didn't go inside, and I didn't start the golf cart. Instead, I walked down to the dock and stopped in at the Lazy Pot. I sat on a sofa with a couple of old timers and sipped on my instant coffee while I waited.

Before long I saw young Jimmy pull up short of the space reserved for the government ferry. He was low in the water and peered over the concrete dock to wave his two-way radio at me. I pulled my radio off my hip and waved it back. Chase Hutchinson had assured me the batteries were full and would last a week and would keep us all in contact better than any cell phones, especially out on the water.

After about twenty minutes, I saw Rusty Reels arrive at the dock. He glanced around but less like a bad spy this time. Now he wasn't faking anything. I sat in the dark of the coffee hutch and watched Jimmy speak to Rusty, then the older man climbed down a ladder into Jimmy's boat. Jimmy pulled out wide into the middle of the channel and headed east toward North Eleuthera.

I was still sitting in my sofa when Ken Corrigan arrived. I pulled my radio off my hip again and called Captain Augie to come on down. Ken sat opposite me in a polo and shorts rather than his uniform.

"Did he take it?" I asked.

"Hook, line, and sinker. With a wrinkle."

"Wrinkle?"

"I told him last night the plan to ship him to a medical center had been put on hold and we couldn't release him until we confirmed his identity."

"Right."

"And I told him not to worry. He wouldn't spend another night in our cells after tonight, as we'd ship him to Nassau and we had lockup facilities there with better medical care. For his own protection."

"So?"

"You were right. He did spend the night thinking, or maybe he just got miraculously better."

"How so?"

"This morning he says that his mind has cleared and that he remembers who he is."

"I thought he might."

"But you didn't anticipate another identity."

"What?"

"He claims his name is Mark Shimano."

"Shimano? Like the fishing reels?"

"Right. Imagination is not his strong point."

"But how does he think he can prove that he's not Rusty Reels?"

"Remember, we found no ID in Rusty's accommodations. The superintendent says to him, 'You're not Rusty Reels?' and he says he doesn't know who that is. He claims he was on a fishing trip and rented the boat and had a slip and fall."

"Okay."

"He says he left his passport behind for safe keeping, and he can get a friend to text us a photo of it. We give him his phone—it's a burner—and he calls his 'friend,' tells him he's in a little pickle and he's at the police station, and can they send a photo of his passport. He says he'll explain later, just to send it. A minute later he gets a text with a photo of a US passport in the name of Mark Shimano."

"He's got a fake identity. So he was trying to disappear."

"It looks like it. Anyway, the boss lets him go. He tells 'Mark' that he might want to get out of town because this Miami Jones guy is around and seems to have a beef against this Rusty guy, and he must look a little like Mark, so he doesn't want to end up in a dark alley with this Jones fellow."

"A dark alley? How many of those do you have?"

"Not many. Or any. Mark says he's planning on leaving, it's been a trauma, and so on, and the boss says we can have a local water taxi take him wherever he wants to go, and since we know he doesn't have any cash on him, the police force will cover the cost to apologize for the inconvenience. He had the biggest smile as he left, like he'd gotten away with the great train robbery."

"Good."

"But he can't honestly think we're that dumb, can he?"

"He's not thinking you're dumb. He's not thinking about you at all. You planted the seed last night, and he spent the night in a cell letting that seed sprout. His well-laid plan wasn't going well, and he was desperate for a story to sell you that not only got him out but also kept his escape plan alive. He could have just told you he was Rusty, and that would have been it for the cell, but then he's admitting he's still alive. But if he could sell the Mark Shimano story, then his plan still lives, and Rusty Reels does not. You gave him an out, and he was too busy jumping at it to think."

I stood and stretched, and as I did, I saw Captain Augie pull up in his charter boat. The guy pouring the coffees took my cup, and

Ken and I walked out into the sparkling sunshine and climbed down into the boat.

"Beautiful day for it," I said.

"For what exactly?" asked Augie.

"For a spot of fishing, of course."

# CHAPTER FORTY

Captain Augie moved along the channel, making no wake. I sat back and took in the smell of ocean and diesel and fish guts. It put a smile in my mind but not on my face. I was wearing my game face.

We weren't in any hurry. We reached the end of the island and could see the deeper water of the channel spreading out toward Gene's Bay. The rocky outcrop at the end of the island reached out like a finger in the low tide, and Captain Augie gave it a wide berth.

I sat on the stern bench and called Hutchinson on my radio.

"Rusty is away," I said.

"The fleet is in place," he replied. "A few out from the sand bars north of the island, and the rest around the sound."

"Just make sure they're not all lined up like the Spanish Armada."

"They'll keep it low down, don't worry."

"I'll keep you updated."

I watched the water as we neared North Eleuthera, then a voice crackled on the radio.

"*Exotic Days*, this is *Fly Flight*."

"Roger, *Fly Flight*."

"I have eyes on your man. They're headed around North Eleuthera."

Captain Augie turned the wheel, and we eased toward the top end of the island. We kept well back so we didn't spook Rusty, and reports kept coming in from anglers on the water describing his movement into the sound and past Mann Island and on toward Harbour Island.

As we were rounding the northwest point of North Eleuthera, I heard Jimmy calling in on the radio.

"Exotic Days, this is Taxi Boy." The kid had a sense of humor. "Your man has just disembarked at government dock on Harbour Island. Should I follow?"

"Negative, Jimmy. Now we know where he's going. Head for home."

"Roger that."

The problem with following someone from an island is that there are literally 360 degrees of escape. By directing him into Jimmy's small boat, we effectively cut out the west options, so we had eyes on most of the other angles. Now that he had made landfall on Harbour Island, we knew where his accomplices were and where to focus our eyeballs.

But we didn't get moving any faster. Captain Augie was navigating our way through the channel between the top of Eleuthera and the reef. The water below us looked plenty deep, but the waves were crashing into the coast hard, just a few yards to starboard, and equally across the reef to port.

As we turned out into the sound, I saw what I was hoping for. There was a loose line of flatboats and bass boats running parallel with Harbour Island down its length. The boats were a couple hundred yards offshore and give or take a hundred yards apart. If they were a soccer defense, they would have been yelled at by their coach to tighten up their line, but for my purposes, they were perfect. They had every inch of the island in view but didn't look like they were doing anything more than fishing.

I saw Jimmy puttering away toward Spanish Wells as Captain Augie slowed us down in the middle of the sound. We didn't bother joining the line of watchers—I didn't want Rusty to recognize me.

Then we waited. And waited. I figured things would take a while to get moving, but I really didn't see Rusty hunkering down. He was in a jam and on unfamiliar ground, but maybe whoever he was meeting might have had a cooler head. So we waited.

Eventually my radio crackled.

"Jones?" she said, dispensing with the use of vessel names.

"Molly?"

"What's going on?"

"We're waiting."

"Jones, if you've sold me a line . . ."

"Hey, I see something," said a male voice. "A large vessel, sixty-footer maybe, blue hull. It's flying a Jamaican flag."

"Where?" I asked.

"Coming out of Valentine's Resort."

Captain Augie pointed out the general area of the resort.

"Can you see anyone? Reels? Richmond?" I had sent a mug shot of Desmond Richmond to Chase Hutchinson, who had distributed it to his competitors. They already knew Reels.

"Negative. The bridge is enclosed. Do you see it? It's turning south."

"I see it," said Molly. "Definitely heading south. Toward the south channel."

I turned to Captain Augie. "What's the south channel?"

"At the end of Harbour Island, there's a deeper channel between it and a peninsula off Eleuthera."

"If they get out there, we won't catch them," said Ken. "That's the Atlantic. Those flatboats aren't designed for that stuff."

"Follow the blue cruiser," I said into the radio. "Report anything." Then I said to Ken, "We need to confirm if they're on that boat."

"How?"

Captain Augie hit the throttle, and Ken and I were nearly thrown off our feet. "The dockmaster will know."

He sped across the sound, and I saw the line of fishing boats moving south to track the big cruiser. It was an impressive vessel and certainly the kind of thing that could sail all the way to Jamaica —or to the US for Rusty Reels to meet with me without leaving a paper trail.

Captain Augie came into the dock making waves, which drew some abuse, but Ken and I paid it no mind as we clambered up onto the decking and ran toward a desk under a pergola. Another guy in a nice polo and shorts watched us coming.

"What do you guys think you're doing?"

Ken flashed his police ID. "That blue cruiser, Jamaican flag. Who's on it?"

"I don't know. Two guys I think."

"Black or white?" I asked.

"One of them was black, for sure. He was on the deck, threw the lines in. But the other guy was on the bridge already."

"Who's the registered owner?" asked Ken.

"I don't know. We don't write that down. Just the number."

"Does it belong to a guest?"

"Of course."

I looked at Ken like we were working to get blood from a china cup.

"Who?" demanded Ken.

"Mr. Richmond."

I got on my radio. "We need to stop that boat," I said to anyone.

"It's headed for the channel," said Molly in reply.

"Can you corner it? Form a blockade?"

"Are you asking us to put a fleet of bass boats in front of a sixty-foot cruiser and get mown down?"

I was, but I realized how ridiculous it sounded, so I looked at Ken for inspiration.

"We gotta do it," he said, bolting back toward our boat.

I was pushing away to follow when I heard a loud roar—the sound of a boat taking off at great speed—which was not something normally heard in a dock with a no-wake zone around it.

As I glanced around, some guy yelled, "Hey, that's my boat!" and I saw a flash of metal from a fishing tower as it zoomed by.

Then my eyes caught up with the movement and settled on the cockpit and the man at the helm, who looked back at me with a wide smile.

The nasty leer of Desmond Richmond.

I hadn't seen him in a long time, and the last time he had a gun on me, but I recognized him as if he was my freshman-year college roommate. You didn't forget a face that pointed a loaded weapon at you. Sitting in the seat facing backward was the pasty visage of Rusty Reels. His eyes were on the guy whose boat they had just stolen—that guy watched in frozen horror as his boat screamed away.

I didn't freeze. For better or worse, freezing wasn't really something I did. I never knew why, but momentum was always what I was looking for, when I felt best. So I didn't stand there watching the boat tear away.

I sprinted.

I pumped my arms hard to get up to speed, then I drove my legs to keep me there, and I charged down the length of the dock. Richmond was going to have to go around the end of the dock to get out to deeper water, so I pushed with every fiber in that direction, the way I had all those years ago on a practice field in Coral Gables. I felt the blood flow through every limb, and my lungs punched the air into me, and I pushed as hard as I could and ran as fast as I could make my large frame move. I saw Richmond reach the end of the dock and turn around it to head out and away, and I put in my last effort and then, with absolute clarity but no idea, I hit the end of the dock, and not for the first time, I jumped out into the ether, launching myself at a moving speedboat.

# CHAPTER FORTY-ONE

I HIT HARD. WATER LOOKS SOFT, BUT WHEN YOU DRIVE YOURSELF FACE first into it, there's more give in a grass field.

The boat zoomed by as I descended from my leap and then I splatted into the wake behind it like a clown. I heard the roar of the outboard as the wash pummeled me from both directions. My face stung from my inelegant landing, and I was momentarily dazed, but then I popped up above the water and shook the stars out of my head, and felt another wake push against me.

"You wanna ride, or you gonna swim all day?" asked Captain Augie.

I looked up and saw him smiling at me. I stroked around to the stern and climbed aboard, and before I was half in, Augie hit the gas and shot off like a rocket. Against the momentum of the boat, I crawled forward.

"Where's Ken?"

Captain Augie stuck his thumb back toward the docks.

"You wanna go back and get him?"

"Where's Richmond?"

Augie pointed forward.

I didn't answer. I just peered through the spray-splattered windshield. I saw a boat well ahead.

"Is that him?"

"Uh-huh."

"Can we catch him?"

"He's got a Merc 100, and we've got twin 250s."

"Is that a yes or no?"

"Give it a second."

Captain Augie already had the throttle down, and we kissed the top of the water as we sped forward. We were gaining. I grabbed Augie's radio from the console—mine had been claimed by the deep —and made a call.

"Any boats able to block the north end of Harbour Island. The north channel."

"We're coming," said Molly, "but we're all behind you."

And there were no vessels ahead. Everyone had moved in formation south to follow the big cruiser. The rest of the fleet was around the main island near Spanish Wells.

It was just Richmond and Rusty and us.

Captain Augie gained on them, and as we reached the northern end of the barrier island, he cut in and pulled alongside to block off access to the north channel.

My eyes caught Richmond's. His black hair had gone gray, and he had lost the mustache he had when I had known him. But he still had those eyes that held an intensity that eluded most people. He had been a schmoozer, a politician in the mafia sense, a broad smile under calculating eyes.

Richmond snarled and yanked hard on his wheel, and before Captain Augie could react, the other boat cut away from us, instantly putting a hundred yards between us.

As Augie turned to follow, I looked back, wondering if Richmond was planning to backtrack to the south. I saw a flotilla of fishing boats spread out across the sound like the blockade I had called for, only this one was against a boat more their size. I cast my eyes across each boat and saw that they were all doing running commentary to camera as they sped toward us.

Richmond must have seen them also because he didn't double

back. He sped across the sound toward the top of North Eleuthera. Captain Augie caught up but dropped in behind. We reached the tip of the big island, and as we got alongside Tay Bay beach, Captain Augie pulled the throttle, and we practically braked on the spot as Richmond sped away along the north coastline.

"What's wrong?" I asked.

"I'm not going through there at full throttle," he said. "Too dangerous."

"But he's getting away."

"The cops are over near Spanish Wells, right? There's nowhere else to go."

As we moved along the north edge of Eleuthera, I saw that the ocean had become a washing machine. Waves were breaking in all possible directions, into the coastal cliffs and the beaches and then seemingly rebounding back into the ocean.

As Captain Augie navigated our course, the boat was tossed from side to side, and I had to hang on for fear of flopping over the edge.

Richmond was gone. I hoped Superintendent Bridges had a boat that could keep up with a one hundred-horsepower Mercury. I wasn't sure what the alternate plan was if Richmond managed to evade capture. How far could he get in a speedboat? If he was to rendezvous with the bigger cruiser, he was going to have to go all the way to the south end of Eleuthera—a good 110 miles away— since they were now on opposite sides of the thin but very long island.

Then as we jostled around the top end of the island, I looked toward Spanish Wells and saw an armada. There was a large police launch surrounded by a collection of flatboats, charter boats, and dinghies at the end of the channel. There had to be fifty vessels in total. It was like the entire town had come out.

Richmond saw them too. He was closer and must have spent a moment or two mulling his options. An armada ahead and a flotilla behind. I waited for him to pull back on the throttle, but like me, he seemed to prefer momentum. So he cut to starboard, a hard right turn, out toward the endless ocean.

"I wouldn't go that way," said Captain Augie, as if Richmond had ordered a sandwich that Augie knew not to be the best on the menu.

"Why?" I asked.

"Devil's Backbone."

"They're flying across the top of the water. There's practically no draft under that hull."

"It's not the hull I'd be worried about."

"Then what?"

"It's the—"

Captain Augie never got to finish that sentence.

The propellor of Richmond's boat hit the reef at what Augie later estimated was approximately sixty miles per hour. The Mercury engine exploded off the boat like an Exocet missile and had well and truly left the vessel behind when it exploded in the air. It was like watching the death of a star.

The bow carved into the water and then the boat flipped nose to tail, ejecting Desmond Richmond and Rusty Reels into the reef. The hull continued on doing cartwheels like the worst IndyCar crash I had ever seen. I counted three more flips but later some claimed it was just the additional one, and others suggested as many as ten. I figured that was par for the course for a group of anglers.

The hull came to rest with a massive final splash, upside down in the middle of Devil's Backbone. Captain Augie eased forward in the choppy water but made no effort to cross the reef. We were joined in the tight channel by a few other boats, including the police launch, searching for anyone to rescue. We were presented with a dark ooze drifting across the water.

"Oil?" I asked.

Captain Augie shook his head. "Blood."

# CHAPTER FORTY-TWO

WE STAYED OUT LONGER THAN WAS NECESSARY. I SAW A FEW OF THE bass boats come into the channel for a look, but the chop was breaking across their decks, and they beat a hasty retreat. Captain Augie followed the rest of the smaller boats back to the docks in Spanish Wells. The crowd who gathered at the ferry terminal didn't disperse. People were talking and recounting the tale and sharing video they had taken.

Ken Corrigan arrived on a fishing boat, and we waited for the tide to come in some. Lizzy and Mrs. Albury and some ladies from the church arrived at the dock with cake and iced tea, and I gave them the CliffsNotes version of what had happened. No word arrived about anyone having been rescued.

Once the tide had risen enough, Captain Augie took Ken and me back out to the reef. Ken had arranged a local flatboat to come in from the other side, around the sand bars, to retrieve the debris. They tied onto the remains of the hull and dragged it off the reef. The pieces of the engine were sacrificed to the not-so-deep channel.

The competition anglers had quickly arranged better boats for the conditions and jostled for the best vantage points to stream the aftermath to their audiences.

They filmed as another flatboat came across the shallows and removed the bodies from where they had been skewered into the reef. I saw the ragged remains of Rusty Reels dragged from the water and then covered in a plastic tarp. Desmond Richmond came on board in several pieces.

Once their bodies had been retrieved, Captain Augie headed back to the dock. He dropped Ken and me off and then headed for home. Ken and I couldn't find any words, so we shook hands and headed in opposite directions.

I walked back to Mrs. Albury's and stopped in the front yard. Something felt different, and it took me a minute to realize that the missing conch in the border was missing no more. The gap had been filled with a conch shell newer and cleaner than those around it, but I figured some tropical wind and rain would fix that in short order. I looked up and saw Mrs. Albury standing at the front door.

"It's a miracle," she said.

Perhaps she was right. I wandered inside to get some water, and Lizzy told me she could organize afternoon flights out if I thought I had any chance of getting my passport back. I thought the chances were solid, and I told her to book it.

I wandered down to the police station. The young cop who had picked me up the first time was at the duty desk and offered me a smile. I nodded in return and walked into the main office as if I belonged there. Ken Corrigan was at a desk doing paperwork.

"A cop's dilemma," I said.

"What's that?"

"The more crime you solve, the more paperwork you have to do. Detective Ronzoni likes to keep a balance and not overdo either."

"This needs doing. We've got two bodies at the seafood cold store, but they can't stay there."

"Red Lobster would not be happy."

He shook his head.

Superintendent Bridges appeared from another room and came over.

"That didn't quite go to plan."

"I'm not going to lose any sleep."

"No. We got the big cruiser, by the way. Two men were on board. You recognize this guy?"

He showed me a mug shot.

"No."

"What about this one?"

"Him, yes. That's the dude who brought me here on the speedboat when I first arrived."

"Figures."

"What happens now?"

"They'll be deported. The cruiser is registered in Jamaica, and we made a call. It's not officially missing, but it should be in port down there, so it seems like your Mr. Richmond has a friend at the dock."

"A friend?"

"An associate. We'll work with the insurance company and get it returned."

"That's good and all, but what I really meant was what happens now for me?"

Ken opened a drawer and pulled out a bag with my wallet, phone, and passport in it.

"You're free to go."

I shook hands with the superintendent and then he turned and walked back into the other room.

"He's a very emotional guy."

Ken laughed and stood, and we shook hands.

"Thanks for everything," I said.

"Back at you. It's not normally this interesting here."

"I like that about it."

"Me too. And guess what? People are reporting that their conch shells are mysteriously reappearing." He raised an eyebrow, and I put my palms in the air.

Ken walked me outside, and we stood for a moment in the shade. I handed him a piece of paper.

"What's this?"

"Elise asked for my lemon vinaigrette recipe."

"I hope she can make it for you one day."

"I'd like that."

"So you're not turned off by us and our little island?"

"I hope you're all not turned off by me. It feels like the trouble arrived with me."

"When you put it like that . . ."

Ken smiled and patted my shoulder, and I walked away in the sunshine. I wandered down the main drag and stopped off to see Phil the mechanic and paid him what I owed. I only had US dollars, and he shrugged.

"Spends the same."

Lizzy had arranged our flight and was packing when I got back. We had tea and cookies with Mrs. Albury, and I thanked her for her hospitality.

"My pleasure, dear. It was nice to have some company. And thank you for fixing the cart."

"Be careful in it, okay?"

"Oh, I've sold it."

"You sold it? To who?"

"Young Jimmy. He's starting up a seniors' taxi and grocery service. He's a very enterprising young man."

"That he is."

As if on call, Jimmy arrived in said golf cart and took Lizzy, me, and our suitcases down to the ferry terminal. I didn't ask if he had a license, but I told him to be good, and he winked and drove away. As we waited for the ferry, Lizzy asked about our client.

"Since he's definitely dead now, and you didn't do it, I supposed we could bill his estate."

"I'm not sure his estate is going to be worth a pile of fish bones. But knock yourself out."

I saw the ferry chugging along the channel toward us when I heard my name and turned to see Chase Hutchinson striding toward me. He looked like the big man on campus again and wore a grin to match.

"They told me you were leaving."

"Things to do."

"Well, I just wanted to let you know, we broke the internet."

"What does that mean?"

"It means servers were literally crashing with all the traffic. All the videos and reels from this morning. The chase and all that. Record numbers. The whole thing's gone viral. Molly's stream has had thirty-five million views around the world since this morning. Can you believe that?"

"I barely understand it, let alone believe it."

"The buzz on the tournament is through the roof. I mean, you said you could deliver some buzz, but boy oh boy."

"Two men died, Hutch."

"Sure, yeah, I get that. Very sad. But they weren't very nice people, were they?"

"No, they weren't."

He slapped me on the back. "All right then. Listen, the cops had a word. Since there was never any cheating investigation and Rusty wasn't murdered or anything, the cops have closed the case. And because I was the last holder of it, they've given the cash back to me."

"Lucky you."

"But it's not mine. I figured you earned it, and since your actual client is now shark bait . . ."

He handed me the envelope, and I flipped it open for Lizzy to see the cash inside, then handed it to her.

We said goodbye to Chase and then I helped Lizzy onto the ferry. A deckhand took care of our luggage, and we stowed it at our feet and headed across the beautiful turquoise water toward home.

# CHAPTER FORTY-THREE

THE UMBRELLAS WERE OPEN TO THE SUN-SOAKED SKY WHEN I WALKED into the courtyard at Longboard Kelly's. Muriel was pouring Ron a beer and flexing her guns as she did it, and she broke into a wry grin as I approached the bar.

"Jailbird," she said.

Ron was enraptured by the amber liquid filling the glass before him and hadn't noticed me, so he spun around and smiled.

"I heard you did time," he said.

"It was a setup, see," I said in my best gangster voice.

Ron slipped off his stool and hugged me; then he quickly remounted his steed. "Dear barkeep, a beverage for our boy back from the war."

I got up onto my stool and felt my buttocks slide into the shape worn in the wood that was all me. It wasn't any softer than a lockup cot, but it was mine, and I was free to leave any time, which made me all the more likely to stay.

Muriel dropped a beer in front of me. "You really did go to jail."

"I did. For murder."

"That's going to give you some street cred around here," said Ron.

"Pulling off a Ponzi scheme gives you street cred in Palm

Beach."

"Maybe they'll make a movie about you," said Muriel.

"The *Shawshank Rethink*," I said.

"Or *The Miami Mile*," she said.

"That sounds like a shopping district in Coconut Grove."

"Or maybe—"

"Could I drink my beer now?"

Muriel shrugged. "Suit yourself."

I took a long drink and then sat the beer on the bar and let out a loud sigh.

"You want some porridge with that?" asked Ron.

"What?"

"Porridge. You know, prison."

"You've lost me." I picked up my beer again. "How was Cape Cod?"

"Hot and humid."

"Like here then."

"And expensive."

"I'm sure you were doing it hard."

"It was a great crew. Lots of white wine spritzers and long sunsets. The light was amazing."

"Who are you?"

"But I was dying for a beer when I got back."

"Ah, there he is."

We touched our glasses and drank.

"I would have come back, you know," he said. He looked a little ashamed that he hadn't.

"I know that. And if it had gotten desperate I would have called. But we had it under control."

"So Lizzy came over?"

"She did."

"She scare them into submission?"

"She certainly sorted out my lawyer in no uncertain terms. But the others . . . I'd say despite them being very different in every visible way, she got them and they got her."

"So she did okay."

"She saved my bacon, so let's call it better than okay."

"Where's Danielle?"

Muriel slid a tray of glasses under the bar. "I heard the British PM was off to California today, and the president was already back in DC."

"So will she come back, or will you go to Tallahassee?"

"I am not going to Tallahassee. I need to stay home for a while, you know? Ron, remind me I said that. If a case comes up further north than Fort Pierce or further south than Lauderdale—"

"Or further east than Palm Beach," said Muriel.

"Right. Just remind me to pass."

"Will do," said Ron. "Is your house ready?"

"I'm told the paint might smell a bit, but, yes, Sally left a message to say it was done."

"Does he know about the jail thing?"

"Not yet."

"He's going to be very impressed. Does that make you a made man?"

"No. Can we just drink in silence now?"

"I would have thought you'd had enough of that, you know, in the big house."

"It really wasn't that big. Two cells, and a roast dinner from the local restaurant."

"So basically, free accommodation in paradise."

I shrugged.

When I finished my beer, Muriel asked if I would like another.

"A wise man once said, one is one too many, and one more is never enough."

"How will you get home?" asked Ron.

"I'll drive," I said. "Because I'm done."

I was flagging and longing for a comfortable bed in an air-conditioned house. I was confident the AC would be connected, but I wasn't so sure I had any furniture. But having seen Muriel and Ron and sent Lizzy home with orders to take a couple of days of leave, I felt replenished in the soul the way only good friends can do. Now I needed to take care of the body and get some sleep.

I gave Muriel a fist pump and Ron a handshake. I told Ron to give my love to his wife, and Muriel to offer a grunt to Mick.

"If I see him, I will."

I walked out of Longboard Kelly's feeling exponentially better than when I had walked in. That kind of therapy was a bargain.

I drove back north and along Blue Heron and over into the island and then I slowed as I cruised through the small shopping area on Singer Island. For reasons I couldn't pin down, I felt nervous. My home had been lashed by a hurricane and fixed and then burned to the ground and rebuilt, but part of me knew it wouldn't be the same. Not the place I left, even before our stint in Miami, before the house had been rented out. And suddenly the idea of that change knotted my guts in a way that left me uneasy.

I turned down my street and headed toward the house at the end, right on the water. The McMansions around it all looked as they had, blights on the skyline, and my place still looked out of place, a ranch among wedding cakes.

When I pulled into the driveway, I noticed the first thing. The window frames were vinyl, not wood, which looked better and was more efficient but just served to make me think: *different*.

I didn't have a key, so I tried the door and found it unlocked. As I stepped inside I smelled the new paint, not overbearing but like a new car. The shag carpet was gone and replaced by engineered wood, which echoed as my suitcase rolled across it.

The kitchen looked amazing. It was white with solid stone counters—the Formica was long gone—and the appliances gleamed like a DeLorean. Opposite, the sunken living room had been replaced by a great room with wide sofas and oil paintings of old Florida scenes: Weeki Wachee Springs and Alligator Alley and the Cape Canaveral Dunes.

In pride of place, right where a normal person would put a big-screen television, was a large photo of Danielle and me. I could not recall ever having seen it before, nor it being taken. It was clearly at

Longboard Kelly's—even with the blurred background I knew that courtyard—but it wasn't a posed shot. Someone had snapped it from behind the bar.

We were both in motion, turning toward each other. Perhaps we had each been talking to someone else and had said something at the same time, I didn't know. But the shot was snapped at the exact moment our eyes met. Danielle was smiling as if in the beginnings of a great laugh. I looked amazed, as if I'd just learned I had made it into the *Guinness Book of World Records*.

I stood for the longest time in front of the photograph. I couldn't stop looking at our eyes. Somehow, someone had captured a moment I didn't recall and would never get back, but a moment in which no other human being on the planet existed. Just me and Danielle, looking into each other like we'd both just found home.

Eventually my legs began to wobble from standing still. I still had the sensation that I was tossing around between the Caribbean and the Atlantic, so I walked out through the sliding doors.

The patio was new, made from some kind of artificial wood, and wide and open toward the Intracoastal Waterway. There was no furniture, so I watched the gulls for a moment, the tink tink of yacht rigging ringing across the sky. This was my place, and this was my view, but I still felt uneasy in the guts. I couldn't shift the feeling they had rebuilt a house but had taken away something else.

Then I heard the sliding door open, and I turned to see Danielle leaning against the frame. She jinked her head and gave me that half smile she does.

"This place looks so amazing."

I shrugged.

"Come here."

I stepped over to her, and she kissed me and then wrapped her arms around me, so my face was in her hair. Then she pulled away and smiled.

"I'm so glad you're home. Aren't you?"

I nodded. "I am now."

# IF YOU ENJOYED THIS BOOK

One of the most powerful things a reader can do is recommend a writer's work to a friend. So if you have friends you think will enjoy the capers of Miami Jones and his buddies, please tell them.

Your honest reviews help other readers discover Miami and his friends, so if you enjoyed this book and would like to spread the word, just take one minute to leave a short review. I'd be eternally grateful, and I hope new readers will be too.

# ALSO BY A.J. STEWART

**Miami Jones series**

Stiff Arm Steal

Offside Trap

High Lie

Dead Fast

Crash Tack

Deep Rough

King Tide

No Right Turn

Cruise Control

Red Shirt

Half Court Press

Past The Post

The Ninth Inning

Big Thaw

Devil's Backbone

Three Strikes

**John Flynn series**

The Compound (novella)

The Final Tour

Burned Bridges

One for One

The Rotten State

Lost Luggage

**Lenny & Lucas series**

Temple of Gold

**Danielle Castle novella**

Little Packages

**Baskin Island Mysteries**

Clearer Waters

# ACKNOWLEDGMENTS

Thanks to David and Lisa, and Stacey for her eagle eye. All the wonderful people of Spanish Wells but especially Sharon Albury for showing me around the land and Sheldon Pinder for showing me around the sea.

As always, all errors, omissions, and fictionalizations are on me, except for the results of the Dizzy Budda at Budda's Snack Shack. That's not my fault.

# ABOUT THE AUTHOR

A.J. Stewart is the USA Today bestselling author of the Miami Jones mystery series and the John Flynn thriller series.

He has lived and worked in Australia, Japan, UK, Norway, and South Africa, as well as San Francisco, Connecticut and of course Florida. He currently resides in Los Angeles with his two favorite people, his wife and son.

AJ is working on a screenplay that he never plans to produce, but it gives him something to talk about at parties in LA.

You can find AJ online at www.ajstewartbooks.com.

Lightning Source UK Ltd.
Milton Keynes UK
UKHW041829030922
408285UK00003B/290